Other Titles by Quentin Carter:

Hoodwinked

In Cahootz

Contagious

Amongst Thieves

STAINED COTTON

By Quentin Carter

Compilation and Introduction copyright © 2008 by
Triple Crown Publications
PO Box 6888
Columbus, Ohio 43205
www.TripleCrownPublications.com

Library of Congress Control Number: 2008928911
ISBN 13: 978-0-9799517-1-8
Author: Quentin Carter
Cover Design/Graphics: www.MarionDesigns.com
Typesetting: Holscher Type and Design
Editorial Assistant: Dany Ferneau
Editor-in-Chief: Mia McPherson
Consulting: Vickie M. Stringer

First Trade Paperback Edition Printing May 2008

10 9 8 7 6 5 4 3 2 1

Printed in the United States of America

Dedication

This book is dedicated to Tashawna Owsley, who lost a long battle to cancer on May 19, 2007. She was my daughter's mother and a long time friend of mine. And she will forever be missed.

If there is enough room in heaven for a gangsta girl, then I know she up there getting on god's nerves.

Sleep in peace!

Love always,

Q. Carter
Brianna Carter

Acknowledgements

First, as usual, I would like to thank god for holding my hand and walking with me through this lengthy bid I've done. I know he had to be with me because I've had more blessings than I could ever count.

Usually I would start by thanking my family and friends. After five novels I figured you're familiar with them enough that I won't have to name them. So this time I'ma do something different and acknowledge all of those whom I've encountered because of my books, who've reached out to me and touched my life in their own way. Each of you had a hand in making my bid a lil' bit easier than it was supposed to be. And y'all should be acknowledged.

To some very special friends of mine and fellow authors. Venesha, author of Mistress Me. Renita Walker, author of Like Night & Day. Toy Styles, author, excuse me, best-selling author of Black and Ugly. And Cynthia White, bestselling author of Queen.

Some of the members of my loyal fan base, Kim White of Coast to Coast Readers. Ashleigh Porter (NE), Tasha Turner (STL), Joanne Mukome (PA), Stephanie Grier (NC), Joi Johnson (PA), Dorothy Wiley (Ohio), Terry Crenshaw (MN), Tameka Holloway (NC), Latoya Workman (VA), Tanisha Ruby (Ohio), Nikki D (MD),

Africa Samone (STL), Phyllis McClendon (FL), Addison Johnson (GA), Victor Bowie (FL), Arsheena Looney (KCK), Tracy Wynder (LA), Catricia Taylor (Chi-Town), Sonya Williams (VA), Ashley Hamilton (VA), Monique Jeffries (KY), Christopher Benefield (FL), Yufeesa Johnson (WV), T. Crenshaw (TN), Tameka Gilmore (VA), Trimika Jones (OH), Keisha Glover (Joliet, IL), TiJianna Kelly (LA), Tim'Esha (OH), Sarah Morning (Brooklyn), Jacole Jackson (CO) and Laterra Washington (MI).

My typist Cynthia Parker.

And the wonderful staff at the #1 leader in Urban Fiction, Triple Crown Publications.

Thank you so much!

CHAPTER ONE

June '01, Kansas City, Missouri. It was hot and humid outside. I was standing outside the American Pub in the Westport area, drinking Rémy and Coke from a plastic cup.

The Westport area is blocks and blocks of nothing but pubs, clubs, restaurants and bars. It was originally designed for whites to come out and have a good time. But you know how us blacks do it. You let us in on something, we bring our boys, they invite some hoes, who invite some more niggas. Next thing you know...it's a black party.

What happens next? As usual, niggas don't know how to act and get out of line. They gather outside the clubs in small crowds wearing gang attire. Shootouts start occurring. Cars get broken into and stolen. You know the drill.

Sheeit, so many people started hanging out in the area that the state was talking about letting the beer taps out on the sidewalk because nobody was going into the clubs anymore. Most of them were too young to get in, so they just hung around outside. This particular night, I was out hunting for a pretty pink-toed white girl to take home.

I had on the usual D-boy garb—wife-beater, Air Forces, baggy shorts and a red fitted ball cap. I had money so you know I was blinging. Back then I thought I was the birdman of KC.

I was walking down the strip, staggering slightly. Bitches were as far as my drunken eyes could see. I mean they were everywhere, wearing tight capris, boy shorts, skirts, halter tops, you name it. The D-boys were hanging around their whips while music videos played on the many TV screens that shone from their interiors. Trucks, cars, Jeeps, vans, old schools, new schools—everything that came through was sitting on 20s and up. Even some of the bitches were coming through on thangs.

A short-haired freak wearing jeans and a loud halter top passed me. She was jocking the chain around my neck, but I like to think that it was my looks alone that attracted her. I ignored her because I wasn't feeling that big-ass tattoo of a dragon on her back, and her stomach had more stripes than a drill sergeant. That alone told me that she had kids and was out soliciting a new baby's daddy. So I kept walking. I sensed that her fake green eyes were staring a hole through my back, but I didn't turn around to find out.

I crossed the street. Loitering inside the parking lot of a Chinese restaurant were my boys. My burgundy Rover was parked on the grass, showing itself off.

Jawan, that's my nigga, his chubby ass spotted me coming. "There Qu'ban go!" he shouted. He and the rest of my crew were surrounded by females. They were just hanging out, drinking and shooting the shit.

"Hey, Qu'ban," the girls said as they waved in my direction. Once I made it over to them, it was all hugs and handshakes. Now do you think I was getting that kind of attention because they loved me or because I had money? Now I know the real, but at the time I thought it was because they loved me.

Before I go any further, allow me to introduce myself. My name is Qu'ban Cartez. I stand 5 feet 8 inches tall, with a muscular build and brown skin. I wear my hair wavy 'cause I got that good shit. I rock a mustache with just that little triangle that grows under my bottom lip. No beard.

O'ban is my older brother. He's the lucky one. He peaked at 6 feet, got good hair and green eyes. If bitches didn't already know I had the most money, he would always have first choice, like he did when we were kids. Times changed. I was a young 22 now and he was an old 25.

Skatterman is the rapper. He sells about 30,000 units underground with ease.

And then there's Terry. He's older than all of us by several years. He's the one who first put me on. But after a lot of late night grinding, stacking and going without while they all partied and kicked it, I soon escalated above him. Then he caught a two year bid and left me with the plug. When he returned home from the joint, I was on. And me being the grimey nigga that I was, I refused to give him the plug back. But I put him back on, and that's the only reason we're still cool.

After all the greetings, they all resumed back to what they were doing before I walked up. I had just turned my cup up when something caught my attention. I cocked my head to the right and instantly became angry.

My black on black flawless '72 drop Cutlass strolled by on gleaming 22 inch chrome Daytons. Instead of me and my niggas occupying it, my baby mama, Lady, and three of her freaky-ass friends were flossing in it. Drunk. I could tell by the huge stupid grins on their pretty faces.

I wasn't pissed because she was out there. I was pissed because she was out there flossing my Sunday's best. After the light that held her up flashed green, she hit the gas. *Scurrrr.* The wheels spun as she rounded the corner. You could hear the 442 engine blowing through the dual exhaust.

I ran to the corner to see if I could find out her destination. As she strolled up 41st, a big blue Tahoe on big rims pulled out in front of her, cutting her off. The driver leapt his lanky frame from the truck. His long gold chain dangled around his neck. He smiled, flashing a set of diamonds on gold teeth as he made his way over to holla at my girl. She was a big flirt. I trusted her, but she loved niggas with paper, so I decided to intervene.

Immediately I ran over to my truck, strapped on my vest and grabbed my thumper from under my seat. The police were all around, but I was heated, drunk, and wasn't concerned about the consequences.

"Bro, where you headed?" O'ban asked.

"Be back," I hollered just before I pulled off. I drove away, careful not to damage my chrome feet on the curb. Traffic was thick, so I had to hit the turning lane.

Three guys had exited the Tahoe and were all leaning over my shit talking to the hoes. I saw the driver reaching for Lady's titty, but she swatted his hand away.

Pissed, I hit the gas a little. One of the dudes looked up and saw me coming. It was dark outside, but the lights from my TVs allowed him to see my face. He frowned. I could tell that he could tell that I was angry.

When I pulled up next to my Cutlass and parked, I could see dude reaching for something. I slammed the gear in park and jumped out, leaving my door wide open. The weight of the Glock protruding from my pocket caused my shorts to sag even lower than they were.

Lady looked up in time to see me coming. Her eyes grew as wide as my rims and her mouth fell open. She was in trouble and she knew it.

"Wha's going on here?" I yelled.

"Nnothin'," she replied nervously. "We was bored, so…"

She got quiet when my eyes fell down, peeping out her attire. Her little fast ass had on coochie cutters and her top was cut so low that I could see the top part of her brown nipples. She was only 5'1" and petite, but her titties were as big and firm as Pamela Anderson's.

"A ride, huh? Well what the fuck you got all these suckas around you for? Especially in my car."

"Them dudes ain't for me, they hollering at them." She was referring to her friends. "Besides, I'm a grown-ass woman. So don't come up here frontin' on me like that."

I scowled. "Bitch, I'll…"

"Hold up, cuz," the driver of the Tahoe said, then placed one hand on my shoulder.

So I took a step back. "Nigga, I ain't yo' mutha fuckin' cousin. And keep yo' fuckin' hands off me."

"I'm just saying, dawg," he went on, "you ain't gotta be all up in…"

"This my bitch, nigga!" I hollered as I gripped the butt of my gun. "You need to mind yo' own fuckin business."

He turned his hat around on his head and balled up his boney fists. "What you tryin' to do, cuz?"

Lady hurriedly emerged from the car. "Unt unh! It is too many police out here for y'all to be fighting." She placed her hand on my chest. "Please, y'all!"

I pulled the gun from my pocket and jacked the hammer back.

"No, Q," Lady said as she clutched my arm. I could see his boy inching toward me.

The crowd sensed an altercation in progress and began moving in our direction, which attracted the attention of the police.

Whoop Whoop.

Two patrol cars sped in our direction. The crowd began to disperse.

Whoop Whoop.

He stared me down. I thought about mirking his ass right there, but I'm not a complete idiot.

"Break this crowd up!" the police ordered through the loud speakers.

"I'll see you again," I said as I began backing away.

"No doubt." He and his boys hopped back into his truck and took off.

I peered at Lady. "Meet me around the corner at Popeye's. Now!" She watched me peel away in my Rover.

My first mind told me to rid myself of Lady, but I loved her. Plus she was good in bed.

Popeye's was crowded as well. Cars were double-parked and the drive thru was crowded. Everybody stared as I pulled in the entrance. My beat wasn't on, but my rims were getting the respect that they deserved.

All of a sudden I heard loud pipes roaring as Lady pulled into the back entrance. She stopped abruptly, then jumped out, storming toward my truck. I got out and met her halfway.

"Fuck was that all about?" she yelled, like it was my fault I caught her out acting a tramp.

"Lady, don't play with me," I replied in a serious tone. "I'll beat the shit outta you out here." She knew I would've.

"Why you wanna go there? Huh?" She got all up in my face. "I don't say shit about you hangin' out, all up in hoes' faces. Do I?"

"Calm the fuck down."

"Nah, you calm the fuck down." She could be feisty when aggravated. "I'm tired of you always…"

I snapped and grabbed hold of her throat, then thrust her back up against my truck.

"Who you talkin' to like that? Huh?" I yelled into her face. She fought to get loose, but my grip was too strong. "Now take yo' ass home and park my shit. Now!"

Her friends saw us tussling and ran to her rescue.

"Let her go, Q!" Toya screamed as she clutched my arm. Lady's tears were flowing.

"Stop fighting," Muffy pleaded. I had already fucked her a few times, and I smacked her a time or two, so she knew how crazy I could get.

Terry just so happened to drive his Jag up in the lot. He had two freaks with him. Upon seeing me choking Lady, he parked and jumped out.

"Q!" he hollered. "Let her go." He grabbed me from behind and pulled me backwards. I finally released my grip.

It took her a while to catch her breath, then she tried to attack me. Lucky for her Toya and Muffy stopped her.

"Let me go!" Lady cried. "I'ma kill this pussy." I heard all that before. "Don't come home, either, bitch. All yo' shit is gon' be out on the yard!"

Terry laughed as he held me back. He liked to see Lady act an ass. She knew how to put on a show.

"Put my shit out in the yard and you'd better sit out there wit' it. Think I'm playing if you want to." Terry guided me to my truck. "Keep fuckin' wit' me. Every bitch out here wish they could take yo' place, be with a nigga like me."

"Ooh, I do," a tall, leggy broad who was sitting on the passenger side of a green Jeep said. "I know how to be a real lady. Can I roll wit' you, ba-by?" Her loud voice slurred from whatever she was drinking.

Lady shot daggers at her. "Bitch, you better roll on, 'fore you get rolled over."

The leggy girl stepped from the Jeep. "Bring it on then, bitch," she challenged. "This'll make twice tonight that you get ya ass whooped."

Lady kicked off her heels. "C'mon, bitch. You gon' get fucked up over some dick you ain't never had."

I drove down to where the leggy broad stood in a bow-legged stance, ready to do battle. She took her eyes off Lady, and gave me her attention.

"Wha's up?" she asked.

"If you're rollin', you better come on." She hurriedly snatched her purse from her friend's Jeep and got in.

"No he didn't," Toya said as she released Lady. "Muffy, let her go, 'cause this nigga is trippin' fo' real."

I made a left out of the parking lot. That's when I heard two gun shots.

CHAPTER TWO

"Shit!" I spat. I couldn't believe that bitch had shot at my shit.

I gained a little distance, then pulled over on a back street to get a look at the damage. The bitch sitting next to me was shaken up as she stared out the back window.

"You aight?" I asked.

"Um-hum. You need to check that bitch. She's gonna fuck around and get you caught up one day." I could tell that she was scared shitless.

I got out and ran my hand over my truck, searching for holes. It took me going over it twice before I found the two tiny holes from Lady's .25 in my back bumper.

While I was bent over crying about my car, the bitch got out and joined me. I looked up, and for the first time noticed how pretty she was. She was rocking a tight-fitting pair of camouflage low riding capris, a green wife beater and some tan high heel sandals. Her arms were folded across her chest.

"Hi," I said.

She looked my way and blushed. "What?"

I straightened up, then said, "I'm Qu'ban." She giggled as I shook her hand.

"I know," she replied. "I'm Erica. Great. Now that we know

each other, where are we headed?"

"You're headed home if you ain't tryin' to go."

She frowned. "Tryin' to go where?" She really knew what I meant.

"You know what I mean."

"Yeah, I think I do," Erica admitted. "You can get the pussy…but it ain't free."

My eyes fluttered, because I was at a loss for words. I couldn't believe that bitch…nah, hoe, had the nerve to charge me for some snatch. But the bitch was too fine to pass up, so I found myself asking, "How much?"

Erica stepped over to me and gently kissed me on the nose. "I'll let you decide after it's over."

Erica stayed in a small house just off 27th Street. On the way there, Lady had been blowing my phone up. She was hoping that her bugging would stop me from getting some pussy from ole girl.

I parked in Erica's driveway behind her purple 4Runner. Before we went inside I called Terry and gave him the address to her crib. You never know, I might have needed him to get there in a hurry. I didn't trust stray hoes. I knew a lot of niggas that would've loved to catch me slipping.

Her house was furnished with fairly new cheap furniture. A big screen sat along a wall. The place smelled like scented candles. It was something fruity.

I sat on the couch and waited for her to make her move. Erica glared at me when she saw me lounging on her sofa.

"Unt unh," she said. "I don't allow nobody to sit in my living room. Especially not on my furniture. Get up!"

I peered up at her face like she was playing. The serious look on her face told me the opposite. Ain't this about a bitch,

I thought. She wanted to preserve that cheap-ass shit. I started to say something foul, but I didn't wanna hurt her feelings.

"You wanna drink?" she offered.

"Yeah."

"Good. There's a bar downstairs. That's where we'll be spending the night at. I'll be down shortly."

A sense of caution came over me. I was too paranoid of a nigga to be hanging out in a hoe's basement. Erica must have sensed my paranoia because she rolled her eyes and said, "Boy, it's all good. Ain't nobody here to do you no harm."

"I'm not trippin'. Ain't no nigga that me and my nogga can't handle." I brandished my gun.

Erica looked at my crotch and smiled. "That wasn't what was down there making you bulge like that, was it?"

"Quit playing," I said as I headed downstairs.

The whole basement was redone. The floor was black and white tile. A gold dancing pole was in the middle of the room. A small snake-shaped box was to my right. To my left was a carpeted area where a huge bed rested.

I fixed my usual, a cup of Rémy hit with a splash of Coke. As I glanced around the room I couldn't help but wonder how many asses had been on that bed. The number was probably somewhere in the hundreds. But her past didn't bother me. Ya gotta let a hoe be a hoe.

Bzzzst.

My phone vibrated on my hip. It was Lady again. I said, "Fuck it," and answered.

"Hello."

"Pussy! You…" *Click.*

Bzzzst. Bzzzst.

"What?"

"Don't hang up on me." Lady was being civilized now.

"Wha' sup?"

"You coming home tonight?"

I hesitated. "…I don't know. I'm pissed at you right now." I heard footsteps, so I faced the stairs and let my fingers caress my nogga. "Hold on."

Erica came strutting down the steps wearing a two-piece Burberry thong outfit and five inch stilettos. I clutched my nogga after I saw a pair of white Nikes trailing behind her. Had to be my nigga's shoes. The guy reached the bottom of the staircase before I realized that it was Terry. A smile crossed my face and my body relaxed.

"Qu'ban," Lady called. "Are you with that bitch?"

"Nah, I'm with Terry."

Terry stared Erica up and down. He got the chance to palm one of her ass cheeks before she slapped his hand. Lady was babbling in my ear while I watched Terry press Erica for some ass. Fuck how I felt about it.

"I'm sorry," Lady was saying. "Please, come home."

I giggled, "Aight. I'll be there in 'bout an hour."

Erica seemed relieved to see me get off the phone.

"Would you please get rid of yo' boy," she said.

"Terry, what the fuck're you doing here anyway?"

He fixed himself a drink. "I let Tanya keep my Jag."

I grunted as I dug the keys to my Rover out of my pocket. "Pick me up early tomorrow. Fo' real, man."

"Aight," Terry replied. "I'll be here early." He was speaking to me, but his eyes were on Erica.

I turned to see just what Erica was doing that had captivated his attention. All of a sudden I heard Joe singing, "*Taking you from the bed to the floor.*" Erica had her left hand

and leg on the pole, and was circling it. While staring at me, she stopped and clapped her hands two times. The lights went out.

I said, "Terry."

"Huh?"

"Beat it."

"Fo' what? I think she wants to fuck us."

Facing him now I said, "I said, beat it, nigga."

He frowned. "Sucka. I'm out." He turned to leave, but I stopped him. "What?"

"Come back." I didn't like the idea of being over Erica's house without my ride. What if the bitch got mad and threw me out?

Erica flipped upside down on the pole. Her legs were spread as she slid the pole in between her ass cheeks. She looked delicious. She managed to motion for me to come over.

Immediately I dropped my shorts, pistol and all, removed my vest and eagerly walked over to her.

~ ~ ~ ~ ~

Lady was relaxing in the tub, sipping on a glass of Chardonnay. Next to the tub rested a dildo, handcuffs and some sex lotions. She was prepared to play sex games when Qu'ban returned home. He was very kinky. He loved to jam the dildo into Lady while she performed her super head job on him.

The doorbell rang.

Lady took a quick sip from her drink, then set it down. She was all smiles as she hurried out of the tub and into her robe.

"Yes! My baby came home," she said excitedly.

When she reached the front door, she opened her robe so

13

that her hairy pubic mound and her breasts could be seen. It never dawned on her that if it was Qu'ban at the door he wouldn't ring the bell. Why would he?

Lady opened the door. Suddenly her smile flipped upside down.

~ ~ ~ ~ ~

"Turn over on your stomach," Erica ordered me. She had just finished riding me like a Ducati and my dumb ass shot cum all up in her. I wanted to pull out but the feeling was too intense.

Bzzzst. Bzzzst.

My phone was vibrating on the floor, but I didn't bother to stop and answer it. It was probably just Lady. Whatever she had to say would have to wait.

So I was on my stomach. My face buried deep into her sheets. Once again I wondered how many other asses had been where my face was at that moment. I felt her taster wiggling around on my back. Ahhh! Shit! It felt so damn good. She worked her tongue ring all the way down to the crack of my ass. My body jerked, but she held me down. She was used to guys squirming under her touch.

Erica used her hands to spread my cheeks, and I found myself in the doggy style position. Gently, she ran the ball of her ring up my crack.

"Whoa," I said. I faked an attempt to get up, but she held me down. Next she put her tongue in my ass. "Ahhh!" I know I sounded like a bitch, but it felt so good that I had to let it out. "Fuck me!"

She giggled briefly, then continued to work her whore magic on me. One hand jerked me off while she continued to lick my ass. I didn't want it to end.

Finally she stopped and said, "This is gonna hurt a little bit." Then she bent my dick to where it was pointed back toward her. Are you supposed to bend a hard dick? I didn't think so. I was just about to protest until I felt her place me…most of me, inside the warm confinement of her jaws.

"Shit!"

When she felt my dick pulsating, she pulled it out in time to watch it shoot her neck and face, where she wanted it.

"Can you go on?" she asked, cum dripping from her chin. I flipped over, panting, and said, "Gimme all you got."

She stood, inviting me back over to the pole.

~ ~ ~ ~ ~

"Terry, what are you doing here?" Lady asked as she closed her robe back up. She wasn't shy about him seeing her body because he had seen it before.

Terry happened to bump into her one night while she was out at the club, drunk. Qu'ban was at the room with some other hoe. Lady hadn't known that until Terry had dropped a dime on Qu'ban.

Anyway, as the night went on, Terry kept feeding her shots of vodka, which led to her accepting his offer to suck her pussy. Her first orgasm was so explosive that she went ahead and gave up the pussy, which wasn't part of the plan. Afterwards she felt bad, but she gained solace by telling herself that Qu'ban was just as guilty as she.

Terry held up his phone. "You texted me," he lied.

Lady scowled, "What? No I did not."

Terry showed her the LCD screen which had her number in it. "Somebody did." He had texted himself from her house early that day when he was visiting Qu'ban. All he wanted was an excuse to come see Lady while Qu'ban was out tricking again. It worked before.

"Mm?" Terry grunted. "Uh, well. Where Q at? It was probably him."

Lady sneered. "I thought he was with you?"

~ ~ ~ ~ ~

Goddamn! It was too much. I was lying on the floor with the pole between my legs while she slid up and down on my shaft.

"You like that, baby?" she mumbled. "Huh? Huh? Tell me. Tell me. Say you like that." She slammed her body against mine. Her cheeks clapped against my thighs.

By then I had busted countless times, and I was running on Rémy. The next time she rose, I slid out from underneath her.

"Wha…what's wrong?" Erica asked in between breaths. Beads of sweat rolled off of her hard, brown nipples. "You're not through, are you?" There was a worried look in her eyes.

"Naw. My turn to drive," I said as I walked over to her bed. My swipe was dangling, and my ass was dripping sweat all over the floor.

~ ~ ~ ~ ~

Lady picked up her cigarettes from the table and placed one between her lips. She set fire to it, took a few puffs, then slowly exhaled. Cutting her almond-shaped eyes at Terry, she saw that lust-filled look in his hawk eyes.

"I know why you're here, Terry," Lady said.

Terry stepped toward her. "Then ain't no need in beating around the bush, is it?" He carefully removed the stick from between her fingers, then stubbed it out in the ashtray. "It ain't too late for me to tell Qu'ban what I caught you doing."

Lady shook her head in disgust. "How long are ya gonna

keep dangling that bullshit over my head?"

Terry shrugged. "I 'on't know. Shit, Qu'ban deserves it anyway. He's out cheating right now, while you're sitting here looking stupid, thinking that he's coming home."

"How do you know he won't come home?"

Terry raised the keys to Qu'ban's Rover up in the air. "Because, I left him stranded until I return."

"Boy, you're some friend."

"You gotta lot of room to talk."

Lady unlaced her robe and let it fall to the floor. "What're you waiting on?"

Terry smiled deviously. "Unt unh. I wanna do it in his bed."

"Fuck nah. Who the fuck do you think you are?"

"Do you want Qu'ban to find out what you've been doing?"

"Fake-ass nigga! You ain't bluffing nobody. He'll fuck you and me both up. It'll kill him that you blackmailed me for sex."

Terry slumped over so he could look her in the eyes. "Friends like me and him expect bullshit outta one another. That's how we do it. Now you...he'll put you and Q Junior out on the street." He peered up the steps. "Speaking of Junior, where is he?"

"Next door."

Gently taking her hand, he said, "Then we'd better try to keep it down."

CHAPTER THREE

Bzzzst. Bzzzst.

My phone scurried across the floor. Erica had her head resting on my chest. She snored lightly, but it didn't take away from her beauty.

Bzzzst. Bzzzst.

"Hmm," Erica mumbled. "Fuck is that noise?"

I parted my dry lips. "My phone. Get it for me."

"What?" She raised her head. "I look like your damn maid?"

Bzzzst. Bzzzst.

"Just get it."

"You just wanted to see if I would do it," she said as she rose from the bed. Her naked ass jiggled across the room.

"No, I didn't. I just wanted you to get that stank-ass breath outta my face." I laughed.

Erica frowned, then cupped and blew air into her hands. "It don't stink." She got back in bed with the phone in her hand. "What if I answer it?"

"I'ma slap you."

"Please!"

I snatched the phone and answered it. "Yo?"

"Mornin' dog." It was Terry. He was in a cheery mood. "I fucked the shit outta this broad last night. A straight hoe."

"Aw yeah?" I sat up. Erica started caressing my inner thighs with her lips. I looked down and saw last night's lipstick and dried up cum stained on my dick.

"I'll tell you about it. I'm on my way." The line went dead.

Fifteen minutes later I was dressed and standing in front of the fridge with the door open, drinking juice from its container. As banging as her body was, it was a wonder why she had so much junk inside there.

Erica walked past on her way to the shower. She stopped suddenly after she saw what I was doing.

"Excuse me," she said in a smart tone. "Don't you think you're getting a bit too comfortable? And while we're at it, where's my money for last night?"

"I got it."

"Place it on my table, please." She walked to the bathroom. I found my way into her bedroom. I was clean, but also cheaply furnished. Inside her drawers were dozens of thong outfits. Then it hit me. The bitch was a call girl and the basement was where she turned her tricks. I thought about leaving without paying.

Under her underclothing I came across her diary. After opening it, I saw that every page was filled with dudes' names, like 200 of them. I spotted mine at the end of the list. I put it back, then left the room. If I would've looked four names up I would've spotted Terry's name. Unknown to me, he had already been up in her.

A fake Louis Vuitton purse rested on the TV. The shower cut off. The doorbell rang. Damn!

I saw a shadow through the closed mini blind that hung

on the front door. My hand was an inch away from it when I heard the bathroom door open.

"Is somebody at the door?" Erica was standing in the middle of the floor, soaking wet.

Shrugging, I said, "I don't know."

Ding Dong.

"Urggh!" She pouted. "Answer it."

"This ain't my house."

"Boy, get the door." She went to her bedroom.

"Hold on," I yelled through the door.

Fumbling through earrings, keys, make-up kits and the maxi pad inside her purse, I finally found her wallet. She had a knot of bills. I slipped a few fifties from the roll.

Ding Dong.

"Q, what're you doing?" Erica yelled. "Get the door."

"Sup, dog." It was Terry. He had a slick-ass grin on his face. "You ready?"

"Hell yeah."

Erica stormed into the living room. "I know you wasn't about to…"

"I got you." I handed her the three 50s that I had just stolen from her purse.

"Thank you."

We hugged briefly, exchanged numbers, then I was out the door. We were on our way to the car when Terry announced that he had to piss. He went back inside.

She was standing in the doorway with her hand out when he entered her house. Terry handed her five 20 dollar bills.

"Thank you," she said. "It's a good thing that he came to Popeye's. I had been looking all over for him."

"Yeah, yeah. Thanks for keeping him on ice for me. If it's

one thing that boy can't pass up is a good shot of white pussy. It'll get him in trouble every time."

"And I love a big colored dick up in this pussy." She frowned as she rubbed her crotch. "And damn it's sore."

When Terry came out we both jumped into the Rover. He drove. 27th Street was damn near empty, with the exception of a few patrol cars. My stomach was turning from the alcohol I drank the night before.

Out of the corner of my eye I saw Terry snickering. He had done something slick behind my back. I didn't ask him what. Whatever it was, I'd get him back. That's how we did it. We still had love for each other.

Terry passed a burning roach to me. I hit it a few times before tossing it out the window.

"I fucked the hell outta that bitch last night," I bragged.

Terry chuckled. "I know."

"What?"

"I hid behind the bar and watched for a minute." He made a left when we reached Prospect. "I got so horny watching y'all that I had to go fuck somethin'."

A group of females in skimpy clothing walking up the street grabbed my attention. I reached over and honked the horn. They started jumping up and down, yelling for me to turn around. It was the Rover. The chrome thangs had them jocking. I sat back and relaxed. At that time my life was good. I was the owner of five rental properties, a small sandwich shop, and had a bad bitch. I was doing aight.

Bzzzst. Bzzzst.

"Hello."

"I just know yo' scandalous ass didn't go through my purse," Erica yelled in my ear. "Why you steal from me, Q?"

I laughed. Terry laughed too, because he could hear her yelling through the phone.

"Q," she said. I hung up on her. Fuck that hoe. Terry drove to Geno's Barber & Beauty and parked behind a brand new Benz.

Terry started stuffing wads of money into my console, then he locked it.

I asked, "Why you carry all that money around? What you gon' do if you get pulled over?"

"I carry it because I got it. And if I get pulled over, I'ma tell 'em I play for the Chiefs. Why would they question it when I drive a $70,000 Jag?" He exited the car.

On the way inside I walked past the Benz. I recognized the guy in the front seat. He was talking to a fine-ass Puerto Rican broad. It was my man, Keith Banks. He was a hustling mutha fucka. I respect him, and gave him a holla every time I saw him.

"I'll be in in a second, T," I said. "I'ma holla at KB real quick." I tapped on his window.

"Wha'sup, Q?" Keith said coolly. "Give me a minute. Let me holla at my honey real quick, then I'ma walk in with you."

When he finished he got out. Then she slid over into the driver's seat, barely able to see over the wheel, and pulled off.

We shook hands and made small talk as we walked inside. There were about 20 females up in there, not including the beauticians, and at least 14 niggas, my crew included. Skatter was sitting in the chair next to O'ban, who was currently getting pretty. Jawan was talking to Tish. Geno saw Keith and immediately cut off his clippers and followed Keith to the back. Geno doing illegal business was new to me. I made my rounds, shaking hands and hugging. The females were checking me out. They loved me. Don't get me wrong, Keith was the nigga, but he was in my 'hood where I was the big dog. Kansas was his stomping grounds at that time.

After snatching up a magazine I copped a seat next to Terry.

Bzzzst.

"Hello."

"Where you been all night?" It was Lady. She sounded pissed.

"Baby, don't start." Terry cocked his head so he could hear me speaking. "I been with Terry all night."

"With Terry? No, you wasn't. Terry stopped by here last night. So tell another lie."

My lips tightened as I faced Terry. All he could do was drop his head. Then I knew why he had been so cheery all morning. The nigga was at my house trying to fuck my woman.

"Ooh! You lie too fuckin' much," she hollered. "I've been up all damn night waiting on you. You should have just told me the truth."

"Told the truth?" I was hot now. "What you want me to say, that I was out fucking another bitch?"

"At least you would've told the truth. I swear, nigga. One of these days...urggh! Pussy eatin' ass..." *Click.*

Childish-ass bitch. I faced Terry. "What you got to say for yourself?"

"C'mon, man. I was just testing ya game." He had an embarrassed smile on his face. "You suppose to be a playa."

"At least you could've warned me, chump." I shook my head. "I know you can't fuck my bitch, nigga. I got that bitch."

"Okay." His tone was too nonchalant for me.

I stared at the side of his head. "You fuck her?"

"Get the fuck outta here."

"Fo' real, man. Don't let me stay shacked up with a hoe and you know and won't tell me."

"I didn't fuck ya broad, man." He chuckled. "Have more faith in ya bitch, dog."

CHAPTER FOUR

Terry was lounging on his overstuffed sofa, sitting in front of his huge TV, watching "*Blow*" with a joint in his mouth. His eyes were on the screen, but inside his head he was replaying the episode that he had with Lady the night before.

Qu'ban's a goddamn fool, he thought. Housing that no-good-ass hoe. Terry would have told Qu'ban, but since he had stolen his plug, he said fuck him. Let him find out on his own.

When the phone rang, Terry reached over and picked it up. "Yeah?"

"Hey, T." He recognized the voice as Monique's.

"Heyyy. What you up to?"

"Me and my girlfriend Lakia are over here bored and try-ing to get into something. Why don't you bring some weed and drink over and kick it with us?"

Terry ran his hand over his curly head. "If I set it out, y'all gon' set it out, too. Y'all ain't gon' smoke and drink up all my shit, then send me home. Dick hard an' shit."

Monique giggled. "I ain't never called you this late without offering you some pussy, have I?" He said nothing. "Okay den. Nigga, get up…and bring ya ass." She hung up.

Terry hadn't hung the phone up good before he received

another call. "Yeah?"

"It's Twan. If you getting out tonight, bring me a nice piece."

"Meet me in front of Monique's in about 30 minutes."

After Terry ended the call, he grabbed an ounce of 'dro, a nine piece soft and his strap. He anxiously ran to his Jag and headed south.

Terry stopped and picked up a couple sticks of wet first. He broke the two sticks up in pieces, then mixed them in with the three blunts of weed that he rolled. He had a little something planned for Monique's girlfriend as well. And the wet laced blunt was sure to make her come up out her draws. He loved pussy and would do almost anything to get it.

Terry flew up Prospect. He was so anxious to get to Monique's crib that he forgot that he was riding dirty. It was a Saturday night so everybody was out riding, including the police.

Once he got out south, the traffic had gotten heavy. Store parking lots were crowded with youngsters who were either hanging out or buying liquor. Loud music pounded out of almost every car that passed.

He glanced at Club 6902 as he strolled past on blades. It was packed. If nothing popped off at Monique's, he planned on coming back through. A blue Ford F-150 pulled into the parking lot of Good-to-Go carrying a flat bed full of young white girls sporting colorful halter tops.

"Damn!" Terry exclaimed as he rode by. One of the girls saw the Jag passing and flashed her huge, pink-nippled jugs at him. He took his eyes off the road and didn't notice it when his car crept through the red light.

Errk!

A black Durango coming from the west jammed on its brakes to avoid collision. Terry swerved left, then regained control after he passed Gregory Boulevard.

"Shit!" Terry watched for any signs of 5-O.

Whoop. Whoop.

Terry was about to hit the gas, but a group of youngstas showing out up ahead had traffic jammed up. He was left with no other choice but to pull over and hope for the best. He left the engine running just in case the traffic cleared before the police exited their car.

Two tall, young black officers with broad shoulders stepped outta the car. Terry watched as they approached from both sides.

"Fuck! Fuck! Fuck!" Terry let down the window.

"Step out of the car, please," the officer stated.

Terry scowled. "For what? I ain't did nothing, Brown."

Officer Brown then tried to open the door, but it was locked. "Open the door. Now!" When Terry put his foot on the gas, Brown took out his stick and busted the window.

"Stop the fucking car," the second officer, Dulow, commanded.

Terry stopped. Brown reached in and dragged him out by his neck. His chin slammed against the concrete after being thrown on the ground. Dulow came up and kicked him in the back.

"Ow!" Terry bellowed.

Two minutes later the two were tearing up his shit while he sat on the curb, cuffed up. Dulow set the weed, dope and pistol on the hood of the car. Officer Brown returned carrying six thousand-dollar stacks in his hand that he retrieved from the glove box.

Brown whistled while holding up the cash. "Look at what we have here." He counted, "One, two, three, four, five, six," as he tossed the stacks onto the hood.

Dulow peered down at Terry, who was fighting back tears. "Is this drug money?"

"No. I used to play football for the Kansas City Chiefs."

"Yeah?" Brown asked. "When?"

"Two years ago."

Brown laughed heartily. "Officer Dulow, can you believe this fool? Boy, you should know that we pass out football cards to kids. And we know every player from the first to the third strings."

"You must think we're idiots," Dulow added.

Brown said, "Or damned fools. We used to play football in high school. And as mad as we are that we turned out to be some fucking cops, you chose to try and mind fuck us. Let us keep half of this money, then we'll let you go."

"Sheeit, y'all can keep it all. Just let me go."

"Uh, ohhh! Now you're also being charged with attempting to bribe an officer," Brown stated.

"Stupid," Dulow added for insult.

While they were loading him into the back of their car, Brown asked, "You're gonna tell us where you got the drugs?"

"Fuck you," Terry spat.

"I didn't think so."

CHAPTER FIVE

Katrina and Nancy Miller were two white girls from the suburbs of Kansas. Katrina was the older of the two sisters at just 22. Nancy was right behind her at 21. Both were taking a break from the private all-girls college that they went to. It was the summer and they were ready to let their hair down and pull their dresses up and get wild.

Not wild like they were used to at spring break where pretty white boys hung out. This summer they were looking for a different kind of fun. A black experience would be a better way to word it. They'd watch all the black shows like "*Girlfriends*" and "*Soul Food*," and saw the movies "*Baby Boy*," "*Booty Call*" and "*The Wood*." From what they learned, they came to the conclusion that blacks had more fun, going through all the violence, drama and whatnot.

All their lives they had been pampered, loved, protected and well taken care of. They were starting to feel common. They wanted to go through what black people went through. Experience some of their troubles. Hang out with them. Get to know a few of them. And most of all, have sex with a couple of black men.

It was Friday night. They dressed in some strapless summer dresses and platform sandals, then jumped into their mother's Benz SUV. Their destination was to cross the state line over into Missouri and find a club where the thugs played.

Their parents, Michael and Kathy Miller, would kill them if they knew that their daughters were going to hang out in the ghetto rather than to a movie like they were told.

~ ~ ~ ~ ~

Me and O'ban were in my Rover singing along with Mannie Fresh while he sang, *"Everybody get ya roll on. Everybody get ya mutha-fuckin' roll on."* We pulled up to the club Life two-deep.

I jumped out and handed the valet what was left of my blunt for a tip. He smiled and got inside. O'ban was brushing the wrinkles out of his Polo shirt when I walked up to him. We both had on Sean John jeans, Air Forces and Polo short sleeve tops. As usual, our necks, fingers and ears were froze, 'cause that's how we do it when we're on the hunt for hoes.

The club was pumping that new Fabolous and Nate Dogg. *"Y'all can't deny it, I'm a fuckin' rida. You don't wanna fuck wit' me."*

I strutted through the crowd, bobbing my head. Here and there I'd give a nod or throw my hand up at somebody that I recognized. Strobe lights were twirling. Bitches were up in there getting loose.

The waitress bypassed me carrying a bucket of champagne bottles and approached O'ban.

She smiled at him seductively. "Your usual?" O'ban nodded coolly. The beautiful red-bone took a bottle of Moët out of her bucket and handed it to me, the other to him. "Yours is on me."

"Thank you," I said, knowing damn well that she was talking to O'ban. Then I shot through the crowd before she could respond.

I was moving through the crowd in a slow pace like a nigga in a video. Everything was going in slow motion, so I pretended. "*I Gotta Be*" by Jagged Edge came on. "*I gotta be the one you touch. I gotta be the one you love. I gotta be the one you feel.*"

That's when I spotted them. A club full of hoes and I could only concentrate on the two who were swaying from side to side before me. They looked out of place. Preppy. Stuck up. I could tell that they didn't know what they were doing because their feet were stuck in place.

Both women were white. Built like those girls that you see on those exercise shows. Both were tall with fresh tans, slender legs, full lips and the one I was attracted to had blond hair. The other had black hair.

O'ban approached me from behind. "What do we have here?"

"Pink toes," I said with glee. "Pretty pink toes."

We approached them. "Hello. I'm Qu'ban and this my brother, O'ban."

They smiled and introduced themselves as Katrina, the blonde one, and Nancy, the dark one. They were siblings as well.

"Why don't we get a table?" O'ban requested.

Nancy shrugged. "Okay."

We settled at a booth. Katrina and Nancy took the inside. Me and O'ban took the outside.

The girls didn't know what to order. Neither did we, because we always drank champagne. So we ordered them a bottle as well. After a couple drinks they began to loosen up.

I said, "So what brings y'all here?"

Katrina scratched her cheek. "Well, we decided that we wanted to hang out with...um...in a black environment tonight." She looked at both of our expressionless faces. "Does that sound right?"

I shrugged.

Nancy cut in, "What she's trying to say is we've been partying with stuck up white people for so long that we decided to do something different tonight."

Katrina shook her head. "Yeah. What she said."

"We're trying to experience what it's like to be black women, like project bitches."

O'ban spit out his drink. "Are you serious?"

Katrina didn't see nothing funny. "Well, yeah. We were hoping to come down here and meet a couple of nice black guys like yourselves. Have a good time. Ya know?"

I said, "So you're doing an experiment on niggas? What, is this for your college course or something? Act like a nigga week?"

"No," Katrina said, then took another sip of her drink. "We just want to be taught how to be cool."

Nancy smiled.

O'ban said, "What's in it for us?"

"Lots and lots of sex," Nancy said. "Great sex."

Katrina was tipsy now. "Show 'em your pussy, Nancy."

"No. Show'm yours. You're the one with blond pubic hairs."

I was in awe. Out of all the white girls I'd laid, I'd never laid a real blonde, let alone one with a blond pussy.

Nancy reached over and pulled up her sister's dress.

Katrina put her drink up to her mouth. When Nancy pulled her sister's panties to the side, we feasted our eyes on a triangle shaved blond pubic mound. I was in love.

The waitress appeared. "Will there be anything else?"

"Yes," I said. "Get these bitches another round."

Nancy frowned. "Did you just call us bitches?"

"Sho' did. That's what we call ghetto girls, bitches and hoes."

Katrina peered at me with a drunken smirk on her face. "Well…I guess I'm your bitch."

"You guys know what they say, don't you?" Nancy asked.

"What they say?" O'ban inquired.

Nancy looked down at the bulge in his pants. Slowly she lowered her hand down to his crotch.

"Tell me what they say, baby."

Nancy gazed up at him. "They…sayyy…once you go black, you never go back."

Katrina looked at me. Not at my eyes, at my crotch.

"Is that true?"

"From my experience," I answered.

"Why don't we…" Nancy unzipped O'ban's pants, "introduce big black to some of this tight white?"

"I don't mind if I do." O'ban finished his drink and stood. "Let's go."

Nancy stood. She slung her arm over his shoulder. "Once you go white…you'll be in it all night." She giggled all the way through the club.

"Your sister is crazy," I commented.

Katrina gazed at me through seductive gray eyes. "You're going to worry about my sister? Or are you going to give me some of that black dick?" Her breathing was so heavy. "I've seen Mr. Marcus fuck Superhead, so I know how brothas get down."

I smiled devilishly as I picked up my drink.

We had them follow us back to the 'hood to a crack head named Odessa's house. O'ban gave her $10 to let us use her bedroom.

Nancy and Katrina had disgusted looks on their twisted up faces when they entered the house. Crack heads were lying around tweaking. Some were gathered in the dining room passing around a loaded pipe.

We led them upstairs. An old cum-stained mattress sat on the floor. Katrina and Nancy looked at each other and frowned.

"What are we doing here?" Katrina asked.

"This is what we do with bust downs. Ain't no use in spending all that money on a motel," I said.

"We have money."

"Shut up." I pulled her close to me and started kissing her. She resisted until the fire inside her hormones lit. I raised her dress and slid my fingers under her panties.

"I can't...believe I'm...doing this," she said while we were kissing.

Katrina pulled her dress over her head. She was braless. Big, perky, pink-nippled jugs dangled in my face. She dropped her panties with no hesitation.

Me and O'ban laid them both on the stained mattress. They cocked their legs up and open, eagerly wanting to get fucked.

We pulled our pants down to our knees and let our hard dicks stretch out before their eyes. Both of us fought hard not to look at each other's dick. Both afraid to see whose was really the biggest.

"Sss. Ooh," Katrina howled as I entered her without a rubber. We figured that they were preppy white girls, so they had to be clean.

When I heard Nancy over there oohing and ahhing, I knew that O'ban had entered her. After we got our rhythm down, we started thrusting to see which one would scream the loudest and cum the hardest.

"I'm really not...ooh...like this," Katrina uttered.

"Neither am I."

She grunted as she giggled. "You...are...so...ohh...not telling...ooh...the truuuth." I went in deep. "Oh, god. It's big."

I heard pussy juices slurping and skin slapping. Nancy grabbed her sister's hair. Katrina yelled, grunted and grabbed O'ban's back.

I could tell then that we were in for a long night.

CHAPTER SIX

Erica was home in her basement sorting out laundry. The red thongs went into one pile. The white in the other. She began turning them all inside out before she placed them into the washer. When she picked up the pair that she'd worn the night before, she noticed little brown spots in the crotch area. She held the drawers up to her nose and sniffed. Whew, they smelled bad. "What the fuck?" That's when she realized that it was discharge. Caused by none other than an STD. Her third. "Oh-my-god. What trifling mutha-fucker done burned me?" It couldn't have been Qu'ban. It had only been 24 hours since they'd had sex. So Erica had to have passed it on to him. "He's gonna kill me." She picked up the phone and dialed Qu'ban's phone number.

~ ~ ~ ~ ~

After Terry finished talking with the detectives about the dope, gun and money that was found inside the car, he was escorted back to the bullpen. He was tired, hungry and the fact that he had a criminal background made him afraid. Life was too good for him at that point to be sitting in no jail for probably 20 years.

He had money, cars, women and a little real estate. How

would anyone expect him to just give all that up? He knew from past experience that when you got locked up, everything—your possessions, money and women—seemed to just disappear.

When the food cart came around at 3 a.m. passing out coffee and danishes, Terry just shook his head in disgust. *This shit is beneath me*, he thought.

"Finch, you want coffee?" the turnkey asked.

"Hell naw."

A crack head asked Terry to get it for him.

Terry accepted the food. Instead of giving it to the crack head, he walked over and dropped it in the toilet. Then flushed it away.

"Dig it out since you want it so fuckin' bad," Terry said coldly.

"That was uncalled for, man."

"You ain't that hungry then." Terry picked up the phone.

~ ~ ~ ~ ~

"Ah! Ahhh!" Nancy howled.

"Oh! Oh! Ohhh!" Katrina moaned.

Both howled at about the same level. Katrina was working on her third orgasm and me my second. Her pussy was just too good for me to pull out when I came. She didn't care where I put it as long as she came.

Tears started running from her right eye. I tapped O'ban on the shoulder so he could see. He brushed me off. Nancy had her legs wrapped around his waist. His hands were cupped over her titties while he worked her at a steady pace.

My phone buzzed. I had to slow down so I could dig it out my picket.

"Hello-o."

An operator came on the line. "You have a collect call from *Terry*. To accept, please dial 3 now."

I stopped humping completely and anxiously pressed 3.

Katrina shot me a disturbed look as she brushed her hair out of her face. "Why did you...stop?"

I held one finger up, signaling her to shut up.

"They popped me, dog," Terry stated in a solemn tone.

"Dammit! What happened?" Katrina gazed up at me with concern. Terry told me everything that happened.

I sighed. "The Chiefs player thing didn't work, huh?"

"Yes. Yes. I'm 'bout...to...cum!" Nancy screamed. "Ahhhhh!"

Katrina stared at her sister, breathing deeply while she watched her experience an orgasm. "Oh, my god!"

Katrina's body shifted as she began to hump my limp dick.

"I'm on my way." Shit. I hung up.

I pulled out of her, pulled up my pants, then sat in a chair, trying to catch my breath. Katrina sat up, clearly frustrated, and pulled her dress back over her head.

O'ban and Nancy lay there, one on top of the other, while they caught their breath.

"That was the bomb," Nancy boasted. "Mom would freak out if she knew I had sex with a black man. I mean, god, she'll probably smell you on me."

O'ban said, "A nigger sniffer."

"She hates blacks," Katrina chimed in. "She believes that blacks bring white people down, if they're in a relationship. Stained cotton, she calls it."

"Stained cotton?" I said.

Katrina shifted her gaze to me. "It's a worthless white woman that's been tainted by a black man, or vice versa."

Me and O'ban shared a laugh.

I said, "We gotta go get Terry's ass."

"Drop me off first," O'ban replied. "I'm exhausted."

The girls both looked disappointed.

Katrina said, "Are we…is this like…you know, the end or what?"

O'ban pulled up his pants. "I know y'all weren't serious about what y'all said earlier?"

Nancy said, "Yes…we were."

"Aight," I said. I logged my number into Katrina's phone, and hers into mine.

We said our goodbyes.

After I dropped O'ban off I went to see Shakur, my bail bondsman. He made a few calls to prove that Terry's story was real. Then we went to pick him up.

I sat in Shakur's car smoking weed and drinking beer while he went in and got Terry. About 45 minutes passed before they finally came out of the building. Terry climbed into the back seat. During the ride he never uttered a word about what he said to the detectives. I was skeptical about the entire situation. But I kept telling myself that he had done one bid without snitching, so why couldn't he do another?

I remembered when Terry gave me my first key of dope. He said, "If you ever get caught, don't tell'm nothing. If you don't say nothing…they ain't got nothing." I had lived by those words ever since. I hoped he wasn't a hypocrite.

Shakur spoke, "Y'all have to be careful. I've done a lot and seen a lot. One thing's for sure, only one in a thousand women do bids. And those who do are usually married, or their men still have money to support them."

I wanted to tell Shakur to shut the fuck up, but I had a lot of respect for the old dude.

"See, a broad is only as good as her nigga," he went on. "You treat her like shit, that's exactly how she's gonna treat you when you're down. They're not fools. As long as you're up, she's gonna take all the abuse you can dish out. But when you fall off, she's gonna introduce you to the real her. The woman that was created inside, built by years of abuse that you took her through." He chuckled. "It's gonna fuck you up, too."

"It ain't gon' fuck me up," I replied. "Nothing that a bitch does surprises me."

"Has either of your broads asked you to leave the game? If they haven't, with all that money you got…it's because they really don't care about what happens to you."

I thought about Lady. She had never said nothing even close to that. I was starting to wonder, was I really sleeping with the enemy?

Terry exited Shakur's car. As I was doing so, he placed his strong hand on my shoulder. I shot him a questioning look, because I wanted to know why had had touched me.

He pointed a finger at me, then said, "You be careful, Q. You understand what I'm saying?"

I peered out the window at Terry, who was standing next to my truck, smoking a cigarette with his head down.

"Yeah, I hear ya."

I hit the alarm as I walked over to my RR. Inside I popped in a freak video on the TVs to help sooth Terry's perverted nerves.

"Don't worry, man," I said. "I'ma get you a lawyer, and hopefully we can beat this shit. If need be, you can keep that $15,000 that you owe me."

Terry spoke for the first time. "I got plenty of bread put up.

It's the timing that's got me fucked up."

I could feel what he was saying. Everyone wanted to make fast money, but no one wanted to suffer the consequences.

"What was you doing riding like that at night for anyway?"

"Maaan, trying to get some pussy."

I turned on my block on 74th Street. Unlike others, I refused to leave the 'hood, like scared niggas do after they get a little piece of change. So I bought my dad's old house and the two next to it, then had them all torn down and built one big crib from the ground up. Some say I was a fool, others commented that I was stuntin', big time. Lady said if somebody wanted to kill me, then I wouldn't be hard to find.

All the lights were out in the house, except for the bedroom. Lady was still awake.

I followed the concrete path that circled my house, leading to a three car garage. In it I kept my old school, a four-wheeler and my Rover.

Lady's Yukon didn't get any privileges. It remained parked outside. Terry left in my truck.

As I entered the back door to the kitchen, I smelled Indo weed burning. It was loud. I stopped by the fridge to grab a snack before the bout.

Lady was sprawled on our bed reading a magazine when I stepped inside our bedroom. She quickly glanced up at me, then back to her *Vibe* magazine.

I expected her to jump up and act an ass, but she didn't. Good. I was too tired anyway. Since she was feeling dramatic, I took a shower, then fixed myself a nightcap.

The lights were out when I returned, and she was under the covers. I downed my drink, then slid in bed next to her. The heat from her body was soothing. Her being so damned quiet was starting to annoy me. So I felt in between her legs to see how she would react. To my surprise, she was naked. I fondled her clit.

"I didn't know you knew how to find it," she commented.

"It's mine, ain't it?"

Silence. Then, "I can't tell. She's been craving your loving all week, but you let her starve."

"I'm ready now."

"Stop!" I kept on. "Unt unh." Soon I felt her legs part. "Ummm. Ooh. Boy, I hate youuu."

Lady rolled on top of me and started nibbling on my neck and ears. My dick stood up between her ass crack. Slowly, she moved her ass up and down on it.

"Lady?" I mumbled.

"Mmm. What?"

"Do you think I should quit hustling?"

She stopped. "Why? What's wrong?" Concern was in her voice.

"Nothing." I caressed her butt cheeks. "I was just thinking. I got a little business, houses, money. I mean, if I keep going I'ma end up in a bad position."

"Like what?" All the concern had left her voice. Now it sounded more like alarm.

"I could end up in jail. Then what would you and Junior do?"

"Please, man. Junior doesn't even know that you live in this house. So g'wan with that." She kissed me. "And as for you giving up the hustle," she kissed me again, "that would be stupid. If you go to jail, I got ya back."

All her talk about having my back made up for her telling me not to quit hustling. I wasn't gonna do it anyway. I really didn't feel like fuckin', so I pushed her off me.

"Wha's wrong now?" she inquired.

I rolled over in the opposite direction. "Leave me alone."

"Ain't that a bitch?"

I laughed silently to myself.

~ ~ ~ ~ ~

"Mmm, uhh," I moaned. Something felt good. "Mmm!" When my eyelids fluttered open, I saw Lady's lips running up and down my shaft at a steady pace. She did it with perfection. Her eyes raised to meet mine. So I started squirming because that's what turned her on. Control freak.

Lady picked up the pace. Slurping, wet sounds came from her mouth. I could feel her tongue wiggling around inside. The second that my dick started pulsating and I was about to unload, Junior walked into the room.

"Shit!" I gasped.

Lady hummed while she jacked it. I pushed her face off me. "Wha…" I pointed toward the door. She looked to her left. Pre-cum and slobber dripped from her lips, while Junior stood there watching. "Shit!" She dipped her head under the covers, leaving my dick exposed.

Junior walked all the way over to the bed with index finger stuck in his mouth. Then touched my shoulder.

"Yeah?"

"Can I go with you today, Daddy?" he mumbled because he's shy when it comes to me.

My heart melted. "Yep."

"Okay." He headed for the door. "Hi, Mama."

After Lady heard the door shut, she peeped out from under the cover. "He gone?"

"Mm hmm."

"Damn. My son caught me with a dick in my mouth." She gazed at me. We both busted out laughing. "It ain't funny."

Bzzzst. Bzzzst.

Just when I thought nothing could ruin my morning, some fucked up shit happened.

"Hello," I answered. I watched Lady throw on her robe and walk out the room.

"Can you talk?" It was Erica.

"Kinda." I could sense some bullshit going on. "Wha' sup?"

"I tried to call you last night."

"Girl, wha' sup?"

"I," a quick sigh, "I think you better go get yourself checked out."

"Checked out? For what?" I knew exactly what she was saying, but I had to be positive.

"Qu'ban, I have gonorrhea."

I had fucked Katrina the night before. Then I woke up with Lady's mouth slobbering all over my dick. My infected pre-cum caked around her mouth. I dropped the phone.

CHAPTER SEVEN

Lady and I lived together, but we hadn't spoken in weeks. After she found out that she had gonorrhea of the throat, she stabbed me in my shoulder. She had every right to be angry, but that didn't stop me from kicking her little ass every time I thought about her stabbing me. Finally she moved into the other bedroom just to avoid me. She was too money-hungry to leave.

Of course I had infected Katrina with the disease as well. But by her being eager for the "black experience," she found it amusing that she encountered her first STD. As long as she wasn't gonna die from it, it was all in the game to her. I liked the broad. So I decided to go ahead and put the cuffs on shaw-ty and make her one of mine. From there on out she and her sister Nancy, who we eventually named Nah Nah, a much cooler name, belonged to us.

They must have misunderstood us because that very weekend we caught them hoes out in the club without us knowing about it. We embarrassed their asses in front of the whole club.

I found Katrina over by the pool table. She was dressed in low-cut jeans, a white blouse and black boots, a white Kangol hat on her head and a pair of tinted Cartier shades. She was holding a drink in her hand, laughing and giggling with some baldheaded, tall nigga like she was cool.

You should have seen the look on her face when I walked up on her. The drink damned near fell from her hand.

"What the fuck you doing?" I barked at her.

Her mouth opened, but nothing came out. "B…"

I slapped her across her face. The glass that she held fell out of her hand onto the pool table. She grabbed her cheek. When I nodded at the dude that she had been talking to, he just held his palms up and backed away.

I clutched a handful of Katrina's hair and literally dragged her through the club.

While I dealt with Katrina, O'ban put a lid on his situation as well. He threw a drink in Nah Nah's face, then made her stand in a corner for an hour while he mingled with other hoes. He wanted her to feel how he felt when he saw her up in the club mingling.

I made Katrina get into the passenger side of her own SUV, then I pulled about a quarter ounce of Dro out of my pocket and handed it to her.

"What do you want me to do with this?"

"Hold it in case we get pulled over."

She was confused. "And then what?"

"If the police search you and arrest you, which they won't because you're white, call me in the morning after I wake up and I'll come get your monkey ass."

"Qu'ban, I…"

"Look, bitch. After the way you made me act up in there tonight, I shouldn't be hearing no complaints from you." Katrina huffed, but didn't respond. The entire left side of her face was red from me smacking her.

"Take that bag and put it in ya pussy before we drive off."

"Why do I have to p..."

"Look, bitch. You wanna learn how to be a down-ass gangsta bitch, then this is what it takes." She didn't say anything. In fact, she did as she was told. "Next week I'ma teach you how to hold an ounce of crack in that pooter."

Katrina secured the weed, then sat back in her seat like an obedient child. I clutched her face and pulled her toward me. She trembled as I reached in and planted a kiss on her lips.

"I love you, girl," I said softly.

Katrina sniffed. "I love you, too."

It took all of the energy that I had to suppress the smile that was trying to bust its way through. I wasn't used to humble broads. I was used to drama queens, ghetto-ass hoes that did nothing but breed babies, hate and cause me grief. Katrina was just the opposite. She was submissive, humble, willing and best of all, white. I decided from then on that if me and Lady ever broke up, I would never house another black woman again.

For about a month we took those broads through a rough orientation period. I'm talking about everything from beatings, stealing from them, introducing them to ex-pills, teaching them how to steal clothes, measure drugs, do credit card scams. Basically we taught them how poor blacks survived with nothing in a white man's world.

They taught us a thing or two as well. They took us out to the gun range where all four of us learned to pop them things for real. We got to play golf with them at the Irish Golf Resort in Lee's Summit. Experience our first steam room and massage. We even agreed to go with them to see the stage play,

"*Cats.*" Ain't that a bitch? We kicked it though. We got a chance to see what the white folk did for fun.

For the summer I hired Katrina to work at my sandwich shop. I even had it switched over to her name so the feds wouldn't find out about it.

Me and my son drove out to my restaurant on Blue Ridge Boulevard. I wanted to show him that his daddy did work for a living, despite what he may hear his grandma say.

A sign was hanging on the front of my restaurant. It read "Back in 15 minutes." I unlocked and opened the door. My angry eyes scanned the room for my new manager, Katrina, who was supposed to be working, not on break.

"Katrina!" I called out. Then I heard the toilet flush. Katrina wore the work uniform like it was a new fashion statement when she strutted out of the restroom. She was shocked to see me.

"Hi, boss," she said, timidly. On the job I was boss.

"What the fuck're you doing?"

"I used the restroom."

"Using the restroom? Naw, you don't use the bathroom until Ebony gets here to assist you."

Customers started filing into the store. That gave Katrina a chance to escape my wrath by easing behind the counter. I followed.

"Taking a shit on my time," I went on complaining in front of the customers. "Now you wanna use the same shitty-ass hands to make sandwiches."

"Okay—boss," Katrina said, sounding frustrated. She was both angry and embarrassed. I didn't give a fuck. It was my place of business, not hers.

I fixed Junior a meal, then helped Katrina get caught up.

For the last three days it had just been me and him. Lady had left the house three days ago and we hadn't heard from her since. If she didn't have a good excuse for where she had been, like being killed, then she was gonna get it. Big time.

~ ~ ~ ~ ~

Lady pulled her Yukon into the parking lot of Quick Trip Gas station on Longview Road. Right on time she saw Terry drive up in a blue Chrysler 300M. He parked beside her and got out. She unlocked the doors so he could get in.

"Wha' sup, girl?" he said with a smile. His voice was loud as usual.

Lady frowned, clearly frustrated by his presence. "Why you talk so goddamn loud? Shit. Giving me a fuckin' headache."

"My bad. My bad. I know you don't like me. Where's the stuff at?"

Lady retrieved a duffle bag from the back seat and handed it to him. He peeped inside. Terry held the freezer bag of cocaine up to his face. Lady pushed it down toward his lap.

"What the fuck is wrong with you, Terry? You trying to get a bitch busted or what? Man, give me the money and get yo' junky ass up outta my truck."

"Bitch, I oughta take this stolen-ass dope from yo lil' thieving ass. Stealing from ya own man."

Lady produced a .38 revolver from under her leg. "And if you do I'ma shoot the fuck outta yo' ugly ass."

Terry regarded the gun cautiously. "Damn. Ain't no need in all that. I came in peace." Terry pulled a brown paper bag from out his pants, then handed it to her. "Fourteen grand for a brick. I can't beat that."

"Yeah, yeah. Get the fuck outta my truck."

Terry opened the door, then looked back at her with a serious look on his face.

Lady put the money bag inside the console. She put the gear in reverse, hit the gas, and then quickly slammed on the brakes.

"No, he didn't," she said to herself as she gazed out her rearview mirror at the three agents that had surrounded her car, pointing guns at her.

That was three days ago. Since then Lady had been sitting inside the city jail waiting to see if she would get out on a signature bond. She couldn't call anybody because she was both scared and embarrassed. But she was tired and ready to go home. Her stomach cramped from holding in her bile for too long.

"Save yourself," the cops had told her. This would all go away if she just simply agreed to cooperate.

Why steal, Lady? she asked herself, *when shit was already being handed to you?*

~ ~ ~ ~ ~

I don't know how Junior felt about his mom's disappearance. He never spoke on it. So I went on like everything was everything's.

Lady's Yukon was parked in the driveway when we returned. It was filthy, and that was a first. Usually it was immaculately clean. A lot of questions flowed through my head.

I found her in the kitchen about to dial a number into the phone. When our eyes met, she just rolled her eyes at me. I shook it off and walked to the bedroom. I took out my cell phone and started dialing numbers. The floor creaked behind me. She was standing in the doorway looking a mess when I looked up.

"Ain't you gon' ask me where I been?" I could tell by her attitude that she was prepared for a confrontation.

"No," I stated as calmly as I could.

"Hello," Jose answered.

I said, "How's the weather up there?"

"No nieve," he replied. And that was it. He hung up.

Lady stormed over to where I was standing. "I think you should leave my m..."

I slapped her across her face with the phone. She fell back onto the bed. She was holding her jaw, gazing up at me with a stunned look on her face as I approached her.

"You wanna keep fuckin' wit' me, bitch?!" I grabbed at her legs, but she kicked me away. "C'mere you fuckin' slut." I clutched her ankle, then pulled her onto the floor. Her head hit the carpet with a dull thud.

"Ouch! Oww!" she cried.

I picked her up off the floor. While ducking her wild punches, I took a few of them, but managed to seize her throat and push her up against the wall. Since I wasn't a fan of rearranging the face of the woman I slept with, I shot a blow to her stomach.

"Ooh!" she groaned as she balled over in pain. Suddenly she collapsed on the floor. When I looked down my heart skipped a beat. Blood soaked the crotch of her pants.

"Lady, you aight?" I asked. My attitude did a 360. "Lady?" I kneeled down next to her.

Lady shook her head no as her eyes looked out into space. "I think I'm having a miscarriage."

"Huh?" I peered over in the doorway and saw Junior staring at me. He had tears in his eyes.

I don't know how many hours we spent at the hospital, but we didn't get back home until after midnight. Lady turned out to have been six weeks pregnant. It was her little secret because she never told me.

We had a hell of a time getting the doctors to believe that she'd tripped and fallen down the stairs. But they had no other choice but to accept it. We stuck to our lie.

The hardest part was me having to explain to Junior why I hit his mother. Wasn't no use in lying to him. I said that Mama had it coming. I was worried sick when she was M.I.A. and Daddy had to punish her for that. And the same would go for him if he ever just up and disappeared for too long. Still I apologized to him, though I felt no remorse. I was just happy that she didn't die on me.

Lady lay in the bed without speaking to me. She could rest for the moment, but soon she would have to produce some kind of excuse for where she had been. I was still in love with her, but I was also still a man.

CHAPTER EIGHT

After all the drama I went through with Lady, I needed a drink to unwind. So I went and picked Katrina up and took her to the casino. She was looking good for her to have gotten ready at the spur of the moment.

She sat next to me at the bar with her legs crossed, facing me. Her blond locks hung down past her shoulders. Her full lips shone under what looked like seven coats of lip gloss. I lit up a cigarette and smiled at her. She smiled back.

"So how do you like being black?"

After a long sip from her drink, she replied, "I like it. It's been very interesting so far."

I shook my head in disapproval. "See, you got it fucked up already. You don't say, 'It's been very interesting.' You say, I can dig it, baby. Or, I'm wit' it. Ya know?"

Another sip from her glass. "Okay, I got it. Ask me something else?" She seemed to be excited about her lessons.

"So how you doin'?"

"I'm okay, I guess. No!" She covered her eyes. "That's not right." She took another drink. "I would say, I'm good. Chillin'. Wha's been up with you, homie?" She stuck her tongue out her mouth and laughed. "That sounded cool, right? Right? I know it did, man. 'Cause I am the shiznit. I keep it one-hundred, on the rizneal. Niggas ask me how I do dat dere." She giggled.

I glanced around the room. "Girly, you better hold it down with that nigga shit. You'll be done gotten yo' ass kicked and mine."

She looked embarrassed. "Ooh, I feel you on that. My bad. A bitch was slippin'. I'm on point now."

"You on point now?"

"Yeahh," she said in a cool voice. She approached me and placed her lips up against mine. "I'm on point because you're lacin' me, baby."

I smiled. "You're being laced, but you won't be ready till you're laced and tied."

That one drink appeared to have gotten her tipsy. She grabbed my ass as she gazed up at me. "Sprinkle me den, nucca. That's what I'ma say. Nucca. Instead of you know. That way won't nobody be knowing my business an' shit."

There was this Mexican cutie across the bar who had been peeping my game ever since we walked through the door. She was with five of her home girls. They were all drinking, laughing and having a good time.

Katrina kissed me one more time. "Mm. I'ma swallow that dick up tonight." She giggled. "I gotta go pee pee...ho-mie." She picked up her purse and walked out the room, talking to herself using black slanguage on her way out.

The Mexican cutie was still on me. So I motioned for her to come over. She stood, adjusted her skirt, grabbed her drink, then headed my way. It took a refill of her drink and about three minutes worth of game for me to hook her. I had literally forgotten that I was there with Katrina.

"Excuse me!"

I peered up through glassy red eyes and saw Katrina. Her eyes were narrow and one hand was pressed firm against her hip. The Mexican chick, whose name was Liza, was standing between my legs with her hands on my shoulders. One of my hands was around her waist. The other held my drink.

"Bbbaby," I stuttered.

"Don't baby me," she yelled as she threw down her purse. "I can't even go to the bathroom without you disrespecting me behind my back. Especially with a fucking wet-back bitch."

Liza turned around and straightened her 5'2" frame, minus the five inch heels that she had on. "I'm Chicano. Okay? So don't be confusing me with no goddamn wet-back."

Katrina gazed down at the smaller woman as if she was a child. "I really don't care what you is, but you had better get the hell outta my face, and away from him…" The Mexican girl reached up and slapped Katrina across the face before she could finish her sentence. Katrina held her cheek where she had been hit. Then she drew back and hit the girl with a closed fist. Liza fell back onto my lap. I pushed her off me, back toward Katrina, who clutched her hair and slung her into the bar.

I closed my eyes and took a drink. By the time I opened them back up, the four other Mexican girls ran around the bar and was hitting on my baby.

First, I grabbed one by the hair and pushed her away. Then I mauled the one who had her by the arm. One of them came at me swinging. I caught her little fists with one hand, then slapped her face with my other.

That done it.

Security, who just happened to be Hispanic as well, popped up and started working me over. One threw me down while the others kicked at my back and sides.

"You like hitting señoritas?" one shouted.

"Man, I…"

"Shut up! Why would you hit a lady?"

"I'm trying to…"

"Shut-the-fuck-up! I'm not gonna repeat it a third time."

Finally I gave up and waited until the negro was asked to speak again.

Thanks to the bartender, who explained to the police that it was not our fault, they released me and Katrina, after informing us that we were not to step foot back inside the place for at least a week.

Fine by us.

On the way out to the car, Katrina was acting all excited. She would stop, hold up her little fists and start jabbing at the air.

"We beat the crap outta those dip eatin' ass bitches, baby." She punched at the air. "Bam! Bam! Bam! I can't believe it, my first bar fight." She ran and jumped into my arms. "We kicked some ass to-night, baby."

I kissed her. "You did good."

"I know." She gazed at me. "Who's your bitch?"

"What?"

"C'mon, tell me? Who's your bitch?"

"You are."

She laughed with glee. "You better say I am."

CHAPTER NINE

That night I slept on the couch. I didn't get much sleep because my phone was blowing up. Wasn't no need in answering it because I still hadn't heard from Jose. But I had to pay my bills, so it was time to get grimey.

I called my man Jeff down in Houston.

"Yeah," he answered. "What up, Q?"

"Is it poppin' down there or what?"

He sighed. "Well, the weatherman said there's a chance of light snow."

I rubbed my naked chin. "How light?"

"Mm? Seven to ten inches."

"And the temperature?"

"Mm? 'Bout 15 degrees."

"I'll be down tonight," I assured him.

"Aight. I'ma hang in today and watch channel 27." That was code talk for "I'll be at Days Inn in room 27."

"Holla."

Then I called my dad. He would have his broad get me a couple of rental cars. Pops was cool like that. Ever since my Cuban whore of a mother ran out on us, it's just been him, my brother and me.

My final call was to O'ban.

"'Sup, lil' bro?" he answered.

I stalled by sucking my teeth. "Eh. I need you to call up Ill Will and place an order for me."

"On how much?"

"About a quarter million."

"Damn. For what?"

"Jose's still dry and I'm getting thirsty. So cut all that bull-shit out, 'cause I can hear it in your voice. Get back with me today." I hung up.

After I took a shower, I fed my son and played the PlayStation2 with him. Then O'ban called back telling me that everything was set up.

I unlocked the small safe behind the downstairs bathroom mirror. It was supposed to be $175,000 inside. But for some strange reason there was only $155,000. Either I thought I had more bricks than I had or Lady was stealing from me. Drunk as I used to be, I might've thought I sold 8½ bricks but only sold 7½.

Anyway, I bagged $125,000 of the money up and stepped out on my front porch. My hoodfellas were out on both corners pumping the block. Fast-ass girls were pacing the block like the rollers. I saw lil' TT leading the pack. Her lil' fine ass couldn't have been no more than 15, but you could tell in another year or so she would be knocking 'em dead. A straight A student, but for some reason she loved to hang out on the corner amongst the thugs.

The cops crept up on the block eyeballing me. They wanted to find any excuse to run up in my crib. Never. I kept no drug dealer company. I even wore my restaurant uniform to let them know I had a job.

They chased me as a corner hustler. Tried to set up stings when I was selling weight. Now it was too late. I had made it to be one of the big men. That's why I built my house on the block, to throw their failures and my success up in their faces.

I felt like Hoover himself. I had taken lives, produced babies, and I had the one thing that made the world go 'round—money.

Two brand new Mustangs pulled up in front of my crib. I ran back inside, grabbed my vest, Glock and the bag. Pop was driving one car, O'ban the other. I waved at him just before I jumped in with Pop.

"'Sup, old man?"

"Youngsta." He was pulling on half of a Benson & Hedges menthol. He pulled off. The Gap Band was playing out the stereo.

Bzzzst. Bzzzst.

"Wha' sup?"

"Where're you off to?" It was Lady.

"I'm going to Texas to holla at Jeff."

"When you coming back?"

"In the morning."

"Be careful." It's amazing how young couples break up and make up so quick. She hung up.

Bzzzst. Bzzzst.

"Wha's really?"

"You straight?" It was Terry.

"Not yet, but I'm headed to H-Town as we speak. I'll be back tomorrow." What was I thinking? I had just done a no-no. You never let anybody know when you're leaving or coming from buying some blow. They could either plot to rob you or set you up to get busted.

Terry said, "Hit me tomorrow."

It took us about 20 minutes to get to Ill Will's crib over in Kansas. Two brand new trucks and a BMW were parked in front of his run-down old house.

Two rough looking dudes were standing out front. O'ban got out and walked up to our car. I handed him the bag through the window.

"If you ain't back in eight minutes, I'm coming in," I stated.

Six minutes later he returned carrying the bag. I checked it, then locked it inside the trunk and we were off. We took Highway 35 South. Pop turned on his driving music. I took out my phone and started calling hoes. Katrina was up first.

It was half past eight when we reached the city limits. Pop cut the A/C on high because down there the temperature was up by 10 degrees.

Before we hit the rendezvous, we stopped at a diner and got a bite to eat. After we ate, I had a drink to calm my nerves. This would be my second time hitting a lick on a Texan with counterfeit money. I wasn't sure if word had gotten around about me beating niggas. For all I knew, it could've been a set-up. In the past I had put my life on the line for much less, so fuck it. I did it again.

We left the diner and drove to the motel. Before I went in, I strapped on my vest and tucked my Glock. O'ban did the same. Pop parked around back with the car running.

O'ban and I found the room. I knocked twice with my left hand while my right remained on my gun.

"Who is it?" a voice yelled from behind the door.

"Qu'ban."

"Hold up." Ten seconds later he answered the door wearing a robe. He regarded me curiously when he saw the bulge from my vest. "Everything aight?"

I peeped around him and saw a fine older woman standing in front of the TV. Jeff was older too, only 38 and already bald. But still he was a real suave dude.

"Yeah," I responded. "You know how it is."

Jeff stepped back to let us in. "I know, but it shouldn't be like that between me and you, Q."

The room smelled like lotion, cologne, weed and cognac. His girl excused herself to the bathroom while we took care of business. Jeff clapped his hands together.

O'ban dumped $225,000 worth of counterfeit money on the bed. I kept the other $25,000 to blow at the strip joint. Jeff scanned the money, then opened the closet door. He removed a black bag, then emptied its contents onto the bed. Then he removed another bag and did the same. Fifteen bricks of tight white stared us in the face. At least I hoped it was good. I was scamming Jeff because the last time we did business he scammed me by selling me some bunk dope. Shit had me up for weeks trying to dump it. It was repercussion time.

"What y'all getting into tonight?" Jeff asked.

"Heading back to the city," I lied. If at some point that night he found out I had burned him, he would've definitely come looking for me.

"I heard that," Jeff said as he loaded the money back into the bags. "Y'all cool?"

"We're straight." I handed one of the bags to O'ban, then shook Jeff's hand. "I'll be getting back to you."

"Do that, player." He followed me to the door. "Sorry about what happened last time. That shit was fucked up, but that's how I got it. Ya know?"

"It's all good. I'll get back at you." I left without another word.

That night we kicked it at a strip club. Lil' Flip and some other stars were up in there kicking it, too. I gave O'ban and Pop $7,500 apiece to throw around. Me and Pop ended up going in half on three freaks. We hit them all with a grand like they were high class hoes. They really thought they were amongst super stars. I was lying. One minute I was a rapper, than an actor, a producer, etc. Those country-ass hoes were eating it up.

I wasn't sure but I think the white girl that left the club with me had me snorting cocaine. Fuck it. I was living for today, and the future was a mile away.

The next morning I was throwing up and shitting every 20 minutes. Pops' gray chest ass was still asleep with two hoes in the bed with him. O'ban was sleep on the floor with two. And my white chick was asleep on the couch where I'd left her. Texas had been kind to us.

I cleaned myself up, then called my family and told them that I would be leaving soon. Terry had left me a message. I texted him back saying that I was on my way back home.

After I woke Pop and O'ban, we put the hoes out. I sat for a moment and smoked, like I always did before I hit the highway riding dirty, while they got ready.

As I was doing so, I started wondering about Terry and his case. Why had I informed him about what I was doing? Stupid. I couldn't trust him with that kind of information while he had a case pending.

The feds were probably on to me already, I thought. They could've been at the strip joint I'd kicked it in. One of the hoes, or the dude in the loud orange suit that sat next to me at the bar. Or…I had become too paranoid. I had to put the weed down before I ended up leaving without the dope.

Pop asked, "You ready?"

"Yeah. But we gotta stop by the rental car place first."

"Why?"

"Because I gotta bad feeling."

~ ~ ~ ~ ~

Jeff was up early. He and his girl had spent almost an hour in the shower going at it. After they climbed their wrinkled bodies out of the tub, they both collapsed onto the bed.

Breathing heavily, Jeff told his girl Sandra to get some money out of the bag to go re-rent the room, and then go grab some breakfast. She did as she was told. An hour later she called Jeff, saying that she had been arrested at the gas station for trying to buy gas with a counterfeit $100 bill.

Jeff dropped the phone and snatched open the bag. After a careful inspection he finally found the flaw. All the bills had the same serial number on them.

"I'ma kill that nigga!" he shouted as he threw a stack of bills at the TV. "Scandalous-ass nigga!"

~ ~ ~ ~ ~

Hours later I was behind the wheel of the Mustang and O'ban was following. We communicated through our Nextel walkie-talkies.

I said, "Bro, you aight?"

"I'ont know. I gotta Camaro on my tail that has been following me ever since we left Texas."

"Let's see if we can shake 'em."

I waited for an opening in the left lane, then I hit it. I bounced back and forth from the left to the right lane, weaving past cars. O'ban followed. The Mustang really handled well. I thought about purchasing one.

To my right I saw flashing lights ahead. The state troopers had a van pulled over. Four Mexican men were standing with their hands on the hood of the police car. I slowed down until I was at least a mile ahead.

"Bro, talk to me," I said. "Where's the Camaro?"

"Behind me. Now there's two of 'em."

"What?"

All of a sudden I saw flashing red lights. I looked in my rearview mirror and saw that they were coming from behind O'ban.

O'ban said, "They're pulling me over." One of the cars pulled along side of him.

"Shit!" I knew it. Terry had dropped a dime on me. Jeff was also a suspect.

"What should I do?" O'ban asked. "Want to hit it?"

I didn't respond because I had spotted two Camaros in front of me, driving at a slow pace, holding up both lanes. Their lights were flashing as well.

"Bro?" O'ban asked.

"Pull over," I said. "What else can we do?"

The four Camaros led us off the next exit and had us blocked in when we pulled over. Eight white guys jumped out, guns drawn, yelling, "Shut off the engines! Now!"

I obliged. I assumed that O'ban did, too. They rushed our cars, snatched us out of our seats, then sat us down on the hot concrete.

"Qu'ban Cartez?" one of them called. "Would that be you?"

"Yes, sir," I replied with respect for the older gentleman who wore sergeant stripes on his shoulders.

He stood me up, shoved me against my car, then searched my person. He found nothing. They did the same to O'ban, once again coming up empty handed.

The sergeant asked, "Y'all mind if I search your vehicles?"

"Why? We didn't do shit."

He sighed briefly, looked around, stared in my eyes, and then said, "Son, I'm gonna be straight with you boys. We were instructed by the FBI to stop and search every blue late model Ford Mustang that came up or down this highway until we found one Qu'ban Cartez. Then I'm supposed to detain you while the feds come have a word with ya." He paused to spit. "Now until they get here, we're gonna search these vehicles for any drugs or weapons." He spat again. "Now do you have a problem with that?"

"No, sir."

"Thank you." He peered at his men. "Boys."

O'ban and I were both cuffed and seated on the curb while they searched our cars. One time I peered up and saw the seats and door panels being taken out.

"You called money," O'ban whispered to me.

Finally two FBI agents showed up on the scene. They introduced themselves as Special Agents Trilogy and Dixon.

"Where's your dad?" the older of the two agents asked.

"We dropped him off in Houston. That's why we drove down here," I answered.

"You two needed separate cars for that?"

I shrugged. "We both wanted to drive," I retorted.

"Unh huh." They walked away.

"It wasn't Jeff that told," I whispered to O'ban.

"How you know?"

"Because Jeff didn't know about Pop coming with us."

After three hours of searching, questioning and harassing, we were released. If Jeff would've told they would've had a case and never released us. No question, it was Terry. Mutha fucka tried to do me in for a time reduction.

Back on the highway, I told O'ban to stay off the air until we reached Missouri. Pop had rented another car before we left Houston and was traveling alone with the package.

I called him, then hung up. Then he texted back saying that he was okay.

CHAPTER TEN

That night when I got home I was tense as hell. O'ban headed home. I instructed Pop to hold on to the package until the next morning. Inside the comfort of my own castle, I couldn't get comfortable. I had to release some pressure.

When I entered my bedroom Lady greeted me with a warm hug. "Baby, you alright? I've been calling you all night. Did something go wrong? Did…"

"Calm down. Everything's cool. I didn't call because I didn't wanna use my cell phone while I was driving."

Though I was exhausted from the drive, and the orgy we had the night before, I needed to relieve some tension. Those feds scared the shit outta me, and I needed to calm down. I kissed Lady's lips passionately.

"I can't, Q. You know I'm still sore and bleeding."

"So what. I'll be gentle."

"You want me to bleed all over your dick?"

I produced a condom from my pocket. She offered little resistance when I pulled off her top. She kicked off her bottom, then removed the pad that the doctors had placed over her womb. It was caked with blood. She left briefly to go wipe it clean. When she returned she sat on the edge of the dresser.

"Be gentle, baby."

She reached inside my sweats and pulled out my stiff rod. Gently she placed it at the opening of her pussy. Lady kept her hand on it as I slid in. Then her hands slid down to my hips, just in case I got too rough, so she could hold me back.

"Uuh. Don't dig too deep. I'm scared."

"Don't be. Just relax."

I picked her up, palming her ass, while gently guiding her up and down my shaft. Damn her pussy felt good. No matter how many times I had beat it up, it always seemed to retract itself. My dick started to feel real sticky from all the blood.

"Try it in my ass," she mumbled.

Lady got down on the bed on all fours. I used a little saliva to lubricate her ass, then I guided myself inside her.

"That…feels…ooh…betterrr," she howled.

When I went in too deep, she grunted and tried to escape my wrath. I clutched her shoulders and placed one foot up on the bed, then started hunching her like a dog.

"Ooh. Ooh. Ooh. Ahhh," I didn't know if those grunts came from my mouth or hers.

Minutes later I released a hot load of cum somewhere deep inside her. My body quivered as she lay down on her side. I felt relieved and I could tell by her face that she was glad that it was over.

"I love you," she murmured. "I'll always have your back, Qu'ban."

"I hope so."

Lady wrapped her leg around mine. "You have to be careful."

I thought about her last words for a moment until fatigue got the best of me, and then I drifted to sleep. Heart to heart, my hand on her butt check, her leg wrapped around mine was how we lay.

At about 2:00 that morning I awoke from a nightmare. Though I hadn't slept long, I felt relaxed. I slipped out from under Lady, leaving her resting on her face. Then I stepped in the shower and prayed to God, thanking Him for sparing my life that day.

After I slipped into a pair of sweats, a wife beater, a pair of white and gray Air Forces and my new chain, I picked up my keys and Glock and hit the door. A quick wipe down of my Cutlass and I was off.

Vroom! Vroom!

I stopped at the corner and dropped the top. Then picked up my hat from off the seat and placed in on my head. The little homies were still out corner hustling. Lil' TT was right out there with 'em, probably holding their straps. She spotted me and smiled. I waved her over.

"Hey, Q," she said with her bright smile.

"Girl, what're you doing out here?"

Lil' TT shrugged. "Hanging with the homies, marinating, chillin' like a villain. Wha' sup with you, Q?"

I pulled the knot out of my pocket and gave her a $50 bill from off the top. "That's for them A's you got last semester."

She smiled. "Thank you, Q."

"Okay. Now you get yo' lil' white ass off this corner and go home. If some niggas come through here shooting, I'd hate for you to get hurt. Ya hear me?"

"Yes. I will. Bye."

I nodded. Out of my CD case I chose C-Bo's "*Enemy of State.*" When he started rapping I cut the beat up. *Whoom! Whoom!*

The streets were crowded with people when I turned on Prospect. Everybody and their mama was out. They were my people. Some hated me, some hollered when they saw me.

I was cruising down the avenue sitting low in my Cutlass. Fifteen inch subwoofers were slapping, my Daytons were spinning, windows rolled up, A/C on and my Glock was tucked under my leg.

On 70th Street I turned into Good-to-Go and parked sideways, taking up two parking spaces. I was in my territory so I left my beat pumping and my duals growling while I went into the store.

There was a group of young females standing at the counter. One was holding a case of beer in her hand. They all smiled at me.

"Ladies," I said.

"Hey, Q," they all sang.

The chocolate one with the short haircut asked, "So when you gon' get with a real woman?"

"I got one at home," I replied, "who sleeps with me every night."

She seemed to find that amusing. "Not every night," she replied. Then she and her friends sashayed away.

"What will it be?" the clerk asked.

"A bottle of Rémy XO, a cup of ice and a pack of cigarillos." The bill came to over $200. I paid and went about my business.

A blue '93 Cadillac Fleetwood on 20 inch chrome Daytons was parked next to my car when I walked out. The heavy set driver had a white towel draped around his fat neck. He stepped out, smiling at me.

He said, "You got it like that where you can leave your car

running while you up in the sto'?" He gave me dap. "Wha' sup?"

"Shit. Wha' sup, Corn?"

"Out here scouting some fresh game," Corn replied. Three girls walked between us, headed toward the store. "What can a fat boy get for two dollars?"

Lil' mama that turned around was light skinned and petite as a muther fucka. "Honey, you couldn't even suck my toes for two funky-ass dollars." Her girls giggled.

One was light brown with a ghetto gold-toothed grill. She just had to offer her two cents.

"Yeah, nigga," she said. "Don't tell me y'all riding that clean and really ain't got it."

Whoom! Whoom…Whoom! Whoom!

Skatter's Excursion sped into the lot beating E-40's "*Ghetto Celebrity*." I ended up cracking my bottle and pouring the three girls a few drinks. Everybody was having a good time. For a moment it was like I wasn't even there. That's when I thought, this is how shit would continue to go down if I got killed or locked down. Nothing would change. Life would go on. The world would keep right on turning. As big as I thought I was, I was really only what was happening for the moment.

To my right two bubble Caprices on rims and a blue Suburban entered the lot. The occupants were all blued up. A young dude on the passenger side of the Suburban was bobbing his head to the music while brandishing a Mac-11.

Corn was a Crip too, but he was cool with us, so he had a pass. He too had seen them drive up. Skatter was inside a circle of people rapping, while Jawan played hype man. The Crip dudes joined the circle. I made my way over as well.

"My weed supply plenty, so hit me if you want mo'. Gotta

mini one-fo', fo' any nigga that want mo'. The sucka said he was a rida, but - he kept a low pro'. But every time we had some problems, Bud-dy was a no show."

While Skatter was rapping, one of the Crips took off his shirt and licked his lips. Skatter saw the challenge and gave dude the floor.

Dude began. "See I'm mockin' the opposition, dropping all competition. You slobs come in flocks, so I got boxes of ammunition. I minor in knockin' bitches, and major in getting riches. And the slobs that get caught hatin', get buried six feet in ditches."

The crowd was hype.

Skatter hit my bottle, then attacked him.

"I'a pop me a nigga, for the doe ray me. But nigga don't hate me 'cause I'm all about the cash, smoke dancing out my Mac when I blast. Hit a lick, don't even trip about wearing a mask. Crips be claiming savs, but most of dem niggas is fags. Nigga, I'll have you and you, and you, bitch, lying dead in a cas'."

"You hear that nigga, cuz?" a short Crip with long braids hollered. "We oughta buck on these broke-ass niggas."

I pulled my knot from my pocket. "Broke?" I asked. "I got about three g's here." I flung it in the air. "Can any of you niggas do that?"

People started snatching money as it fell from the sky.

Skatter pulled out his gun. "You crab-ass niggas better get somewhere where they love y'all at."

Light skinned said, "C'mon, y'all, see. We was out here...out here." She was too drunk to speak clearly. "Kicking...it. Now y'all wanna kill each other."

"You and yo' friends need to get in my car where it's safe,"

Corn said. He was trying to use that opportunity to get some pussy.

The Crip dudes retreated for the moment. I grabbed my gun off my seat and tucked it.

Skatter asked, "What you about to do, Q?"

"Yeah, what you about to do?" Light skin's friend asked.

"Probably 'bout to…"

Tat tat tat tat tat tat.

When the gunfire rang out, I ducked, ran and dove into my car. I slammed it in reverse, then backed all the way onto Prospect. *Errrrk!* Then accidentally slammed it in neutral. *Vroom!* Damn! I found drive. *Errrrk!* I fired three shots in the air as I pulled away. Skatter fired a few shots as well as he fled in the opposite direction.

On 67th Street I made a quick left and stopped. Seconds later Corn pulled up beside me and let down his window. The three girls from the store were in his car with him.

"What you gon' do?" Corn asked.

Bzzzst. Bzzzst.

I looked at my phone. It was Katrina. "Probably 'bout to head in," I replied. I answered the call, but was still talking to Corn.

"Ah, party pooper," Light skinned complained. "Let's go, Corn. He ain't trying to do nothing."

"I'll catch you," Corn said just before he pulled off.

"Hello," I spoke into the phone.

"You stay around some bitches…don't you?"

My knees guided the steering wheel while I put R-Kelly's "*TP-2.com*" into the deck. "*I Don't Mean It*" was my song selection. After the song came on, I turned it down low so I could still hear Katrina talking.

Katrina said, "You're listening to the wrong song, aren't you?"

"Why you say that?"

"Because, you mean to do all the bad things you do, Qu'ban."

"You like it though."

"I don't mind being put in my place, sometime. But you can go overboard." I laughed. "It is not funny. You need to come over here and stay the night and fuck me to sleep. Can you do that?"

"I might. What you got on?"

"Virgina," she replied. "You like that?"

"Depends on how wet it gets."

"Hold on." Katrina placed the phone between her thighs while she fingered her crevice. The swooshing sounds it made turned me on. "Did you hear it?"

"Um hm. I'll be over in a minute."

"Don't wait until it dries up, baby."

"Bye, girl." I hung up.

For the time being, I felt the need to be alone and just ride and gather my thoughts.

While I was cruising, my mind started shuffling through old memories. About a year earlier I had met this young, petite white girl while out in Westport. She had gotten drunk. I took her to a motel room somewhere down I-70, where I fucked the dog shit out of her. Baby had the warmest pussy that I had ever been in. The next morning I took all her money and threatened to leave her stranded if she didn't let me pee inside her mouth. I was an ornery little fucker back then.

After about 20 minutes of hearing her pleas and cries, she finally agreed to let me pee inside her pussy. I did it, and left her there anyway. She wasn't even from the city. She and some friends had driven from Springfield, Missouri, to kick it in KC. 'Til this day I don't believe I would've done such a harsh thing if I wasn't high on P.C.P.

Another blunt, a half a pint and a trip around the city later, and I found myself pulling into Katrina's driveway.

CHAPTER ELEVEN

Jeff arrived in the city that same morning. Little did Qu'ban know, Jeff had him checked out from day one. He had connections inside the county sheriff's department in Texas, who had connections to the department in KC. So when Jeff saw the sign that read, "You are now entering Kansas City," he already knew where he was going. Because he knew the exact location in which Qu'ban laid his head.

~ ~ ~ ~ ~

I woke the next morning in Katrina's bed. Donell Jones' "*Love*" was crooning through the speakers that sat on a shelf on her bedroom wall. After a slow yawn, I rolled over and planted my nose in the empty space next to me and inhaled. Mmm. There was not a sweeter smell than that of a white woman after sex. The night before, I went down on her. Sucking her pussy was like drinking fresh bath water. I felt purified afterward.

I sat up and examined her room. The pictures of Kid Rock, Shania Twain and her collection of country CDs had been replaced by a hip hop collection. Jay-Z, Omarion, and posters of R & B artists had taken their place. She was really trying to be a sister.

The door opened and in walked Katrina. She was naked. Her pink-nipple jugs danced with each step. "Hi," she said, then jumped onto the bed on top of me. She smiled, then planted a kiss on my lips.

"I've been thinking," she said.

"About what?"

"You. Me…us."

I let my hands travel down her smooth back to her ass. "What about us?"

Her gray-eyed gaze pierced my soul. "I love you."

A brief hesitation. "I love you, too," I replied with a bit more honesty than I wanted to admit to myself.

"Good," she said with a smile. "So you won't be angry when I tell you that I'm pregnant." She shouted. "Oooh! Yes!"

I was temporarily stunned. Never had I imagined having a white girl for a baby mama. Mixed babies are handsome. But what about Lady? She was gonna kill me. Right then I figured that my best bet was to keep this baby thing a forever secret from Lady and Junior.

Katrina's smile faded. "You're angry at me?"

"Nah, nah. I ain't mad. But…uh…what do you think your parents are gonna say? Hmm. A black grandbaby would fuck their whole world up."

Katrina looked out into space and sighed. "I don't know. But I'm having this baby. I don't care what anybody says."

"Congratulations then, Ms. Miller."

Katrina leaned toward me and stuck her tongue down my throat. While we kissed she reached under her and removed the covers from my naked body. Her hand clutched my dick and inserted it into her wet, hot crevice. Slowly she rocked back and forth, gliding herself up and down my pole.

"Ssss. Ahh," she moaned. "Ooooh!"

There was a knock on the door.

Katrina jumped right off my dick, dashed over to the door and grabbed her robe. "Oh, my god."

"Who is that?"

"Shh." Katrina threw on her robe, then whisked out of the room.

It was time for me to make an exit as well. I had spent enough quality time. Business was calling. My phone vibrated in my sweats as I was pulling them on. I answered it.

"Hello."

"Your brother has been trying to get in touch with you all morning." It was Nah Nah. "Hold on." I could hear her passing the phone to him.

A second later O'ban came on the line. "Sup, bro? Fuck you been at all morning?"

"I'm over Katrina's. I'm headed over to Pops' to get that shit after I leave here."

"Pops is at yo' house. Lady called him this morning and told him that you said to bring the shit over."

"Lady did that?" I was confused.

"You didn't know?"

I hesitated. Couldn't let this nigga know that I didn't have control over my bitch. So I lied. "Yeah. I must've forgot. I was fucked up last night. I'll just see you at my house."

"Aight."

"Yeah." I hung up.

Stuck up voices echoed throughout the house as I walked out of the bedroom. As I neared the front room their voices became clear. They were having a conversation about black women, and how lazy they are. A topic given to them based on something that they'd heard Bill Cosby say. When I stepped into the room all conversation ceased.

Katrina's father, I presumed, was tall, blond and blue-eyed with sharp, handsome features. He regarded me with a cold stare from the sofa that he rested on. The woman immaculately dressed in a business suit sitting next to him looked at me like I was a ghost. A clear sign of disapproval. With the exception of her platinum-colored hair, she looked like a 40-year-old version of Katrina.

Katrina sat in a chair across from them with her head tilted forward and her left hand over her face. She hoped I would've remained in bed until they left.

"You'd better be the maintenance man," the woman said in a serious tone.

I was instantly offended. But I didn't want no trouble with these people. "I'll see you later, Katrina."

The woman jumped up. "What's going on, Katrina?"

Katrina took a deep breath, then slowly raised her head. Finally she stood and walked over until she was standing beside me.

"Mom...Dad," she said in a slow voice, "this is my boyfriend, Qu'ban."

Her mother cried out, "Boyfriend?"

"Yes," Katrina said with a bit more firmness. "These are my parents, Michael and Kathy Miller."

I offered Mr. Miller my hand. He stood to his full height of about six-two. "I'm not going to shake that thing, punk. You get the hell out of my house."

My anger got the best of me. "Fuck you!"

"Qu'ban!" Katrina yelled. "Just leave. I'll call you later."

Michael Miller's eyes narrowed on me. "What did you say

79

to me?"

With my lips pressed together tightly, I glared over her shoulder at the huge white man with the stone face.

"Please, Qu'ban," Katrina begged. "Just go."

Bzzst. Bzzst.

I leaned in and planted my lips against hers. Mrs. Miller closed her eyes. Our lips made a loud kissing noise when they parted. Then I placed my hand over her stomach.

"Don't let these people stress you out too bad," I said. "I wouldn't want to hurt our baby."

As I was walking out the door I heard the beginning of a heated argument between the three of them. Her mother said, "You just had to go messing around with one of those nasty people. You weren't satisfied until you went out and got pregnant with one of those little nigglets of your own, were…"

Her voice stopped abruptly when I walked back inside.

~ ~ ~ ~ ~

Lady was angry that morning and agitated. She had been calling Qu'ban all night without an answer. Usually he called the next morning and checked on his home. Lady knew that he had to get there soon or everything would be ruined.

She dressed Qu'ban Junior in a hurry. Then asked Pops to take Junior to get some breakfast. Her reason was she didn't want her son around when Qu'ban began bagging up the drugs that Pops had brought over.

Lady lit a cigarette and peeped out the front window. She didn't see anyone. She crept over to the bags that sat in the cupboard. She took out three keys of dope, and then took them out to her truck. Carefully she placed them under the back seat, and then pulled her truck out of the driveway and onto the street where it would be safe. With that out of the way, she got out and activated her alarm.

When she reached the front of the house, she realized that the front door was open. Maybe she'd left it open, but she certainly didn't remember doing so.

She stepped inside, closed the door, and then was struck by a hard blow. Woozy, her body slid to the floor. Through teary eyes she looked up and saw a tall, baldheaded man with a gun in his hand glaring down at her. He was saying something, but her ears were ringing too loud to hear.

~ ~ ~ ~ ~

I stepped back inside the front door. Mrs. Miller didn't flinch. There was so much hatred built inside her that she could've exploded right there in the living room.

"Bitch, if I hear that nigga word come out of your mutha…"

Michael Miller attacked me. He pushed me toward the glass end table. As I was going down I drew my gun and fired a single shot.

Pow!

The loud, deafening sound echoed throughout the room. Both women screamed loudly. I picked myself back up. Michael was cowering behind the sofa. A big hole was in the wall less than a foot from his head.

Without hesitation I stuffed my gun into my pocket and dashed outside to my Cutty. The tires squealed as I bolted away. Three miles later I felt my phone vibrate. I took a moment to catch my breath, and then answered it.

It was Lady. "Where are you?" she asked. I mistook the tremble in her voice for anger rather than the fear it really was.

"Lady, why the fuck did yo' ass…"

"Qu'ban, listen. You need to come home now."

"I'm already en route."

"Just come home." I didn't speak. Something was wrong, I could feel it. "Somebody stole Junior's Big Wheel."

"What the hell you…" It took me a second, but I caught it. Big Wheel. A code word that we used to alert each other if we were ever in trouble. "I'll be there in a minute. I love you." I hung up and hit the gas, opening up the exhaust on that bitch.

Lady hung up the phone. Jeff stood behind her with a knowing look on his face. "Somebody stole Junior's Big Wheel, huh?" he asked. "That was a good one." He smacked on a piece of gum.

Lady walked away from him and stood in front of the front window. It wouldn't be long from now. The police would be there any minute, kicking down the door, in search of Qu'ban. Instead they'd find Jeff. Which would work out even better. She'd tell them that Jeff was the connect, and hopefully be able to avoid getting Qu'ban in any major trouble.

Jeff looked into the bags at the dope that he made Lady give him. Three keys were missing. A minor loss compared to what he would've lost if he had never come there.

He cut his eyes at the back of Lady's head as he pointed his gun toward her back. "You and I both know damned well that Qu'ban Junior is too big to ride a goddamn Big Wheel." He smacked his gum loudly. "Ain't that right?"

A tear escaped Lady's left eye. She was nervous and couldn't think of a good, convincing response. She closed her eyes tightly.

Pow!

First she heard the blast. But she didn't know that she'd been shot until she felt her temperature rise about 20 degrees.

~ ~ ~ ~ ~

I was flying through the city trying to get home to rescue my family. I had my heater on me driving way over the speed limit. But my family's safety came before me. Nine times out of ten, whatever was going on at the house that had her scared was because of my thug activity.

~ ~ ~ ~ ~

Jeff crept out the back door of the house with the two duffle bags in hand. Quickly he jogged two backyards down, then came out in front of the house where he jumped into his rental car. The last thing he needed was to be seen coming from that house. He started the car and took off up the road.

Four federal agents were traveling at a high rate of speed as they headed north up the 10-block-long strip called Olive Street. They were en route to Qu'ban's house to serve a warrant for his arrest.

Four blocks from their destination, they pulled their masks down over their faces and armed themselves.

"One minute," their sergeant announced.

Lady was lying face down on the living room floor when she came to. It was hot inside the room. Very warm. Sweat was pouring from her head. She raised a hand out in front of her. Her hand clutched the carpet and she tried to move herself. She successfully managed to move an inch before the little energy that she had rushed out of her. Drowsy. Barely conscious. She had about given up because she knew that the authorities would be there any minute. But then she saw something that gave her willpower to make it out that front door.

~ ~ ~ ~ ~

I hit Olive without slowing down and almost swerved into a tree. I sped southbound to my block, then made that sharp right turn headed to my house. A light-colored Buick sedan was headed in my direction at a high rate of speed. My natural reflexes caused me to grab my steel. As the car was passing on my left I slowed to get a look at the face of the person driving.

Me and the driver stared at each other for about a half of a half a second. But it was enough. It took me a second, but I recognized that sucka-ass nigga's face anywhere.

Errrrk!

I heard his car come to a stop. He had gotten the drop on me. In my right side mirror I saw Big Jeff step out of his car with his gun drawn. He fired.

Pow! Pow!

Two bullets entered my passenger window as I whipped up into my driveway. *Pow! Pow!* He fired again as he ran toward my car. I followed the concrete path all the way around to the back of my house. Jeff was still coming. I leaned over and pushed the passenger door open as I stepped on the brake.

Jeff aimed his gun toward the passenger side of the car and quickly fired at the air, thinking that I'd jumped out. During that time I kicked open my door. He heard the old door jam squeal, but wasn't quick enough to react. I fired three times.

Boca. Boca. Boca.

Jeff screamed but didn't fall. Instead he ran back toward the front of the house. I followed. I caught him on the side of the house where I aimed toward his back. He was hurt and running at a slow pace.

I had him set in my sight and was too blind to see the armed task force that had guns aimed at us. By the time I squeezed the trigger I heard several blasts that came from a gun that I know I didn't shoot.

My legs crumbled beneath me as I hit the ground. Woozy and in shock, I heard footsteps come upon me. My gun was kicked out of my hand. I gazed up and a jolt of fear shot through my body when I realized what I was looking at.

It wasn't the smoking hole of the barrel of the gun that I was staring up at. It was the blaze of fire and smoke that busted out of my living room window. Slowly my eyes fluttered. I fought it for a second or two until I eventually fell unconscious.

~ ~ ~ ~ ~

O'ban arrived on the scene. After he recognized that it was the feds in his brother's yard, he spun the Mustang around and tried to speed away. Policemen apprehended him at the corner of the block.

While that was going on the feds stormed up on the porch. They found Lady on the porch face down in a puddle of blood with her hands stretched out over her head. She was unconscious, but she had a pulse.

CHAPTER TWELVE

When I came to I was in the hospital cuffed to the bed. Two officers were sitting on a bench across from me. I thought it was all a dream. But after I saw those two assholes sitting across from me, I wanted to scream.

I sat there for a moment trying to recapture everything that took place. It had only been a couple of hours but it seemed like a couple years had passed. I saw Jeff's face, then saw him running toward me. Me shooting at him. What I saw next brought tears to my eyes. Because I still had the belief that my entire family, including Pops, was still inside the house. The fire broke through the front window.

My head started moving from side to side. "My family," I mumbled. "What h…" I swallowed my spit, "…appened to my family?"

The two officers looked at each other briefly, then one exited the room.

"Where's my fuckin' family, man?" I whined. "This shit ain't funny." I pulled at the cuffs. "Talk to me. Say something. Hey! You ignorant mutha-fucka!"

The policeman entered the room with another police officer in tow. This one was wearing sergeant's stripes. He stood next to my bed gazing down at me.

"Yvonda Smith," he stated, referring to Lady, "was shot one time in her back." He paused. "She died on her way to the hospital."

"And my dad? My son?"

"They're both okay. Your dad and son have been here since we notified them." Then he left. Everybody left. Soon I was alone. Alone. With nothing but my thoughts, and guilty feelings about the way I had abused her.

Her face flashed in my head. Then I had a vision of us having sex; when she had Qu'ban Junior; the time I punched her in the stomach and made her have a miscarriage. Then I broke down crying, with no one around to comfort me.

For two weeks I laid up in that hospital room crying like a bitch with a broken heart. No visitors. No phone calls, no nothing, until I was finally transferred to the federal holding center in Leavenworth, Kansas.

Once I got there my lawyer came to visit me and informed me about my case. From what my lawyer had told me, after Terry got busted he agreed to cooperate and help the authorities out with an investigation that was about to be launched on me. He informed them that Lady had been stealing large quantities of drugs from me and selling them to him at wholesale. He agreed to set her up, knowing that she would roll over on me to save herself. Which she did. And to think I had been crying and blaming myself for her murder for two weeks, and she had been the cause of all my troubles.

Even though the inside of my house went up in flames, they still managed to find $32,000 in cash and two guns that were safely tucked inside the fireproof safe. And an additional $48,000 was found inside O'ban's home which was charged to my indictment.

He also informed me that with my cooperation I would only receive a five-year sentence, and O'ban would not face a conspiracy charge. He would only get charged with the firearm that he had on him at the time of arrest. Without my cooperation, we would both get twenty years for conspiracy to distribute cocaine.

Unfortunately for Jeff, his need for revenge had lured his country ass right into a drug conspiracy that he was about to unknowingly take the rap for. He was going down for murder anyway. Why not blame everything on him so I could walk out of the penitentiary still a young man in five years? Fuck'em.

What fucked me up was the fact that they only found twelve bricks of dope in Jeff's car. And there in Lady's Yukon, the missing three.

Even after death the bitch was trying to cheat me.

I made a statement to the feds that took a little more than an hour. I informed them that I had been employed by Jeffery Taylor for three years and that he brought the drugs that he had on him to my house for me. Who knows, maybe he knew that I was under investigation and was fearful that I'd snitch.

On the other hand, Jeff remained solid. He knew that it was his 3rd strike, and regardless of what he said, a life sentence would be mandatory. So he pleaded the 5th. He had nothing to say. If he had to spend the rest of his life hustling behind the walls of a federal prison, then so be it. He was from the old school, where snitching didn't exist.

Both Katrina and Nah Nah had come up to visit us. It was the first time that I had seen my brother in weeks, being that he was housed in a whole other building. We hugged each other in the visiting room. He was already up on everything that was going on with our case.

Katrina walked into the visiting room wearing a halter top and capri jeans, a Kangol cap on her head and Cartier shades. Only a private institution such as the one we were in would allow a visitor to come in dressed like that. It was at that moment that I regretted giving her as much game as I did. She took a seat and picked up the phone.

I gazed at her through the 2-inch thick glass window that separated us. Nah Nah walked in. Unlike her sister, she still possessed that innocent white girl look and was dressed in a respectable manner. It made me feel as if I'd chosen the wrong one.

"How you doing," I said into the phone.

"I'm fine," she replied without really looking at me. "I'm sorry to hear about your baby's mama, an shit." Her speech had changed.

"Yeah. I'm cool."

"So how much time you facing?"

"About five or so."

"Five years?" she spat. "You better tell on somebody."

I wanted to say, "I did."

Katrina smacked her lips. "Forgive me for sayin' that. Because that would be some sucka shit fa' real doe."

I shook my head, disgusted by her choice of words. "Why you talking like that?"

"Aw, shit. Here we go," she said as her head rolled from side to side. "Don't start that shit. Next ya gon' be talking about you don't eat pork." She held her fist up against the glass. "Wha' sup, Mo?"

"You think that's funny, you big head-ass bitch? Huh?" I glared at her. "Acting black don't mean acting stupid. Now you..."

"Who you calling stupid? Yeah, I'm stupid aight. Stupid for getting pregnant by yo' black ass." She hung up the phone and crossed her arms with her lips poked out.

I would've expected this shit from a black bitch, but not my pink toe. It all boiled down to every hoe reacted the same if you put them in the same situation.

"Pick up the phone."

Reluctantly, she did so. "What?"

"Look, girl. If you plan on having my seed, you're gonna have to conduct yourself in an appropriate manner out there. No giving up the pussy while you're pregnant."

"I'ma do me."

"And what is doing you?"

Katrina took off her glasses and showed me those piercing gray eyes. "What do sistas do after their men go to jail?"

I was pissed. "Aw, yeah. That's how we are now? You gon'..."

"Boy, shut up. I was just playing. I'm here. I'm waiting on you." She gazed at her watch. "I have to go. I love you."

The soft look she gave me seemed sincere. But I knew better. "Yeah. You too." I got up and asked to be taken back to my unit. When she didn't trip on me walking out on her, I knew it was over.

CHAPTER THIRTEEN

Eighteen months had passed. The judge sentenced O'ban to the five years that was promised to him. As for me, I received a fuckin' 12-year sentence, unlike I was promised. The additional seven years came after Katrina's funky-ass mother pressed charges against me for brandishing a weapon inside Katrina's home that day.

Qu'ban Junior was turned over to the custody of Pops by the state. Once a month they came up to visit me and O'ban in the joint. 'Til this day, I've never heard about him shedding a tear for Lady. And she was basically all he had, because I had never been much of a father to him. I guess he had his own way of mourning the loss of his mother.

Katrina had a beautiful daughter that she named Brianna. The baby wasn't accepted by her parents, so Nah Nah was left to care for our child while Katrina stayed out late going from club to club. Don't get me wrong, Nah Nah kicked it and did her thang too, she just wasn't nearly as bad as her sister.

On one particular night both girls had gone out to a club called the European. Jermaine Dupree and Janet Jackson's new duo had the club jumping. "*Maybe we'll meet at a bar. He'll drive a funky car,*" Janet crooned throughout the club.

Nah Nah was out on the floor twirking her thang like one of the sistas that she'd seen on BET. She had every brother in the club ready to catch jungle fever. She was being admired from a distance. It just so happened that she spun around and caught the eye of her stalker.

Snatch was big, about 6'6", 270 lbs. of prison muscle. He looked like the guy that played Damon in the movie "*Friday After Next*." He was suited up in a cut John Varvatos and croc-odile shoes. He casually eased his way out on the dance floor. He stood before her, stepping smoothly from side to side.

"Snatch," he introduced himself. "I just got out."

Nah Nah smiled. "I'm glad," she said in a smart tone.

He admired her body. "Mm. I mean, I did a five-year stretch. I didn't jack off one time while I was in there, baby." He undid his pants and held them open. "Look at this thing. It's huge. And I'm offering you the exclusive rights to experi-ence that first explosion of cum that shoots outta this thing."

She thought he was funny. Something inside her couldn't help but make her take a look. She leaned forward and looked down. His thing looked like a black baby python coiled inside his underwear, like a nest. Nah Nah almost grabbed it. Instead she turned and tried to walk away before she was forced to give in to her desire.

Snatch clutched her arm. "One drink," he offered, "and a word or two. Or three. And I'll leave you alone."

Nah Nah smirked. She couldn't help but want the huge black man between her legs, stretching her womb gate open.

Two drinks and a conversation later, they were sitting at a table rubbing up against each other when Terry walked up. He had a slick-ass grin on his face as he practically eye-fucked Nah Nah.

"Dog, who is this?"

"This here be Nah Nah," he said proudly. "Baby, this is T."

"Nah Nah, huh?" Terry licked his lips. "You here alone?"

"No, she's not." The voice came from behind Terry.

Nah Nah's eyes lit up when she saw her sister standing there with her hand on her hip, checking Terry out. She jumped up and ran around the table, clutching her sister's arm.

"This is my sister, Katrina," Nah Nah said.

Katrina nodded coolly at both men. Her hair was in a bun that stuck out from under her Kangol. She admired Terry through her shades.

Terry removed them from her face and looked into her gray eyes. "I can read your mind, baby. I know what you're thinking."

Katrina bit down on her bottom lip. "Mm. Tell me what I'm thinking, daddy."

"You're thinking that you gotta hell of a player standing before you. And you wanna make a good impression."

Katrina raised her brows. He had damned near hit it on the head. "I'm impressed. But actually it was the opposite. I was thinking that you wanted to make a good impression. And that I was the playa."

Terry admired her. "I love you."

Katrina raised her finger. "At least wait until after you get the pussy before you say shit like that." She paused. "Have you ever seen a blond pussy?"

Terry seemed to ponder her question. "Not in real life."

Katrina grabbed her sister's hand. "Keep ya game tight, playa. And I might let you taste your first one." Then she pulled her sister away from them.

Snatch and Terry followed them outside to their Benz SUV. "Baller bitches," Terry said. "Where y'all headed?"

"Breakfast," Nah Nah said as she got into the truck.

Terry looked at Snatch and gestured toward the Benz SUV. Without being invited, they got into the back seat.

"What are y'all doing?" Katrina said while looking at them in her mirror.

"We going with y'all," Snatch answered. "After the good convo we just had, Nah Nah, I know you ain't gon' just up and leave a nigga?"

Nah Nah turned around in her seat, a big grin on her face.

"I know you want dis," Snatch teased.

"I do," Nah Nah admitted.

Katrina peered at her sister in disbelief. "Nah Nah, chill. Damn." She looked at Terry in the mirror. "Aight. Y'all can roll." Then she went into the console and took out a bag of weed and a Chrome .25 automatic with a pearl handle. "But y'all gotta hold the shit."

Snatch looked at Terry like what the fuck?

Terry said, "Damn, baby. What you think, we're a couple of hoes or somethin'?"

"Hoes ride in the back, Tee. Now either you gon' be a hoe tonight and kick it wit' us playas..."

"Or get the fuck out," Nah Nah added. She winked at her sister.

Terry thought about that blond mound of public hair that surrounded her pink pelvis. That was a sight that he couldn't pass up. Snatch was ready to make an exit until Terry stopped him.

"Let's play their lil' game. We'll win in the end." Terry leaned forward and whispered in Katrina's ear. "Just know that once you start playing man games...you have to be able to take an elbow or two." Then he snatched the weed and the gun from her and handed it to Snatch.

Katrina put the car in drive. "Trust me, Terry. If I can take a dick in the ass, then I can definitely take an elbow or two." Then she pulled away.

Terry leaned toward Snatch. "If we get pulled over, kick that shit under that bitch's seat." Snatch nodded.

They went to Chubby's, an all night breakfast place. Its interior was decked out 50s style like an old malt shop with checkered black and white tiled floors, bright red bar stools and waitresses that rolled around on skates.

Terry and Katrina sat next to each other in the booth, across from Nah Nah and Snatch. Katrina stuck her tongue down Terry's throat and kissed him for close to 30 seconds. Terry slid his hand inside her pants.

Katrina said, "What if you grab a dick down there?"

Terry snatched his hand back out. "What?"

Nah Nah looked across the table at her sister curiously.

"What if I was really a man, and you just had your tongue down my throat, ready to..." she laughed, "caress my Johnson?"

A laugh escaped Nah Nah's lips. Then she said, "I have to go to the bathroom." Snatch stood while she left the table.

"You a dude?" Terry said.

"Get yo' lame ass outta here." Katrina took his hand and placed it inside her pussy. Terry felt her warm velvety clit. "Feel like a dick to you?" Katrina stood. "I gotta go check on my sista." She handed Terry her cell phone. "Put your number in that." She waited until he finished, then she put her phone in her purse on her way to the restroom.

Katrina entered the bathroom giggling. She looked in the mirror at her reflection. "We served them niggas, Nah Nah."

Nah Nah was leaning up against the sink shaking her head at her sister. "You're bad."

"Who's bad?"

"You're bad." They gave each other high five.

Nah Nah faced the mirror and began straightening her hair.

Katrina frowned. "What are you doing?"

"Making sure I look good. I know it's gonna be sweated out in the morning, but..."

"What you mean, sweated out? We're not fucking those lames. Not tonight anyway." She looked at the mirror. "God, you're so naïve."

Nah Nah turned around and looked at her sister. "Hey, I'm so horny I'm about to bust over here. I feel like a nun already. God!"

"Use one of my vibrators, 'cause we're leaving those suckers here."

"That's not funny, Katrina. That's how girls like us end up getting raped. It's called cock teasing."

Katrina brushed her off. "Niggas do it all the time. It's our turn to get off on someone."

Nah Nah shook her head. "You've really been using that nigga term loosely lately. Hello, you're not black. Okay?"

"I know," she said as she admired herself in the mirror. "A black girl could never be this hot." She picked up her purse. "Let's go."

"Let's go have a smoke." Snatch dropped a $20 bill on the table on their way to the front.

As soon as they stepped out of the door onto the sidewalk, they saw Katrina's SUV driving past them. Nah Nah had her naked pink ass sticking out of the front window as they passed. She blew the horn.

Their laughter echoed in Terry's ears.

Snatch said, "You think she know that was her ass, dog?" he asked in a sarcastic tone.

Terry peered at Snatch. They both felt so stupid that they had to laugh.

~ ~ ~ ~ ~

"So I guess you two are not going back to school?" Michael Miller asked Katrina during a heated conversation at his home.

Katrina said, "We're going back to school, Dad. Don't worry." She was drunk. Her body swayed back and forth while he talked to her. Nah Nah was sitting on the sofa with a timid look on her face.

"You said that 18 months ago. Now you've gon' and had a nigglet and…"

"You leave my daughter out of this."

"I stayed out of it and look what happened to you two. Pure white…trash you've turned into."

"Michael, please. They're our kids," Kathy said from behind him.

Michael turned his head halfway in his wife's direction. "Stay out of this, Kathy. I mean it." He turned back toward Katrina.

She stared up at him with a sour frown on her face.

Michael looked disgusted with her. "You're nothing but a drunken whore."

"I hate you!" Katrina screamed in his face. She tried to turn away, but her dad clutched her arm and spun her around, then slapped her across her face.

"Michael!" Kathy screamed as she went to her daughter's aid. She clutched his shoulders.

Michael started shaking his daughter violently until she threw up all over his shirt and the floor. Kathy backed away screaming. Katrina's mouth hung open as she stood there bent over toward the floor. Nah Nah hopped up. Katrina pushed her hair out of her face.

"C'mon, Katrina. Walk with me to the bathroom. C'mon." She held onto Katrina's arms as they began to take slow steps.

Katrina glared up at her daddy as they passed him. They disappeared into the other room.

Michael eyes fluttered while he stared down at the puddle of vomit in thought. Then he slowly lifted his head until he was staring at Kathy. Tears stained her face.

"Those are your daughters," he stated, then headed for the door.

"They're yours, too," Kathy cried out. The front door slammed after he went out it. "You can't just give up!"

~ ~ ~ ~ ~

Michael pulled his BMW into the parking lot of a Quick Trip Gas station. He exited his car wearing a T-shirt and his soiled Polo shirt in his right hand. He tossed it in the trashcan on his way inside. He wouldn't return home that night. He needed to go somewhere where he could smoke a whole pack of cigarettes and be done. First he had to grab some cash from the ATM machine so he could get a hotel room for the night.

His card wouldn't compute inside the ATM machine. It kept on rejecting it. "Dammit!" Michael hit the machine, then stuck the card back in. Same result.

"Excuse me," a female voice said from behind him. Michael turned around. A black woman was standing behind him. She was tall, about 6 foot—6 foot 3 with the heels that she had on. She was honey coated, with long black hair, hazel eyes and a cute little pair of glasses. She had the look of a professional; a lawyer or an accountant, Michael guessed. Whatever she was, he found himself strangely attracted to her.

"Do you need any help?" She spoke with a British accent.

"I just..."

The woman took the card from him, turned it around, then put it inside the machine. It was accepted.

"Thank you," Michael said with a smile.

The woman saw the vomit stains on the ends of Michael's T-shirt. "What happened to you?"

Michael looked down and saw the stains. He blushed. "My d..."

"Nevermind," she said. "Get what you came to get and meet me at my car."

"But..."

"No buts," she said with authority. "I'll be waiting outside." She walked away.

Michael glanced around the store to see if there was anybody in there that he knew. There wasn't. He sighed. What could it hurt to see what she wanted? He grabbed $100 in cash and a pack of cigarettes.

The woman stood behind the open back door of her '99 Jeep Cherokee, opening up a JC Penney's bag. Michael spotted her when he walked out of the store. She heard him approaching from behind. Out of the bag she produced a fresh package of wife-beaters. She took one out.

"Take off that shirt. You're a bloody mess."

"Out here?"

She looked at him as if to say, "Where else?"

Michael sighed, then removed his shirt. His chest was hairy, but he was in great physical shape. The woman slipped the new shirt over his head. Damn, her fragrance smelled good. Almost seductive.

"Yeah. That's better," she said as she adjusted the shirt to his fitting. "I like that. Do you wear wife beatas?"

"Wife what? No. I've never hit my..." He stopped talking. They both stared at each other for a moment.

"I'm free tonight," she said boldly. "How about you? Is there a Mrs. at home?"

Michael looked down at his wedding ring. He hadn't cheated on Kathy since high school. Never had the thought of making love to a nappy head. But for some reason—he didn't know if it had something to do with what was going on in his life—the moment just seemed right. Deep down inside, he was curious of what it would be like.

The woman saw the ring on his finger. "Oh, sorry. I'll be seeing you."

Michael's arm reached out on its own and clutched her arm. She looked at him.

"Follow me," he finally said.

CHAPTER FOURTEEN

As fate would have it, me and my brother O'ban ended up doing our time at the same prison. Thank God for that blessing. If I had to do a bid, I'd rather do it with somebody that I could trust.

Our paper was fucked up. It wasn't long before the feds came and seized the sandwich shop from Katrina. The visits from Nah Nah and Katrina were extinct. Occasionally we got cards or pictures in the mail from them. Luckily we had Pops. He kept our books tight and he and Qu'ban Junior visited on a regular.

We were inside the TV room watching the football game. I was sitting at the table across from O'ban with my feet up in a chair.

"Every time you start seeing those athletes in music videos, it be the end of their careers. They never be the same after that."

O'ban was in a world of his own. "Man, fuck this game. I'm ready to hit the bricks and get my money on."

"I ain't mad at you." I sighed. "Unfortunately it'll be a while before I see the streets again."

O'ban gave me that serious look of his. "If I get money, you get money. Nigga, you should already know that. You my bro. I love you, nigga."

"I'ma hold you to that."

A moment of silence passed.

O'ban said, "What do you want me to do about Terry once I touch down?"

I peered at the TV screen. Then I looked at him. "Kill'm."

"It's done."

~ ~ ~ ~ ~

Bzzst. Bzzst.

Michael stuck his arm out from under the covers and picked his phone up from the nightstand. The caller ID alerted that it was his wife calling. He set it back down on the table next to his wedding ring.

The naked woman lying next to him began to stir. Her eyes opened and saw him staring at her.

"You are admiring my naked bo-dy, are you?"

"No. I was admiring you…"

She smiled. "Kortni. Have you forgotten already?"

Michael shrugged. "I'm just so overwhelmed by last night."

Kortni threw a long leg over his, then slid up under him. "What about last night?"

"You were great."

"Your first piece of kinky bush, eh?"

Embarrassingly, Michael shook his head. "I've never looked at a black woman…sexually."

"Mm." Kortni peered at him. "Well, I guess what they say is true. White men know how to clean a rug."

"Excuse me."

Kortni giggled. "I'm talking about eating pussy, silly."

Michael giggled. "Ya care to have another taste? I hear that it's a lot better the next morning."

A fire started in Michael's loins. He rolled over on top of her and kissed her breast.

Bzzst. Bzzst.

"Mmm," Kortni moaned. "The old lady is calling."

Michael stuck his head up. "What?" Kortni nodded toward the phone. "Answer it."

After a long sigh, Michael leaned over and picked up the phone. "Hello."

Kortni slid out from under him with a devious smile on her face.

"I stayed at a hotel last night," Michael informed Kathy. "I needed to thhh…" When he felt Kortni's cold tongue slither up the crack of his hairy ass, he closed the phone and dropped it on the floor.

Kortni smacked him on the ass. He let out a howl. "You're mine now, Michael. Say," she smacked him hard on the ass, "yes!"

"Yess! Yess!"

With a serious look on her face, she lay on her back and spread her long limbs. "Now get down there and finish sucking this pussy." Michael did as he was told.

"Sss," Kortni squirmed as her arm reached over and picked his wallet up off the nightstand. With one hand and five fingers, she relieved him of one of his credit cards, put the wallet back, then tucked the card inside the pillowcase.

Bzzst. Bzzst.

Kortni said, "You answer that phone again. Sss. Mmm. And me is going to fuck you up something really serious this time."

Michael lifted his pussy juice soaked face. "I won't, mama."

Kortni put his face back down there, tilted her head back and released a loud howl.

~ ~ ~ ~ ~

Six months had passed. It was the summer of 2003. Terry had been balling so hard that he had to make a serious investment. He bought a section of a strip mall on Rainbow Boulevard and opened up a massage parlor. He had twenty-two women of different nationalities working for him. A few of them were imports from other countries that didn't speak a lick of English. All in all, Terry had jumped into a modern day pimp game called an escort service.

He spent a gwap gutting out the interior of the building and having it redone and laid out with all the latest spa, bath and massage equipment. It had an oriental environment.

Besides the hoeing that was going on under cover, one could come in and get platinum spa treatments and massages for a very hefty price. And it worked, because he knew black people. They lived beyond their means. They purchased what they could buy, not what they could afford to buy.

Terry was driving up Rainbow Boulevard headed to his place of business. He stopped at the light on 39th Street, an eye-shot away from Body Workz Spa Treatment. His eyes zoomed in on a beautiful sight.

Katrina exited her truck and voluptuously swayed into Body Workz. She was escorted to a private room, where she was given towels and told to remove her clothing.

One of the escorts was behind the front desk talking on the phone when Terry walked in.

"What about the credit card you gave me?" the woman

spoke into the phone. "I maxed it out. How far did you think a girl could get with only a $25,000 limit? I mean, come on. These days a bloody purse costs a grand. Call me when you've gotten it." She slammed down the phone. She gasped when she looked up and saw who it was standing before her. "Sorry, boss. Can I help you?"

Terry said, "A young lady just came through the door. Caucasian. About my height. Blonde."

"Suite 13."

"Thank you."

Terry slowly eased open the door. An old Asian tune was playing softly. Steam rose toward the air. Katrina lay on a table of hot rocks. She was completely naked. A very young Asian girl stood over her applying a hot oil treatment over her body. When she finished, the woman stuck one pin in each of her ears. Then she removed her robe, revealing her own naked body, and climbed on top. Gently the Asian grazed her body in a calculated circular motion up against Katrina's. It was sexupuncture, a technique designed by Asians to reduce sexual desire. After twenty minutes of that, Terry saw Katrina's body spasm as she released orgasmic fluids onto the table beneath her.

When they were done, the Asian woman put on her robe, accepted her credit card, then left the room, nodding at Terry on her way out.

Katrina wrapped the towel around her body and stood.

"Long time no see."

She gasped when she saw Terry, but quickly regained her composure. "So it has. What are you doing here?"

"I own this place."

Katrina's head cocked sideways. "Really?"

"You know sexupuncture decreases your sex drive? At least it's supposed to."

"That's not why I'm here. I haven't had any dick in a while and I needed to get off."

The Asian girl carried the card up to the girl that was sitting at the front desk. The black woman swiped the card through the machine. A red flag appeared on the screen. She looked at the card and could not believe what she saw.

"You've got to be bloody kidding me," she said to herself. Then she walked around her desk on five inch stilettos on her way to Suite 13.

Terry approached Katrina. "You think I'm soft for letting you leave me and my dog at that restaurant?"

"Soft? No. The way I see it is that you yen to get this pussy, and because you really dig me, that's the only reason that your foot ain't buried in my ass right now."

"You..."

The door swung open. Terry peered over his shoulder and saw the tall woman from the front desk standing there. "What is it?"

The woman was admiring the slender white woman standing only a few feet from her. "Umm...her credit card is maxed out."

"It's not maxed out, honey. My father gave it to me this morning," she said in a cocky tone.

The woman's heavily glossed lips twisted into a smile. "Trust me, suga...this bloody card...is bloody busted."

"Fine. Cut it up." Katrina looked at Terry. "I got other means of payment."

Terry smiled. "I'll handle it, Kortni."

"Right." She closed the door.

Terry took off his cap and approached Katrina. She ran her hands through his curly hair while he removed her towel and attacked her breasts.

Kortni returned back to the room five minutes later and took a peek inside. The room was still steamy from the hot rocks. Terry's pants were down to his ankles. Katrina was sitting on the table with her legs wrapped around him while he gave it to her one stroke at a time.

"Uhh! Uhh! Uhhhh!"

Kortni closed the door, then took out her cell phone.

~ ~ ~ ~ ~

Michael pulled into the driveway of his home. He got out of the car and looked up at his house. He sighed, thumped away his cigarette, then entered the front door.

Kathy was sitting on the living room sofa. A cigarette was burning in her hands. Bank statements, credit card bills and other things of that nature were scattered over the coffee table.

Michael caught a brief glimpse of one of the papers when he walked in. He saw the name of his bank written across the top. He knew then that there was about to be trouble.

"Hi, honey," he said.

Kathy didn't look at him when she said, "Michael, we need to talk."

Michael stopped in his tracks. He took a deep breath as he stared down at his keys. "About what?"

"Well…for starters we can talk about the last six months of our lives. You've been distant. You leave and come home at strange times. Some of your underwear is missing. I noticed that you switched from T-shirts to tank tops, from trousers to jeans. You've dyed your goatee." She paused. "All those signs point to another, younger, more exciting, outgoing, sex-crav-ing woman. I mean for Christ sake, you haven't even touched me while we're in bed together."

"I don't…"

"I know I'm not the woman that I used to be physically. Don't you think I realize that, Michael?"

Michael gazed at her in a questioning way. "Enough!"

"No! It's not enough." Her eyes began to water. "I found out this morning that you withdrew $7,000 out of our savings account. You didn't even bother to tell me."

"Look…Kathy. I'm…" the phone buzzed. Kortni's number appeared on the screen. "I gotta go." He turned back toward the door.

Kathy ran to the door and covered it with her body. "Michael, please don't leave this house." Her voice was full of desperation. "We can discuss this. I'm sure that something can be worked out."

"Move away, Kathryn. I have to go."

"I'm not moving away from…oww!"

Michael shoved her aside. "You have no idea what's going on." He opened the door.

"Michael! Michael!" Kathy ran after him. "Please don't go. I can learn."

Michael became enraged and grabbed her by her shoul-ders. "Don't you get it, Kathy? I'm…I'm in love with another woman."

Kathy's face twisted up. She fell to her knees crying. "Michaelll!"

Michael shook himself free of her and got into his car. He peered back at Kathy, who was on her knees with her face in her hands. If this was what he really wanted to do, then now was the time. He started his car, backed out of the driveway, then sped up the road.

~ ~ ~ ~ ~

"How do you know?" Michael asked Kortni.

"This is how." Kortni showed him the credit card that Katrina brought into Body Workz. She was supposed to cut it up, but kept it when she recognized Michael's name on the front. In fact, it was because of her that the card had been maxed out.

"I only took an interest to it," Kortni continued, "because I thought that you had another one of your bloody bitches spending our money." Kortni stood up from the sofa that they were sitting on. She had on a bathrobe with a towel wrapped around her head. "When she said that she was your daughter, I was like whoa. And for a minute there I was starting to feel guil-ty. Un-til I caught her getting greased in the steam room."

Michael breathed in, then let it out slow. It hurt his heart to hear that his daughters had turned into the tramps that they had. They were a complete disappointment to him. He wanted something bad to happen to them. Not something as serious as death or anything like that, but enough to wake them up and realize that they were headed in the wrong direction.

He stood up and kissed her. "I'm going to take a shower." He nodded toward a small black bag that was sitting on the table. "Check it out and tell me what you think." Then he walked away.

Kortni dropped to her knees in front of the table, then ripped the bag open. She snapped open the box that was inside. "Ooh! Michael!" It was the ring that they had seen in the jewelry store a week before when he'd purchased her three carat bracelet. "Mama always said knowing how to give a good blow job would carry me a long way in America." She kissed the ring. "You just have to find the right dick to suck."

~ ~ ~ ~ ~

"Ain't nobody been doing nobody in no steam room, Dad," Katrina yelled into the phone. "Where are you getting your information from? Is it that skanky-ass tramp that you left mother for?" Katrina passed the phone to Nah Nah, who was sitting on the passenger side of the truck. "Talk to that ass-hole."

Katrina thought back to her encounter with Terry. The black receptionist was the only one who saw her come in to the spa. *Could that be the woman he left mom for?* Katrina quickly dismissed the thought, knowing how her father felt about black people. She cranked the music up to where Nah Nah could barely hear. "My neck, my back, lick my pussy and my crack," Katrina sang along. "Do it now, lick it good, lick this pussy just like you should."

"Dad. I'll…I said I'll have to call you back. Bye." Nah Nah hung up the phone. Then she reached over and cut the music down. "The baby is back there."

Brianna was screaming at the top of her lungs in the back seat. Katrina turned her head around. "Shut up!"

"You shut up." Nah Nah reached into the backseat, undid the seatbelt, then picked Brianna up and bounced her in her lap. The baby stopped crying. "There we go. Good girl."

Katrina noticed how her daughter had taken to Nah Nah better than she did her own mother. It would've taken her a half hour to get her to be quiet. Katrina may have gotten wild, but she hadn't lost her good sense. She was fucking up. When it came to her child, she was gonna start being a better parent.

That was a promise that she made to herself.

Nah Nah examined the interior of the H2 that they were riding in. "Terry let you drive his truck, huh?"

"Yep," Katrina said as she bobbed her head to the music.

"You fucking him?"

Katrina gave her sister that look. "Do you honestly believe that I would be driving his truck if I wasn't fuckin' him? Hello."

"I was just asking." She gazed down at Brianna, who had just fallen asleep in her arms. "What happened to his friend Snatch?"

"Why? You thinking about giving it up to him?"

"I thought about it."

"Please. Bitch, don't think for a second that if you give him some pussy, you gon' be driving around in his whips and shit. Terry gave me $1,500 this morning to spend and we've only fucked once. I got that holla back nooky."

Nah Nah grunted. "So you think your pussy is better than mine?"

"Yes."

"Bet." She held up a fist.

"Bet? Bet what?"

"That after I fuck Snatch I'll get more than $1,500."

"Bet." They slammed their fists together. "If you lose, you owe me a hundred bucks. If you win, I owe you."

"You're on."

"Oops. I forgot to tell you. Snatch is more like Terry's goon, so he might not have $1,500 to give." She broke out into a laugh.

Nah Nah glared at her sister. "You dirty dog you."

CHAPTER FIFTEEN

A week or so later, Kathy had neither seen nor heard from her husband, Michael. If it hadn't been for him keeping in contact with his daughters, he would've been presumed dead. The neighbors had been asking about his whereabouts, but Kathy was too embarrassed to tell the truth. Twenty-seven years of marriage didn't just end like that. Katrina had mentioned her suspicions about the black woman at the spa. It just didn't add up. All this time he had been so adamant about hating blacks, and now he was leaving her for one? What was so special about black people that they were able to take over the entertainment business, take her two daughters and now her husband? Kathy wanted to know firsthand.

She dressed up one night in a sexy strapless black dress, high heel pumps, jewelry and made up her face. Kathy was a gorgeous older woman, no one could dispute that. But that was the problem. She was old.

Kathy climbed into her SUV and drove to the inner city. She didn't know where she was going, she just went. She saw a spot just off Interstate 70 in the heart of the city. It looked like the place to be, so she took the exit.

Satin Dolls was the name on the sign when she pulled into

the crowded parking lot. Small groups of people of all age groups were pulling up and going inside. Kathy smoked a whole cigarette to calm her nerves. Then she popped in a stick of gum and went inside.

Hip hop music crooned throughout the club. It wasn't at all the type of atmosphere that she had expected. Female strippers with exotic thong sets danced on stages, on poles and some walked the room, going from table to table, trying to solicit a lap dance.

Kathy was about to turn around until she was approached by a gentleman dressed in a dark blue off-the-rack suit. He looked to be in his late 30s to early 40s. Tall, with a strong build like he had spent a significant amount of time in prison. He smiled.

"Uh, you come here often?"

Kathy was a bit shaken up from being in the presence of all these black people, let alone one standing less than three feet away from her.

"Uh, no," she said nervously.

The man saw her trembling hands. "Let me get you a drink." When he went to clutch her hand, Kathy flinched and took a step backward.

"I'm not gonna hurt you..." he stated with a big smile.

"Susan," she lied.

"Susan, I'm Ronnie." They shook hands. "C'mon, let's put a couple of vodkas up in you to help ease your nerves."

Three strong glasses of vodka mixed with cranberry juice later and Kathy was loose. She was sitting at the table laughing and spouting off at the mouth about her high school years.

Ronnie didn't hear a word that came out of her mouth. He

was busy sucking on an olive while staring at her in a very seductive way. Kathy was smart enough to catch on.

She smiled bashfully. "Are you attempting to court me, young man?"

"Young lady, I'm trying to do a whole lot more than court you. I wanna…" he leaned in like he was about to whisper something to her. Instead he stuck his tongue inside her ear.

Kathy was ticklish. She cocked her head sideways. "Mmm. I haven't had anybody do that to me in years. It feels good."

Ronnie stood. "I know something that'll make both of us feel real good." He took her hand. "Let's get out of here."

Her danger senses alerted her. Leave with him? Sure, Ronnie was a nice enough guy, but she never planned on going anywhere with him. But what did she expect to happen? She had gotten dressed up, walked into a strip club, had a few drinks with a man, and now it was time to either put out or go home. She knew the game. She was young before. Kathy peered at Ronnie. He had a big smile plastered on his face. Then she looked at the quarter glass of vodka that she had left. What the hell? She downed what was left in the glass, then allowed him to lead her outside.

Ronnie had his hand on her leg as she drove down Van Brunt headed north. Kathy was drunk and as gullible as a lonely fat girl.

"Where're we headed?" Kathy asked.

Ronnie eased his hand up her thigh. Her eyes closed as she exhaled, then opened again. "Make a right two blocks down."

"We, um, it's been a while for me…since I…you know," she said in a nervous tone. "It might be a good idea if we stopped and picked up some KY."

Ronnie allowed a laugh to slip through his lips. Kathy turned toward him. "What's so funny?"

"Nothing. Nothing. Make a right up here."

Kathy made a right. Per Ronnie's instructions, she drove three houses down and pulled over in front of a blue house. Ronnie turned to her.

"Uhh, can I get $20 off of you right quick? I don't keep much cash on me."

Kathy regarded the man with the eager look on his face. She wasn't in a position to tell him no, she figured. So the best thing for her to do was to give him the money.

She opened her wallet, took out a $20 bill and handed it to him.

"Thank you, Susan." He leaned in and kissed her on the lips. She gently caressed his check. "I'll pay you back. I promise."

Kathy watched him walk around to the back of the house rather than using the front door. Her first mind told her to pull off, but she was enjoying Ronnie's company, and didn't feel like being alone tonight. Like all lonely women, she was desperately trying to be held.

Ronnie returned less than a minute later. "I can't wait to get you naked."

Kathy blushed. "I'm...I'm really not much to see."

"What? Woman, you're beautiful. Anybody that tells you any different is hatin' on a player."

She laughed, "Ronnie, you're so crazy."

"Uh! Uh! Uhhh!" Kathy howled. Ronnie repeatedly hit her with slow thrusts in a circular motion as her hands clawed at his back.

Ronnie gazed down at her face while he stroked her. Kathy was in a world of sexual bliss. Her head was cocked back, pressing hard into the pillow, eyes squeezed tight and mouth hung open.

"Sss. Sss. Sss," he hissed. "I'ma knock the cobwebs outta this old pussy."

"Ooh, Ronnie. Ronnie. Ron...nie."

Fifteen minutes later it was over. Kathy fell over on her back, panting and trying to catch her breath. Ronnie got right up, dug his works kit out of his pocket, and set it on the table. Right away Kathy recognized the procedure and knew what was about to happen next. Instantly she became afraid.

While Ronnie injected the poison into his veins, Kathy eased her underclothes on. Ronnie finished the hit and set the needle on the table. His head slowly tilted forward and his eyes closed.

"Ronnie," Kathy called out. He didn't move. She hurried out of the bed and hurried back into her clothes. Then she picked up her purse and keys from the night stand. The keys made a jingling sound.

Suddenly Ronnie's eyes popped open. He saw Kathy making a run for the door. He got up from his chair and tackled her into the wall.

"Where you goin'?" he said in a deadly whisper.

"I...I have to go," Kathy cried. "Please, don't hurt me."

"Nahhh, you ain't going nowhere. I ain't through with you yet." He threw her on the bed, ripping her dress off of her in the process. Her purse and keys fell onto the floor.

Ronnie forced himself on top of her. She kicked and clawed in an attempt to defend herself. After her fingernail scratched him across the eye, Ronnie became enraged. He raised his huge fist and smashed it into her face. Blood squirted from her nose as she lay stunned on the bed.

"Ssstop," she mumbled.

Ronnie brought his huge fist down on her again. And again. And again, until Kathy was no longer conscious. He stood over her glaring down at his work. It took him a second to catch his breath. When he did he got up, relieved her of her jewelry, picked up her purse and keys, then grabbed his works kit on his way out the door. What the fool was too stupid to realize was that he left the rubber that he'd used on Kathy on the floor, with his semen in it.

Chapter Sixteen

Jagged Edge's "*Where The Party At*," crooned through the club speakers. Nah Nah was drunk and out on the dance floor doing her thang, like an out-of-rhythm white girl. She couldn't dance a lick, but her sex appeal more than made up for it.

Snatch, who was dancing behind her, noticed that she was pantyless under her khaki cropped cargo pants. He was high off of a pill and a half of ex, had a serious hard-on, and was tired of playing a song and dance just to get the pussy.

He snapped his fingers on his left hand to the beat. In his right hand was an ex-pill that he held up about face level. Nah Nah spun around and focused in on the pill that was being offered to her. Without even thinking about it, she opened her mouth.

Snatch pulled it back. "You sure you want this?"

She was in a drunken state and giggling like a school girl. "Yes."

Nah Nah clutched Snatch's wrist, pulled it toward her face, then took the pill out of his hand with her teeth. She swallowed, then placed his finger inside her mouth and sucked it.

Snatch started to sweat. "It's like that?" Nah Nah nodded. "It's time for us to leave then."

There was a seductive sucking sound when she pulled his wet finger from her mouth. "Let's do it then."

Snatch took her by the hand and led her through the club. On the way out they stopped by the V.I.P. to see Terry.

Terry was sitting at the booth with three of his working women, including Katrina. She was drunk, giggling and having too much fun to notice that Kortni's hand was on her upper thigh, easing its way up her skirt.

Snatch whispered into Terry's ear, "I'ma take the car. Me and Nah Nah about to go do our thing."

Terry shook his head. "Hell naw. Fuck you gon' do, just leave me by myself? Fuck that. I ain't about to be prey to these niggas up in here because you horny." Everybody stopped and looked at them. Terry picked up his glass. "You better take yo' ass back out there and have a few more drinks until I'm ready."

Snatch was embarrassed. "I'll be by the bar."

As he was leaving he heard Terry say, "Every time. Every time he pop one of those fuckin' pills he loses sight of shit."

Katrina kissed Terry's forehead. "That's 'cause he's stupid, baby. Him and my sister belong together."

Nah Nah stopped and turned around. Then she stormed over to the table, snatched Terry's drink and threw it in Katrina's face. Katrina sat there with her mouth open and her eyes fluttering.

"Take that, you stuck up, superficial-ass whore." She brushed her hair out of her face. "I'm your sister! No one else here cares about you but me." She cut her eyes at Terry, then back to her. "Start acting like you've got some goddamn sense." She threw the glass onto the table, then she walked away.

Katrina swallowed. "Bitch."

Terry decided that it was time to leave. They took Nah Nah and Katrina out to his crib in Grandview, Missouri. Neither sister said a word to each other the whole way. Nah Nah didn't speak because the pill had kicked in and she was up front touching herself. Katrina didn't speak because she was high off the PCP that Terry had laced her joint with. He had his dick in her mouth from the time they'd left the club for the 20 minutes that it took to get to his crib.

At the house Nah Nah stripped her clothes off the second she hit the bedroom. Snatch did the same. Fully naked, Nah Nah jumped into his arms, planting kisses all over his neck and face.

"Mmm. Mmm. I want...you...to...fuck meee," she begged.

Snatch threw her down on the bed. Automatically, she got on all fours and buried her face in the sheets. Her pussy hole was pulsating. Snatch got on his knees and put his big ole rod inside her.

Nah Nah's head snapped backward and she let out a sharp howl. "You asked for it," Snatch uttered. Slowly the big dick penetrated, stretching her womb gate as it did so.

"God! It's...it...it's...b...big."

"I know."

Snatch pulled her toward him. Without mercy he hit her with the longest, thickest strokes that she'd ever been hit with. It felt like it was in her throat, but she took it like a champ. The more he hit it, the wetter it became, making it easier for her to take.

"C'mon! C'mon, Sn...atchhh. Ohh. Ooh!"

"I'ma give...it...to...ooh." Snatch stroked her while he

man-handled her small waist. The pussy was wet, warm and tighter than he expected a white girl to be. Beads of sweat started to roll down his forehead. He spread her ass cheeks wide, then stuck his huge index finger inside her asshole.

"Ahh! Ahhh! Urrrgh! Uhh!" She howled. Her pussy had stretched to its full potential. That's when she placed her palms flat on the bed, then started to push back. "Give it…it…it to…ooh! Ooh!"

Snatch stopped pumping and let her take control. She may not have had much rhythm on the dance floor, but the bedroom belonged to her. While pounding her ass into his pelvis, she moved her pussy up and down, then in a circular motion. Snatch had to lean back and brace himself with his hands.

Snatch's mouth hung open. He let out loud sounds like a howling bear. Nah Nah sped up the pace. Slapping noises echoed through the room as she continued to attack the dick. Up and down, side to side, back and forth, she pushed herself up on him until her pussy squirted her juices all over him. Then she turned around, facing him, and got a good look at the huge dick.

It didn't discourage her. She spat a big glob of spittle onto the huge, veiny thing, then started jerking him off. Her lips sucked the head, then took half of him inside of her mouth. It was way too big to even consider trying to swallow. He grabbed the back of her head. Nah Nah didn't try to stop him. She made her throat open and let his head travel down her throat. The feel of his dick head pounding the back of her throat enticed her even more. Nah Nah shook her head from side to side as she stroked it. She took it out, sucked the spit from the head, slobbered on it, rubbed it across her face, jerked it some more, then put it back inside her mouth.

"Mmm," she hummed. "Mmm. Mmm. Slurrp. Mmmm." She started bobbing like a chick head pecking at the ground for food. "Mmmm."

Snatch's eyes were squeezed together tightly. "Okay. Okay!" He tried to push her forehead back away from him. "Hold on. Na...Na..." She picked up the pace for about ten long seconds, then released him.

"Big Snatch, huh?" she was breathing hard. Spit was caked around her mouth. "You can't handle it?"

Nah Nah climbed on top of him. She placed her hands on his big shoulders, then slid down on top of his love muscle. Her titties jiggled in his face as she bounced up and down on him.

"Yess!" she shouted. She bounced up and down on him for what seemed like forever.

"I can't cum," Snatch admitted.

Nah Nah stopped, caught her breath. "What?"

"That ecstasy. I can't cum."

Nah Nah thought a moment. Then she got up and left the room. She returned a little while later with a trash bag that she had found in the kitchen drawer. She opened it completely up and laid it across the floor, then instructed him to put his ass on it and lay down. He obeyed.

She shook the hair out of her face, then lowered herself onto his manhood. Slowly she rotated her hips back and forward. The dick was huge and felt too good. Her eyes were closed. Snatch caressed her ass while she slow rode him.

Suddenly her eyes popped open. "Sss. You ready?"

"Gimme what you got."

"Sss. Here it co...co...omes."

Snatch felt a hot liquid travel out of her pussy and onto his dick. He couldn't believe how great the liquid felt running down his thick, veiny shaft, to his balls, through the crack of his ass onto the plastic. His dick got real stiff and started to throb. By the time he realized that he was being pissed on, he felt himself exploding inside her. It was so powerful, and so intense, that it drained all of the energy out of his system.

Panting, Snatch said, "Did…did you just piss on me?"

Nah Nah shook her hair out of her face as she gazed down at him. "Did you like it?"

"Did you piss on me?"

"Did…you…like it?"

Snatch hated to admit it, but he did. "Don't ever tell nobody about this."

"Did you like it?"

He hesitated. "Hell yeah," he said in a soft voice. "Can you do it again?"

Nah Nah laughed, kissed him on his sweaty forehead, then got up. "Come wash me up. I'm not through with you."

They fucked again in the shower. When they returned to the bedroom, Nah Nah was laid out on the bed. A big smile was on her face. She was still high. Snatch popped a bottle of champagne and poured it all over her naked body. She stuck her finger in her pussy, then stuck it in her mouth. "Mmm." Her eyes had been closed the whole time.

A tongue traveled up her thigh, up to her stomach, then her breasts. Snatch had to have been a pro, she thought, because he was sucking her breasts like they were supposed to be sucked.

"Ohh, Snatch," she moaned. "Snatch."

Nah Nah started moving her hips. She wanted her pussy

ate. She reached up and planted her hand on top of his head. Her body was feeling tingly and going through a phase where the only touch that she felt was the tongue that lapped the champagne from her body. But her hands were wide awake. The second she touched the head of the person that was on top of her, she knew it was not Snatch.

Her eyes grew wide when she opened them and saw who it was on top of her.

~ ~ ~ ~ ~

Kortni had come home drunk and ready to fuck. Michael popped a Viagra pill and took her on. At that moment she lay between his legs with his dick in her hand, while she gently sucked on his ball sack. Never in his life had he been sexed so good. Sex with his wife was a couple of pumps followed by a dry nut. No head, no ass-licking, no 20 positions, and toys were definitely not an option. Michael was in love.

His cell phone rang.

Being that it was after 3:00 a.m., he figured that it must be important. He reached over and answered it. "Hello." He listened for a moment. "Oh my god! Is she all right?" He listened. "I'm on my way." He pulled his nuts out of Kortni's mouth and stood up. "Kathy's been in an accident." Kortni got up and walked up on him. "I have to...oww!" She slapped him across his face.

"What the fuck did I tell you about answering that bloody phone while we're having sex? Huh?!"

Michael gazed at her. "But she...oww!" She hit him again.

Kortni showed him the ring on her finger. The one he gave her. "Listen, I'm your woman now. So if you plan on being with me...you had better let go of those feelings that you have for her."

"Baby, I didn't mean to…"

"I'm hurt, Michael."

"It's just…"

"You said you loved me." She folded her arms across her chest.

"I do. I do, damn it." He turned her toward him and started planting kisses on her face.

"Stop it. No more bloody sex for you tonight. Grab some sheets and go sleep on the couch."

"What?"

"You heard me. And you'll continue to sleep there until you learn how to treat your la-dy."

Michael started toward the door. She clutched his shoulder. "And don't even think about picking up that phone, because I'm taking the one in here off the bloody hook." She slapped him again. "Now get the hell out of my room."

When he was gone, she slammed the door behind him. "Fucking wanker." She pulled out a 7-inch vibrator from under her mattress, then climbed back into the bed. She had him right where she wanted him. She knew he was ashamed about being in love with a black woman; she was going to have to force his hand if she ever wanted to get her Green Card.

~ ~ ~ ~ ~

Nah Nah gasped softly when she saw the top of her sister's blond head, but she didn't move. Her mind was saying no, but her body wouldn't respond. Katrina worked her way up to her face.

Terry stood over them. He poured champagne on Katrina's hair and back. The cool liquid ran down Katrina's head and onto Nah Nah's face.

Nah Nah's dry throat welcomed the cool liquid. Katrina's tongue was gentle and soothing. It paralyzed Nah Nah's muscles and kept her from being able to object to what was going on. For a second they made eye contact, then Katrina closed her eyes.

Terry stuck his dick between their faces. Katrina immediately started giving it a good tongue bath. Nah Nah felt his balls rubbing against her nose and lips. She opened her mouth and let him teabag her, dropping his sack in and out of her mouth.

Snatch entered Katrina from behind. When she felt her pussy being stretched open she screamed, "What the fuck is that?"

CHAPTER SEVENTEEN

The ringing sound that a cell phone made was annoying when a person was asleep. Nah Nah's face frowned. Her phone rang from the floor. She shifted. There was a body laying next to her. A little too smooth to be a man.

Nah Nah opened her eyes and nearly lost her breath when she saw her sister lying there asleep. She slapped her on her naked ass. Katrina jumped awake.

Her gray eyes focused in on Nah Nah's boobs, then up to her face. Last night's episode came back to haunt her. She put her hand on her forehead and moaned.

"Please tell me that we didn't muff dive?"

Nah Nah said, "I don't think so."

"What the fuck were we on?"

"Ex."

"You sure it wasn't crack?"

The phone rang. Nah Nah leaned over the bed and picked it up. "Hello." It was the babysitter inquiring about when they were coming to pick up Brianna. "As soon as we get dressed we're leaving. Okay. Bye." She hung up.

Katrina sat up again and released a gust of wind that rippled the hair that was hanging over her face. The phone rang again.

Nah Nah put it up to her ear. "Hello." She listened for a second. While she was doing so her face slowly started to twist up. "Oh my god. Are you positive?" She listened. "We'll be right there."

"What's wrong?" Katrina asked.

A tear shot down Nah Nah's face. "Mom is in the hospital."

~ ~ ~ ~ ~

Me and O'ban was up looking at videos on MTV, listening to all the rappers rap songs about the life that we used to live before Terry got busted and took it away from us. Our bid was getting rough. Pops was a working man, not a hustler. He had to take care of home and my son. So there were times when he couldn't send us no money. O'ban was an all around hustler. He started an ironing business. Being the pretty boy that he was, he knew how to iron a fit and make it look like it was fresh out of the cleaners. Me, I had a reputation to protect and refused to hustle anything in that place. It was beneath me. I would rather starve than admit my weakness to one of those suckas inside the joint.

Not a day went by when I wasn't in a bad mood. I was bitter, angry and restless. I needed to get out of there, and my time wasn't going by fast enough. While me and my brother sat in prison, the nigga that caused this bullshit to happen was still out there living life. Don't get me wrong, some of the blame belonged to Lady, but she was dead. There was nothing that I could do to her. The Devil would settle that score for me. Sometimes I did miss her trifling ass though.

"Beyoncé is a bad bitch," O'ban announced as he scratched the beard that had started growing on his face. Our hair had grown so long that we had them in plats. "Look at her shaking that big ole ass of hers."

I couldn't look at that shit. She wasn't my girl. I couldn't fuck her. Every time that nigga saw a bitch on TV he screamed, "Damn, she's a bad bitch."

"I wish you'd get a bitch, nigga," I said to him. "I'm tired of you lustin' off every hoe on TV."

O'ban frowned at me. "Nigga, it's better than you walking around here cranky all mutha-fuckin' day, talking about what you gon' do to Terry."

"I don't be talkin' about what I'ma do to Terry. I be talking about what yo' punk ass better do to Terry when you get out."

"Well, I'm tired of hearing it. We got time to do. So do it and shut the fuck up."

I got up from my chair. I was so frustrated that I wanted to swing on his punk ass. If I didn't think he could whup me, I would've. "Fuck you," I said on my way to my cell.

"Fuck you, too."

I walked into my cell and kicked the chair. I had a picture of Brianna posted next to the bed. Damn, she was beautiful. That was my baby. I would walk the track with my headset on and imagine spending time with her and Qu'ban Junior. It was amazing how a nigga all of a sudden felt like being a dad after he got locked up. I would miss most of their childhood, but I didn't have a life sentence, so I would get a chance to get out while they were still young enough for me to be an influence on them.

~ ~ ~ ~ ~

O'ban stared at the TV. The dark haired white girl that was on the screen singing made him think about Nah Nah. He missed her. She was cool. Somebody that he felt like he could really fuck with. He knew he liked her the night that she pissed on his dick and he didn't slap the shit out of her. He never knew that being pissed on could feel so intense. He came so hard he just knew that she would end up pregnant.

After the video went off, Nah Nah was heavy on his mind. O'ban shook his head. "I want my bitch back."

~ ~ ~ ~ ~

Nah Nah and Katrina rushed into the ICU and were directed to their mother's room. Kathy was lying in the bed unconscious. A blood-stained bandage was wrapped around her head and left eye. Bruises covered her face and upper body. They both broke out into light sobs.

An African American man in his mid-fifties wearing a white lab coat and carrying a clipboard in his hand approached them.

"Are you two her daughters?"

"Yes," they both answered in unison.

Sniffling, Nah Nah asked, "What happened?"

The doctor sighed. "Your mother is suffering from a concussion and a broken jaw bone, due to a number of blows to her head and face."

"Oh my god," Katrina cried out.

Nah Nah put her hands up over her forehead. "Was she raped?"

"According to the authorities, your mother was found beaten unconscious inside a motel room. Some people in the room next door heard a scream and called the police. No purse was found at the scene. There were traces of a narcotic substance on the table and a used condom on the bed. Also a tube of KY lubricant was found on the floor. Police think that the sex part was consensual, but she was the victim of a robbery after apparently picking up a stranger."

Nah Nah started to cry.

"That asshole dad of yours!" Katrina yelled. "It's all his fault. He drove mother to the streets." Katrina was also upset with herself. If she had just kept quiet about her suspicions of the affair with the black woman, her mother would've never been in a place like that.

Nah Nah glared at her sister through teary eyes. "Yeah? Well who drove us?" She knelt down over her mother.

Katrina's face twisted up. "Don't you go blaming all this fuck up on me, you whiny bitch."

Nah Nah straightened up and bolted over in Katrina's direction. "I'm not the one who wanted to spend our fuckin' vacation going to the fuckin' ghetto…trying to meet some fuckin' black guys, so we could get treated like the fuckin' whores that we are."

"Ladies," the doctor said in an attempt to calm them down.

"Speak for yourself, bitch."

"Speak for myself? You weren't the same person that snuck on top of me last night and practically had sex with me, your own fuckin' sister?"

"All right, that's enough!" the doctor shouted. "Both of you stop this right now, before I have you escorted off the premises. Your mother's been attacked and she's in bad shape." He paused to take a breath. "Show some compassion and respect for her, because you obviously don't have any for yourselves."

The doctor looked from Nah Nah to Katrina while he collected himself, then he exited the room.

Nah Nah crossed her arms over her chest, then dropped down into a chair next to the bed. She shook her head as she reflected on how her life had gone from complete order to chaos. Because of their irresponsible actions, their family had been destroyed. Their relationship with their father was rocky, which caused him to leave home, which caused Mom to become desperate enough to have sex with an addict in an attempt to find companionship, and had nearly gotten herself killed.

The only question left for Nah Nah to ponder was, *Is this the life that I really want to continue living?*

~ ~ ~ ~ ~

Terry picked Katrina up from the hospital later on that night, after another heated battle with Nah Nah about not picking Brianna up from the sitter. They were lucky to have such a caring babysitter who would even put up with Katrina's mess. It seemed like when Terry called she had forgotten that her own mother needed her as well.

"Where're we going, baby?" Katrina asked him once she was inside his truck.

"I got something that I need you to do," Terry stated as he pulled away.

Katrina chewed on a stick of gum while looking at the side of his face. "That's cool. You know I'm down for you." She pulled her hair back into a ponytail, then leaned over and kissed his cheek. "What is it that you want me to do?"

Terry just laughed.

The first stop was at her crib. There he had her shower, style her hair, make her face and put on something sexy. Then they were off again.

The drive took them approximately 30 minutes. Terry pulled into the parking lot of a Super 8 motel located outside the city, an area of town that Katrina had never been to. Terry put the car in park, but he didn't cut off the engine. He faced her with the most serious look in his hawk eyes. "Listen, Kat. What I'm trying to do here is get in good with some very important people, white people. I'm trying to expand this escort shit to nationwide clientele so I can leave that drug shit alone. It's important that I get in their good graces. So I had to offer you to them as a token of my friendship."

"But I'm your girl. Why don't you get one of your whores to do it? The ones from Body Workz?"

"I can't just give them any hoe. I gotta give 'em my own personal woman. That spells good faith. I trust them with you." Terry paused to let his words take effect. "I could probably use anybody, Katrina, but I want you to do it. You're perfect. A tall, white, all American, natural blonde woman."

A moment of silence passed while Katrina thought about what was being asked of her. She had grown to like Terry. He was fun and unpredictable in a dangerous sort of way. And he wasn't a bad fuck. She was his girl now, so she was obligated to be the down chick that he needed her to be, and do whatever it would take to help him progress. Because after all, she was his woman, and progress for him meant progress for them.

Katrina took a deep breath, then stuck her hand out. "I need something to motivate me."

Terry smiled. Then he dug a bag of ex-pills out of his pocket and placed two inside her hand. Katrina swallowed them dry, then kissed him in the mouth.

"I'll do it...for you."

Terry handed her a key to a room and a Crown Royal bag. "Go to room 22."

Katrina licked her lips. "Umm...I guess I'll see you..."

"You'll just be a couple of hours. Don't worry. I love you."

Katrina smiled. "I love you, too. Bye." She exited the truck. It wasn't until she stuck the key into the door of room 22 that she realized that Terry kept referring to them in a plural sense. "Their good graces," he'd said. Katrina pushed the door open and gasped.

Eight people stood around the bed wearing suit coats, shirts and ties. None of them had on pants. None of them had on underwear. All wore Halloween masks to shield their identities. All the men stood in a circle jacking their dicks hard, except for one. The odd person, smaller than the rest, was rubbing on a clit.

Katrina looked inside the Crown Royal bag and saw that it was full of condoms. She popped her neck from side to side, then pushed the door closed.

"Who's first?"

~ ~ ~ ~ ~

Kathy's eye slowly opened. Her pupil focused in on the light above. Her muscles ached as she turned her head to the right. It warmed her heart to see her baby daughter sitting there scribbling on a pad. Tears came to her eyes.

"Nah," she stopped to swallow her spit, "Nancy."

Nah Nah's head snapped upward. She caught a glimpse of her mother's eye open and hopped up, letting her notepad fall to the floor. "Mom, you're okay," Nah Nah said with joy.

Kathy nodded as best she could. "Where's your dad?"

Nah Nah lowered her head. She already tried to contact her dad several times. When he finally did answer, he made up a bunch of excuses about why he couldn't make it. But at some time during the short conversation he managed to tell her that he loved her. Nancy couldn't tell her mother that her dad wasn't coming. It would probably kill her.

"Umm...he's downstairs," Nancy lied.

"And your sister?"

Nancy held on to her mother's hand. Once again there was hesitation.

Kathy closed her eye, then opened it. "I'm a big girl, Nancy. I'm old, but I'm grown. You don't have to lie to protect my feelings." She managed to produce a weak smile.

Nancy sighed heavily. "Katrina had to leave. Father...he never showed up."

Kathy turned her head back to its original position. She gazed up at the lights for a moment in thought, then twisted her neck toward Nancy.

"Nancy, what happened to me...I was only..."

"Shhhhh. You don't owe none of us an explanation. What's important is that you're alive. Now please," she kissed her hand, "try to get some sleep."

Kathy smiled. "I love you." Then her eye closed.

Nancy wiped the tears from her eyes. She picked up her notepad, sat down and started back to work on the letter that she had been writing to O'ban. As far as she was concerned, the street life was over for her. She was going to get a job, go back to school, and hopefully be able to settle down with the man who she had once been in love with.

~ ~ ~ ~ ~

Katrina sat straddled across the female's face, humming while she sucked the man's dick who was standing over her. At the same time she had her hands around two other dicks, stroking them to keep them hard. Cum was on her hand and someone's finger was in her ass. She was being treated like a first class slut. But in truth, she was enjoying every minute of it.

Before she would depart from that room the next morning, she would have almost as much experience with dicks as Vanessa del Rio.

CHAPTER EIGHTEEN

Two weeks had passed. Nah Nah had spent every day and night in her mother's room at the hospital. To occupy her time she wrote letters back and forth to O'ban, apologizing for everything. She even asked to be his woman again, promising to be faithful this time around.

Like most men doing time, he gladly accepted her offer, even if he truly believed that it wouldn't last long.

Nah Nah entered the visiting room with Brianna in her arms. Every black woman inside the visiting room made faces at her when they saw that the child she was carrying was black.

"That's why I can't get no man," she overhead a woman saying. "White bitches is always up in a nigga's mix."

Nah Nah ignored those ignorant comments as she traveled to her seat. She couldn't understand why dark skinned sistas were so insecure, if black was supposed to be so beautiful.

For close to 20 minutes she waited, listening to people make indirect racial comments toward her. Finally O'ban walked into the visiting room. He glanced around the room for his visitor.

Nah Nah stood with a big smile plastered on her face, waving her hands for him to see. He spotted her, then strolled as cool as he could over to her. The other waiting women in the room narrowed their eyes on him in lust.

His shiny hair was braided in fancy cornrows. Jail had made him look even better than he did before. His skin shone like a newborn baby who'd been rubbed down with baby oil.

They embraced each other with warm hugs.

Nah Nah moaned as she held him tight. "Mmm, you smell so good." O'ban tried to break away. "No. Just a little longer." She did that to allow all the haters in the room to hate for a moment. Then she released him.

O'ban gazed down at his niece. "Hi, Brianna." Brianna spit her bottle out of her mouth, then stretched her arms out toward him. He picked her up, then sat in her seat.

Nah Nah picked the bottle up. "So...what's been up? You happy to see me?"

O'ban gazed at her. "Should I be?"

Nah Nah frowned. "I guess not."

"So why the change of heart?" Brianna pulled the key ring from Nah Nah's hand.

"It got really bad after you left," she admitted. "I mean really bad. I mean I...let's just say during that time I've experienced enough to say that I'm through. I'm about to get me a job, go back to school and take care of my niece."

O'ban peered down at the child in his lap. "She looks just like that lil' nigga Qu'ban." He giggled. "What I don't understand is why you got to take care of Brianna. Where's her mama? What's she out there doing?"

Nah Nah sighed as a look of sadness came over her face. "She's like really out there bad. She met this dude named…well, actually we met these dudes named Terry and Snatch and shit has been downhill ever since."

O'ban's stomach suddenly started to burn inside at the mention of Terry and Snatch's names. He decided to wait before he said something, and let her keep on talking.

Nah Nah continued. "My dad left my mom, and we're pretty sure it's a black girl." O'ban's eyebrows shot up in disbelief. "Then mom was so fucked up about it that she got dressed up one night, went out and picked up a black stranger from a bar, had sex with him…"

"What?" That was hard for him to believe.

"Yes. And ended up almost getting herself killed. He robbed her and beat her so bad that she has to get reconstructive surgery. Shit's just all fucked up right now." She looked at him. "That's why I came back for you. Hoping that I can salvage one good thing out of this whole…mess that I got myself into."

O'ban said, "Tell me about Terry and Snatch. What are they up to?"

Her eyes widened. "Terry messes with Katrina, and…I was kinda like messing with…well we fucked once I think." O'ban grunted. "Don't do that, O'ban. Please. Anyway, we thought they were cool, but…they've really degraded us in their own little way." She noticed the sour look that O'ban had on his face. "What? You're mad at me now, huh?"

"Nah. I was just thinking. You know ya man Terry is the reason that me and Qu'ban is in here."

Nah Nah's mouth opened. "Quit playing."

"This shit ain't nothing to play about. Believe me when I say that Terry's the one that got us fucked up. So you can just imagine how I feel over here listening to you tell me how those two niggas been carrying y'all out there, while we've been in here fucked up." Brianna climbed down off his lap. She stood at the table gazing at the people that sat across from them.

Nah Nah touched his hand. "I had no idea, O'ban. You have to believe me. Me or Katrina would've never knowingly did no shit like that. That's fucked up. I'm really embarrassed about the whole situation."

"That's from not keeping in touch. Look, I'ma give yo' ass another chance, but you gon' have to shape up. Keep that pussy on lock, and start sending me some money up in here."

"Okay. I will. I promise, baby. I'm here to stay." Her tone was very convincing. "I'm here for you 100 percent."

~ ~ ~ ~ ~

O'ban had been on visit for six hours. That was the first time he went to a visit without me. I was mad because I got up and got dressed after they called for him, half-ass expecting for Katrina to show up as well. I was in desperate need of some affection, and I was hoping to be able to play with my daughter.

When O'ban finally came into my cell smelling like perfume I was so jealous, I couldn't even look at him. I was sitting in a chair with my shirt off getting a tattoo of Brianna drawn on my right arm. I placed a towel over my face like I was in that much pain. But I really just wasn't trying to see his punk ass. Listen to me. Hatin' on my own brother.

"How was your visit?" I said without taking the towel down.

"You ain't gon' believe what's going on out there."

"Was Nah Nah lookin' good?" I asked, ignoring what he had said.

"Nigga, did you just hear what I said?"

I frowned. "Man, I ain't tryin' to hear that shit. Fuck the streets. What's going on in this prison is all I'm concerned with." I paused to catch my breath. "Now...was Nah Nah lookin' good?"

O'ban didn't answer right away. "Yeah."

"Did she mention Katrina? Why didn't she come see me?"

"Don't worry about it, nigga. You don't wanna hear shit about the street. Remember?"

I removed the towel from my face and gazed at him. "Is Katrina the streets, mutha fucka?" I said, being sarcastic.

O'ban removed his shirt and hung it up on the bed post. "She might as well be, from what I'm hearing." He opened up the cell door. "By the way, your daughter came, too." Then he walked out.

"Hold on, man," I said to the Mexican that was drawing on my flesh. He cut the gun off. I jumped up and went after my brother. "O'ban!"

He turned around making a face like I was bothering him. "What, man?"

I placed my arm around his neck and walked him up the hallway. "I'm sorry, man," I said in a pleading voice. "Tell me what happened. Brianna came up, too?"

O'ban smiled. "Yeah, she came. We took some pictures. That's a pretty little girl y'all got."

"That's fucked up. My daughter was up here and I couldn't even see her. Man, that bitch..."

"Eh. Fuck all that," he cut in. "Check this shit out. The whole time we been up in here, Terry and Snatch have been out there treating them bitches. Got'm popping pills and all kinda shit. I'm talking about treating them hoes bad."

"Our hoes? Katrina and..."

141

"Yesss. Nah Nah, too."

My heart started pounding with anger. "Did Terry know who they were?"

He shrugged. "Man, I'on't know. The bitch say since she's been messing with them niggas her daddy don' left her mama for some black broad. Mama went to the 'hood and picked up a nigga and ended up get fucked, robbed and damn near killed."

"Damn. All kinds of shit be happening out there." I turned away from him, walking in circles with my fists balled up. "I gotta get the fuck outta here, dog."

"I'm hip." O'ban leaned up against the wall.

I sucked my teeth. "Terry's like some goddamn infectious-ass cancer that just won't stop eating at my fucking brain. I swear if I don't kill that nigga I'ma have bad luck from here on out."

~ ~ ~ ~ ~

Katrina lay across the bed in her underwear staring up at the ceiling. She wanted to go up to the prison with Nah Nah to see Qu'ban, but was afraid of what would happen. She had changed so much over the last couple of years. Since the transition, she hadn't been much of a daughter, sister or mother. Although she allowed herself to act so irrationally, she was very much conscious of her mistakes.

Ever since that night that Terry made her have sex with all those people at that motel, he had been treating her like shit. When he picked her up that morning, thinking that she had pleased him, she caught a beat down for actually going through with it. He told her that he was just testing her loyalty and that she failed.

It started with a sniffle. Then a tear. Soon Katrina had herself wrapped around a small pillow and was crying like a child.

"Katrina!"

Katrina sat up quickly and wiped her tears away using the backs of her hands. She stood in front of the mirror until her face was free of tears. But anybody with a pair of eyes would be able to easily tell that she had been crying.

"Katrina!"

"Coming, Mom!" She pulled her hair back into a ponytail, put on some short shorts and a T-shirt and left the room.

Nah Nah and Katrina brought Kathy home the day before. The doctor prescribed a bottle of pain pills and plenty of bed rest. Katrina agreed to keep an eye on her while her sister was away.

Kathy was sitting up in bed watching a blank TV screen. Katrina appeared in her doorway. She tapped the bed next to her. Katrina entered the bed on her knees and rested her cheek up against her mother's hand.

"You've been cryin'," Kathy said. "I just wanted you to know how sorry I am for doing what I did." Katrina tried to speak, but Kathy shooshed her. "It's not your fault, or your dad's. The truth is, I have been curious of what it would be like to...to...you know, with a black man since Prince became famous."

Katrina couldn't help but laugh. "No way."

"It's true," Kathy admitted. "Your mother wasn't always a stuck up bitch. I had a little freak in me too. So...I guess you got it, honest." She turned and took Katrina's face in her hands. Katrina couldn't stand to see her mother's face in that condition. "What I'm trying to say is, don't let your curiosity have you ending up like what happened to me...or something

143

much worse." She kissed her daughter's forehead.

Katrina snuggled up in the bed with her mother and fell asleep.

The door creaked when it opened.

Katrina opened her eyes. She turned her head and flinched when she saw that she was face to face with Nah Nah.

Nah Nah raised a finger up to her lips. "Shhh!" Then she motioned for her to follow her out of the room.

Katrina eased out of the bed and followed her out of the room. Nah Nah faced her once they got into the living room.

"What happened up there?" Katrina asked as she placed her hands on her hips. She cut her eyes toward the sofa and saw Brianna lying down on the couch. "Was she happy to see her uncle? How is Qu'ban? Did O'ban mention him at all? I…"

"Katrina! Shut up and listen."

Katrina ran her fingers through her hair, then walked over to the sofa and sat down next to Brianna. "So what happened?"

Nah Nah peered at her and said, "Your new man Terry is the same guy that helped put O'ban and Qu'ban in prison."

Katrina's mouth opened wide. "You've got to be kidding, right? Please tell me you're kidding."

She rolled her eyes at Katrina. "Does it look like I'm kidding? O'ban asked what's been going on. I told him about us and how we've been fucking with Terry and Snatch. He waited until I finished talking, then he told me that Terry and Qu'ban used to be best friends. Somewhere along the line Terry became a stool pigeon." She put her hand on her forehead. "And to think we've been out here kicking it and having kinky sex with the guy who's responsible for putting our men in jail."

"Unfuckin' believable."

"Yes," Nah Nah agreed, "it is." She paced the floor with her arms folded across her stomach.

Katrina gazed up at her sister. "You think they knew?"

Nah Nah shrugged. "I don't know. Probably. You never can tell with those two."

Katrina thought to herself for a moment, then looked up at her sister and said, "Tell O'ban to ask Qu'ban to call me."

~ ~ ~ ~ ~

When O'ban called that night to make sure that Nah Nah had made it home, sometime during the conversation she relayed Katrina's message for me to call her.

The next day Katrina received a phone call from me.

"Hi," Katrina said in a timid voice. She was embarrassed that she had been having a fling with my enemy. I knew that because her voice hadn't been that timid since I got locked up.

It took me a minute to respond. I was angry, and I knew that if I spoke too soon I would've ended up cussing that bitch out and fucking up everything.

Katrina was impatient. "Sooo…you don't have anything to say to me?"

"I do, but what is there to say? I'm fucked up wit' you. I'm fucked up about this whole situation with Terry."

"Qu'ban, you have to believe me. I had no idea that you two even knew each other. I know I'm just a dumb white girl and according to your theory, 'white women fuck their men's friends,' but that's not the case here."

"And the purpose of this conversation is?"

Katrina let out a drawn out frustrated sigh. "I…I wanna make this right. Ya know? This whole thing is…is killing me inside to…to know that I've committed such a disloyal act toward you."

"Man, you don't even know me like that fa real."

"You're my daughter's father, Qu'ban. I...I've been through so much that I'm just ready to bolt down. I want to make things right with you, our child and my family."

Same old song, I thought to myself. "What exactly are you gonna do to make it right? Huh? Tell me that."

Katrina got quiet. "I don't know, but I'll figure something out."

"Well, until you figure it out...you ain't got nothing to say to me." Then I hung up the phone.

CHAPTER NINETEEN

Terry sat behind his big desk inside his office, located in the back of Body Workz. He was talking business on the phone. Katrina sat in a chair on the other side of his desk with her legs crossed, looking sexy in a snug fitting skirt and Cartier shades.

"That is too fucking much," Terry yelled into the phone. Nah, what you need to realize is...hello? Hello? Shit!" He slammed down the phone.

Katrina studied his face for a moment. "You know what your problem is, Terry?"

Terry frowned at her. "No. Tell me what my problem is."

Her legs uncrossed as she leaned forward. "You don't know how to run a real business."

"What? Bitch, I've been handling business since I was 16."

"I didn't say you didn't handle your business. I said you don't know how to run a real business. When you speak to real businessmen on the phone, you don't use words like, 'nah' or 'fucking.' You handle business people with finesse. That's why you need me more than you realize."

Terry leaned back in his chair. "What can you do?"

After a brief sigh, she stood, walked around the desk and took a seat on the edge, facing him.

"I know how to handle people. I need to be the front face for this business. I can go places and deal with people that you can't. My major in college was Business Accounting. I'm good with numbers, and you can trust me."

She kicked off her shoe, then placed her foot on Terry's crotch. The bitch had a point, Terry thought. She had hipped him to things that he should've thought of. She was white, educated and had a little game about herself. A jewel was up under him and he didn't even know it. Until now.

"Okay," Terry said as he stood.

When Katrina saw him unzip his pants, she pulled her skirt up to her waist.

"From here on out," Terry continued, "I want you to show up here every morning at 10 a.m. dressed in the proper women's business attire. "I'ma put this place in your hands to run. Groom the rest of them hoes on how to be professional. Collect all the money and handle the books. It couldn't hurt for me to see how this plays out."

"It's gonna work," Katrina said as she leaned toward him. She pressed her lips up against his.

~ ~ ~ ~ ~

The heels of Kortni's quarter length boots tapped against the floor as she walked through the building that housed Michael's office. She took the elevator to the 6th floor.

The receptionist at the desk picked up the phone when she spotted Kortni coming.

"Don't bother," Kortni said, "he's expecting me."

Michael and one of his colleagues were in the middle of a meeting when Kortni barged into his office. Both men peered up when they heard the door swing open. She stood there, feet spread apart, hands on her hips with an evil glare in her eye.

"David," Michael said, with worry in his voice, "can you please excuse us."

David's head turned toward Michael, who nodded at him. He walked toward the door.

David shook his head as he left the room. As soon as he was gone, Kortni stomped over to Michael's desk and slammed her bag down. She stared at him briefly. Suddenly her hand raised high above her head, then came down striking him in the face.

Kortni screamed, "What the hell are you doing calling my job inquiring about my position there?"

Michael held his jaw where her fingernail had dug into his face. He examined the blood on this fingers.

"Kortni," he began, "I've got some respectable friends. I'm a respectable man in my community." He paused to snatch some tissue from the box on his desk. "I can't have you coming into my place of business with this shit. I think I have every right to know a little more about you other than how much you enjoy shopping and fucking."

Kortni pointed a manicured finger at his face. "I already told your ass that I was a secretary and I liked my job. Didn't I? Didn't I?"

"Kortni, honey, you and I both know what goes on at massage parlors, so why don't we just cut the bullshit."

Her eyes narrowed on him. "Are you asking me if I'm...if I'm a bloody whore?!" Michael didn't respond. Her mouth twisted up as she raised her hand again. When she swung, Michael ducked it, clutched her wrist, then dragged her over the desk, knocking everything over. She fell face first onto the floor screaming. Michael put his foot on her chest, then applied pressure. She squirmed, cussed, tried to move it, but his leg was too strong.

"You have no idea what a man under my kind of stress can do to a woman, Kortni," he said in a chilling voice. Kortni gazed up at him with fear in her eyes. "If I want to have you checked out," he continued, "I'll have you checked out. And if what you told me that you do there doesn't check out...then you're gonna check out. Get my drift?"

When he finally removed his huge foot, Kortni hurried to her feet, still holding her chest, looking at him like he was crazy.

Michael took a seat in his chair and readjusted his tie. "I won't be home 'til late and when I do get there, I want a good meal waiting...and you serving it to me in something sexy. I threw away a perfectly good family for you, so you're gonna have to make up for that. Now go, Kathy...uh...Kortni." He hit a button on his phone. "Send David back in, please."

Kortni didn't take her eyes off him as she picked up her bag and backed out of the room. David was standing at the front desk when Kortni stomped past with a terrified look on her face. He made a devious smirk on his face as he watched her get on the elevator. She was going to have to be extra careful if she was going to get the proposal she so desperately needed.

~ ~ ~ ~ ~

"You what?!" Nah Nah shouted.

"I'm in charge of Terry's business now," Katrina repeated for her.

Nah Nah sat down the pillow that she was holding and stood up from the bed that she was sitting on. She approached Katrina, who was standing in front of the mirror, trying on different outfits for work.

"What part of Terry snitched on Qu'ban and O'ban don't you understand?"

Katrina regarded her, "What part of I don't give a fuck don't you understand?" She held a white blouse up to her torso. "We have to look out for ourselves. The Cartez brothers can't do a damn thing for us right now. What do you think of this blouse?"

Nah Nah snatched the blouse out of her hand, then threw it onto the bed. "I thought we agreed that we were through with all this shit—hanging out and doing drugs."

"I am through. Working as an accountant for Terry's businesses is a real job."

"It's not right, Katrina."

"What's done is done! So just get over it."

The two sisters stared at each other for a long moment. Suddenly, Nah Nah spun around and marched out of the room, slamming the door behind her.

Katrina peered at the closed door for a moment, then turned back toward the mirror.

At 10:15 a.m. the next morning, Katrina showed up for work dressed in a white blouse, black pinstriped slacks and three-inch pumps. She was ready for business. Terry placed her behind his desk and opened his books up to her. Body Workz was a massage parlor that doubled as an escort service, which was really a front for a prostitution ring. Then there was the real estate investment company. Katrina's job was to funnel the profits from the prostitution scheme and the drug money through both businesses without being detected. Being that she had a gift for working with numbers, she knew exactly what to do. By using her dad's name for influence, she would be able to attract professional people in high positions in both Kansas and Missouri as clientele for the escort service. She could hide those funds by writing receipts for massages and treatments that never happened. On the real estate side of things, on paper it would appear that Terry was buying and selling 3 to 4 homes per week, making 20% profits. Off paper, the majority of the homes didn't even exist. Katrina had the skills to route, re-route, and transfer funds so fast and so often, that the trail would be nearly impossible to detect, unless the feds had an inside source.

It turned out to be a great scheme, because fortunately for Katrina, just like the feds wouldn't be able to track the funds, neither could Terry. And he was making so much money that he wouldn't even notice a 5 to 10 percent skim here and there.

For the first two months, business was prosperous for both Terry and Katrina. Like she had planned, the escort service took on a broader, more elite type of clientele. Katrina was also placed in charge of marketing. On their business cards she had the words, "Ladies Will Travel" added on, which attracted a lot of out-of-town clients as well.

By her sixth month Katrina had successfully managed to skim a quarter of a million dollars from the companies' profits.

Ring, ring.

"Body Workz. This is Terry." He listened intently to what was being asked of him. "I've already tol...uh...informed you, Mr. Galanis. We don't have any women available at this time. I'm booked up." He hastened, "I know you're an important..." He listened some more. "We don't have to go there. Let me see what I can do." He hung up, leaned back in his chair, ran his hand over his chin, sighed, then picked up the phone. "Kortni, get in here."

"Right away, Mr. Finch."

It took her all of 10 seconds to come walking through his office door. "Yes, Terry?" She was looking quite sexy in her white ruffled blouse, gray business skirt that complemented her curves, and black knee high boots.

Terry stood, walked around his desk, then sat on the edge of it, facing her.

"Who was it that brought you over to America, on the run from a lunatic husband that thinks that you were kidnapped?"

"You did, Terry."

"And who set you up with a place to stay, a vehicle and pays you a hefty salary to be his secretary?"

"You, Terry." Her hands started to fidget.

Terry leaned forward, wrapped his arms around her, clutched her ass, then pulled her body up to his. Kortni turned her face away. She didn't feel comfortable in that position.

"I did all of that," Terry continued, "and only asked what of you?"

"To…to show some gratitude when the time comes."

Terry released her, then picked up the phone and dialed a number. "Mr. Galanis? I found someone." He picked up a pen. "Go ahead."

While Terry wrote down the address, Kortni turned away and walked over to the window. She had a sense of loyalty to Terry, but she was also afraid that Michael would find out. If he did, it would fuck up all her plans. She was steadily getting him to ease up on his aversion to dating a black woman, and hopefully within the next year his resolve would be gone completely. Then they could get married and she would legally become a U.S. Citizen. She knew that this sort of thing took some time and finesse, but she was confident it was within her reach. That wouldn't happen if Terry decided to contact her husband in London and make trouble. So she was trapped. She had no other choice but to go through with it and pray that she didn't get caught.

Terry hung up the phone. As he was doing so he ripped the piece of paper from the pad, then he handed it to her.

"Take the company limo."

~ ~ ~ ~ ~

The company limo pulled up in front of the Embassy Suites Hotel. Kortni took her shades out of her purse and put them on. When the driver opened the door for her, she bolted out of it with her head down and into the front entrance.

She took the elevator to the top floor. Once she located the room she unbuttoned her trench coat. Two knocks and the door swung open. Kortni had opened up her coat, revealing that she had on absolutely nothing underneath, before she realized who it was standing before her.

~ ~ ~ ~ ~

"Cartez," the C.O. called out.

"Pass it," I yelled.

I watched as my letter passed through three hands before it reached mine. It had been a long time since I'd received anything from anyone but Pops, so you can imagine how shocked I was when I saw that it was from Katrina.

There was no reason for me to stick around and listen to other inmates' names get called. I knew I didn't have nothing else coming, so I dashed off to my cell, where I closed the door and plopped down on my bunk.

"What the fuck this bitch got to say?" I asked myself as I

tore open the envelope. I hadn't heard from her since that last phone conversation we had six months before. The fucked up part about it was that I heard that the bitch was still hanging from Terry's nut sack.

The letter was typed on pink paper that reeked of perfume. It read:

>*Dear Q,*
>
>*I know you're fucked up with me right now, but you have to please believe that everything that I'm doing is in our best interest. I'm your bitch, nigga, and always have been. So start preparing yourself for the streets because I'm coming to get you and I'ma have a gwap waiting on you when you get here. Think I'm playing? Check your account.*
>
>*Who's your bitch?*
>*You better say I am.*

I read the letter three more times before I finally got up and walked to the phone. I entered my four digit code and impatiently awaited the outcome.

The operator lady came on and announced that I now had $10,052 on my account. My first thought was, what the fuck has Katrina gotten herself into? It didn't take me long to figure out that she was stealing from Terry. That was the only explanation that I could think of for her still seeing Terry.

On one hand it was good that she was trimming the sucka's pockets. But on the other hand I knew Terry. He was a snake, and didn't trust nobody, not even the innocent blonde white girl, Katrina. Sooner or later he was going to start sniffing around, and if he picked up on Katrina's scheme, then she was gonna pay everything back ten-fold.

I grabbed some envelopes and a notebook from the cabinet in the C.O.'s office, then took them back to my cell. I had to write Katrina a letter that would hopefully save her life.

~ ~ ~ ~ ~

"David," Kortni said with shocking surprise.

David smiled as he removed his glasses. "Come in, Kortni." She didn't move. "I'm not gonna bite."

Kortni closed her jacket. She entered the room and headed straight for the mini bar, where she took a bottle of Jack Daniels from the cooler.

She popped the top off the small bottle, tilted her head back and downed half of it. The hot liquid made her face twist as it traveled down into her stomach.

David approached her. "You okay?" He was being sarcastic.

Kortni caught her breath. "This is not what you're thinking, David."

"Sure it isn't," David said in disbelief. He took a few steps away from her, then spun around. He smiled at her. "I got you right where I want you, Kortni. I don't know how your little black ass managed to get up on Michael like you did, but I do know that he left his wife for you, a detail I'm sure he wouldn't want to get out. And on top of it all, you're nothing but a skanky hooker."

"I'm not a hoo…"

"Shut up!" He gazed at her.

A moment of silence passed.

Kortni was restless and too scared to keep her mouth closed. "So what is it that you want, David? Sex, is it?"

David cut his eyes at her like the thought alone made him want to vomit. "No. Unlike my colleague Michael, I don't have an interest in having sex with a nigger, even if she does talk fancy."

Kortni's lips were pressed tight together as her anger grew. Her gaze fell upon the ice pick that sat on the bar top. She envisioned herself picking it up and sticking it in his throat. That would keep his big mouth from being able to say anything to Michael about anything ever again.

"So why am I here, David?" She placed her hand down beside the ice pick.

David walked over to the window and gazed out onto the Westport area. "I've had my eye on this one woman since she was fifteen. I used to literally ejaculate in my slacks every time I saw her. So many times I've wanted to approach her, but I couldn't. She was too young. The time wasn't right." He turned around and faced Kortni. "And it simply wouldn't be the appropriate thing for me to do. But now...now it's perfect. I am able to have sex in her, and we'll both keep it quiet." He pointed at her. "And you're going to help me get her in this bed...or I'll tell everyone about Michael's dirty little secret and you can kiss your sugar daddy goodbye."

"Who is this person that you're referring to, David?"

His eyes blinked repeatedly. "Michael's daughter... Katrina."

CHAPTER TWENTY

"So how soon can we make this happen?" Katrina asked the man in the cheap suit who was sitting across from her at the table.

The man made a steeple with his fingers while he contemplated an answer. "Assuming that everything goes right...within the month."

"And on my end?"

"Uh, that's hard to say for sure, but I'd say sometime within the next 60 days everything will be settled."

"Good enough for me." Katrina pulled her laptop out of her bag that sat beside her chair. She placed it on the table and opened it up. "This is what I have." She closed it when she saw the waitress coming in their direction.

"Sorry for keeping you waiting. What will you be having today?"

Katrina said, "Order anything you want. It's on me today." She took a sip from her water glass and smiled.

~ ~ ~ ~ ~

Kortni walked into the front door of Body Workz. She dropped her bag on her desk, then dropped down in her chair. Her elbows rested on her desk and her face in her hands.

"How do I continue to get myself in these bloody messes?"

"Back so soon?"

Kortni gasped as her head snapped upward. Terry was standing there staring down at her through suspicious eyes.

"You done already?"

"Uh, yeah. Un huh. It didn't take long." David told her before she left to keep things discrete. It was her job and her job alone to get Katrina into his bed.

"You sure?"

Kortni faked a smile. "C'mon, Terry. I promised you, didn't I?"

From his hip he removed his cell phone and began dialing numbers. Within seconds he confirmed that Kortni had told him the truth. He sighed a breath of relief after he hung up the phone. Without a word he patted her on the back and walked away.

Kortni snatched up the phone off her desk and dialed Michael's number.

"Hello," Michael answered.

"Hey love."

"Hey," he said with excitement. "How are you doing?"

"Good. Look, I was just sitting here wondering was there anything special that you wanted for dinner tonight?"

While she was talking on the phone to Michael, Katrina walked through the door. She stopped just short of Kortni's desk and started conversing with Terry.

Kortni heard Katrina giggling and looked up. She saw Katrina standing in front of Terry with her laptop up to her chest. Occasionally her gaze would shift down toward her feet, admiring the crocodile boots that she had on.

"Let me give you a call back," Kortni said into the phone.

She hung up and rose to her feet.

Katrina nodded her head at Terry. Seconds later they parted ways.

"Umm...oh yeah. You got some messages." Kortni picked up two small pieces of yellow paper from her desk and handed them to her.

"Thank you." Katrina tried to walk away, but Kortni held her up.

"Katrina."

Katrina stopped and turned around. "What is it, Kortni?"

"I...will you...urggh!" She waved her hand. "Never mind."

Katrina look at her like she was strange. "Okay. I'll catch you later." She walked away.

Kortni plopped down in her seat. "Shit."

~ ~ ~ ~ ~

Katrina picked up her mail from home that night, then drove over to her mother's. Brianna and Nah Nah were there sitting at the kitchen table, eating Oreo cookies and milk.

"Mama!" Brianna called.

"Hey, ba-byy." Katrina dropped her purse and ran to hug her. "What ya eating?"

"Cookies."

"Mmm. Can I have some?"

Brianna held a half of a cookie up to her mouth. Katrina bit off a tiny piece. "Mmm."

Nah Nah experienced a feeling of jealousy run through her. She stood up and clutched Brianna's hand.

"C'mon, Bri Bri. Let's go take a bath."

"Bye-bye," Katrina cooed.

Katrina sat in the chair and looked through her mail. She thumbed through the short stack until she spotted one with

Qu'ban's name on it. The rest she set on the table. She opened it up, picked up an Oreo off the plate and began to read.

Bzzst. Bzzst.

She sighed, set the letter down and answered her cell phone.

"Hello." The operator came on and announced that Qu'ban was calling. She pressed 5. "Hello."

"Wha' sup?"

Katrina smiled as she sunk comfortably inside the chair. "I was just about to read your letter. Did you get mine?"

"I got it. Be careful what you say on the phone, but from what I'm getting out of your last letter leads me to believe that you're raping Terry."

"So what if I am? All that matters is that you benefit from it, right? Because you're the reason that I'm doing it. I want to make sure that we're straight when you get out. I meant you're coming home soon and I want to make you proud. I want you to have a reason to love me."

"I can dig that. But try and understand what it is that I'm saying. I know the man. Okay? If you get caught, he's gonna do a whole lot more than just kick yo' ass. You feel me?"

She ran her hand through her hair. "Listen, baby. On the surface I may seem like a dumb white girl, but trust me when I say I got this."

"You got it?"

"Yeah. I got it."

Qu'ban sighed. "Then there's nothing else to be said. Handle your business, and be careful."

"Thank you. Now let me hear what I need to hear."

"I love you."

"Who's your bitch?"

"You are."

"You better say I am."

~ ~ ~ ~ ~

While I was speaking to Katrina on the phone, I saw my case manager, Mr. Allen, come walking out of his office. He flinched when he saw me. Probably surprised that I was still on the unit, being that everyone else had left for chow.

Without so much as a nod, he walked right past me. When he got down to the end of the hall, he turned and looked at me. I could see him out of the corner of my eye, but I didn't turn in his direction. Suddenly, as if he didn't want to be seen, he made a quick left and disappeared.

The phone made a loud noise when I finally hung it up. I took off in the same direction as Mr. Allen. By the time I got to the end of the hallway, he just appeared out of nowhere, and scared the shit out of me.

"Damn! Mr. Allen," I hollered. "What the hell you doin' snooping around an' shit? You scared the shit outta me."

His wrinkled face cracked a smile. "Just shaking down cells, that's all. You don't have anything in yours, do you?"

"No, sir. I'm trying to get sent to a camp. I ain't doing nothing wrong."

"That's good." He was acting weird.

"Well, I'll see you later." I turned around and started walking back toward my cell. On the way there, I couldn't help but think about what I had just seen on Mr. Allen that wasn't appropriate for him to have at that moment.

~ ~ ~ ~ ~

The next morning Katrina got up and drove out to Lee's Summit, where she met with an agent from J.C. Nichals Reality Co., to make an offer on a house that she had been looking at. She already picked out the furniture that she wanted to decorate the place with. Everything was going to be perfect when Qu'ban finally came home.

For over six months Katrina seemed to be doing everything right. She was moving money from one place to another, skimming a few dollars here and there, making it disappear without a trace. She had gotten so good at it and her ego blew up so big that she thought it was impossible for her to get caught. But what she failed to realize was that she had to cover her tracks at all angles, not just on paper.

Katrina didn't arrive at Body Workz until the afternoon. She strutted into the building wearing an expensive business suit, carrying a crocodile briefcase.

Kortni was sitting at her desk when she saw Katrina coming. She jumped up out of her seat. "Excuse me, Katrina." Katrina stopped and gazed at her. "You mind if I talk to you for a moment?"

Katrina shrugged impatiently. "So talk."

"It's a private matter, really."

A quick sigh, then Katrina looked at her watch. "Okay. Follow me to my office."

Snatch was standing nearby in the midst of a conversation with one of the working girls when Katrina first walked in. He watched the two women converse, then go into Katrina's office. Then he excused himself and went to go talk to Terry.

Terry was kicked back with his feet up on his desk reading a book called *The Art of Business* when Snatch walked in. He set the book down and sat up straight.

"Wha' sup?"

Snatch took a seat in a chair in front the desk. "Something ain't right, T."

"What ain't right, Snatch?"

"Katrina just pulled up in a new BMW 645."

"So?"

"So, when did we start paying her that much? I mean, that suit that the bitch strutted in here in had to cost a couple of grand."

Terry smiled. "C'mon, dog. You know the bitch ain't gone be in control of all that money and not skim a few pennies here and there. You got to expect that for what she's doing for us. Why do you think I pay the bitch so little and she don't complain about it? 'Cause the bitch is getting her chop off the top."

Snatch leaned in toward him. "Yeah? But the million dollar question is…how much chop is she getting off the top?"

Terry reclined in his leather chair. He stared up at the ceiling while he contemplated what was being said to him.

The leather whined as he slowly leaned his chair forward to where he was facing Snatch again. "Keep an eye on the bitch. You might just be onto something."

~ ~ ~ ~ ~

Kortni stood in Katrina's office with her arms folded across her chest. Katrina sat in a chair behind her desk, waiting on her to say what she had to say.

"I'm listening."

Kortni locked her fingers together. "Well, it's like this, Katrina. There's this guy. He called here the other day requesting a girl. There was none available, so Terry summoned me to go to the man's room and entertain the bloody wanker. Anyway, when I got there, I quickly found out that it wasn't me he wanted."

"Who was it?"

"It was you, Katrina," she admitted.

Katrina's eyebrows shot up. "Me? Why?"

"He says that he's had a fetish for you since you were 16 or something like that."

Katrina laughed. "He's obviously crazy. I..."

"I don't think so. He went on telling me that he was the real reason that we've been having so much business. He says that there wasn't a girl available that day because his associates had ordered them all. He...he was banking on them sending me, which they did...and now I'm supposed to get you to go to bed with him."

Katrina stared at Kortni. Kortni looked away from her, obviously avoiding eye contact.

"Why is it, Kortni, that you think he chose you to try to coerce me into sleeping with him?"

Kortni didn't respond.

Katrina rose from her seat, walked around her table and stood in front of her. "Kortni?" Silence. "Maybe it's because he found out about you and my father?"

Kortni raised her head and shook the hair out of her face. She looked up at Katrina with a bewildered expression. She took a deep breath. "So you know?"

Katrina stared at her in disbelief. All of her suspicions were finally confirmed. Then her face suddenly twisted up as she reached back and punched Kortni in the nose. Kortni fell to the ground, holding her face.

"You bitch!" Katrina yelled. She pointed her finger down at her. "You ruined my entire goddamn family."

"Katrina," Kortni cried as she got up on her knees. "Katrina, I swear to you I didn't mean for any of this to happen."

"Do you have any fucking idea what my family has gone through since you walked into my dad's life? Do you?!" she screamed.

Tears flowed down Kortni's cheeks. "I love your…"

Katrina stepped forward and hit her in the face again. "Don't you say it. Don't you dare tell that lie in my face. I know your kind. You couldn't possibly be in love with him. You're just using him."

Kortni sat back up. She wiped away the tears and blood from her face with the back of her hand. She took a second to gather herself, then climbed to her feet.

Panting, she said, "Are you satisfied now? You've beaten me up. Does that make it any better? If you don't do this then David is going to out your father…"

Katrina raised her fist like she was about to strike her, but thought better of it. "Urrgh! Get the hell outta my office!"

A second or two passed before Kortni dug David's card out of her pocket and tossed it onto the desk. "If you should decide to help, that's his card." Then she exited the room.

Although Katrina was angry, she couldn't help but take a look at the name on the card. She snatched it up. She recognized the name on it almost immediately.

"You got a fetish, huh, David?" She snatched up the phone and started dialing numbers. She pushed her hair back over her ear and held the phone up to it. "This'll teach you about thinking with your little head instead of your big one."

CHAPTER TWENTY-ONE

Bzzst. Bzzst.

Kortni removed one of her hands from the steering wheel and picked up her cell phone.

"Hello?"

"I'll take care of it." It was Katrina.

Kortni closed her eyes in relief. "Oh, god. Thank you, Katrina. You aren't going to say anything to your father about the call I went on are you?"

"Why would I do that? He's a grown man. He's old enough to know what he's getting into without any involvement from me." Then Katrina hung up.

On the way home Kortni stopped at the store and picked up some red wine and chocolate strawberries.

When Michael arrived at home, he was greeted with a hot dinner and a bubble bath. Jazz was crooning out of the bathroom radio while Michael sat in the tub, soaking his aching bones. Kortni appeared in the doorway. An unusual amount of makeup had been applied to her naturally pretty face. She had on a two-piece, red, sheer nightgown from Victoria's Secret. A bottle of red wine was in one hand, and a small bowl of chocolate covered strawberries was in the other. Michael peered over at her with lust in his eyes.

"I was hoping that you could show me what to do with these," she said, referring to the chocolate strawberries.

Michael wasted no time getting out of the tub.

The entire escapade lasted no longer than an hour. Afterwards they collapsed into each other's arms panting. Beads of sweat covered both their faces. Kortni rolled over on top of him, their foreheads touching. She gazed into his eyes. She decided to try to move her plans for Michael along at a quicker pace.

"Promise me you'll never let me go, Michael. No matter what happens."

Michael had a serious look in his eyes. "I love you too much for that to happen."

"Enough to get married?"

His eyes fluttered. His mind shot off in a million different directions. "I…I…I don't know Kortni, this has all been so fast. I love you, I do, but you're going to have to give me some time. I promise I will think about it, but that's the best I can do right now."

Kortni smiled. At least he was willing to consider it. It would only be a matter of time before he was wrapped totally around her finger. She eased her body down until the covers were over her head and her face was between his legs.

Michael closed his eyes. "Oh my god."

~ ~ ~ ~ ~

"So what are your plans for when you get out, O'ban?" Nah Nah asked him. They were inside the visiting room in Springfield.

O'ban chewed up the rest of his chicken sandwich before he answered. "What the fuck you think my plan is? I'ma hustle."

"Until when? Or are you going to hustle until you get busted again? You got to have some kind of goal."

"Aw, shit. All the white girl is starting to come outta yo' ass now."

Nah Nah shook her head. "Look, I'm with you while you're doing this jail thing. But if all you're going to do when you get out is do shit to get locked back up, then I can't be with you."

O'ban rolled his eyes. "Well, what do you think I should do, Nah Nah, since you know so goddamned much? Work at McDonald's and hope that I take over the company one day?"

"No. I'm not saying that you can't hustle. I'm just saying to have a goal to go along with it. For instance, while you're just sitting here, you could be learning a trade. Learn how to paint cars or lay brick, then start your own business with your hustle money, so you won't have to hustle no more. No more hustling means no more jail. It's just that simple."

O'ban seemed to think about it. "That all sounds good. And I might even do that. But first I gotta settle up with this nigga Terry. I owe Qu'ban that much."

"Boy!" She sighed out loud in frustration. "You need to leave that bullshit alone. Concentrate on O'ban and what he's going to do with his life. By the time Qu'ban gets out, I'm sure he won't even be thinking about Terry. Hopefully he'll be too busy trying to get his life back in order."

O'ban shook his head. "You don't know Qu'ban."

"But I know you. I'm in love with you, and I want you to get out of here and do the right thing."

"Why?"

"You showed me how to be projectish...now let me show you now to be just the opposite. I left that street shit alone because I don't have the stomach for it. And quiet as it's kept, I don't believe that you do either."

~ ~ ~ ~ ~

Inside her rearview mirror she spotted a blue Chrysler LHS. If she wasn't mistaken, that same car had been following her since she left Body Workz. It was in the parking lot of the nail shop. She swore she had seen it when she'd stopped by the sex store to pick up some sexy undergarments. Now there it was again, three cars behind her. Katrina wondered how long the car had actually been following her. A day? A week? A month maybe? Whoever it was probably knew every place that she had been. Had been there when she met with the agent about the house. When she purchased her hot new car. And knew what bank she had the money stashed in.

She didn't have any enemies that she knew of. But she was doing wrong things. And when you're doing wrong, enemies form out of nowhere. So it was possible that the person following her was an enemy of Terry's. Or maybe even worse. Terry might have gotten wise to what she was doing and was having her followed. If that was the case, then the person who was following her was really an enemy of her own.

Which was a scary thought.

Katrina came to a halt at the stoplight on 39th and Broadway. The Chrysler pulled alongside her. The man behind the wheel was big, fortyish, with a shiny bald head. He put her in the mind of Snatch when she peered at him.

When the light turned green he drove off without looking at her once. Before he got too far ahead, she had enough sense to log his license plate into her phone.

~ ~ ~ ~ ~

Someone tapped on the door.

David dashed a heavy amount of aftershave into the palm of his hand, then smeared it over his cheeks and neck. He gazed into the mirror studying his reflection. He was a young version of Tom Arnold. A dork to anyone else. But he liked what he saw.

When he answered the door he saw Katrina standing there. She wanted to laugh when she saw how he was dressed—a short terry cloth bathrobe and black dress socks that were pulled up to his knees.

"You," she said.

David smiled bashfully. "Yeah."

Katrina shook her head from side to side. "You naughty boy. And to think all that time I thought you were just a dumb geek when you used to come over to our house. But inside you were fantasizing about making love to me. I was just a kid, David."

A slick smile appeared on David's face as he turned around. "Were you now." He walked over to the bar and started preparing two drinks.

Katrina stepped inside and closed the door. "There was a lot of sarcasm in that 'were you now.' So could you please elaborate?"

David handed her a drink. "I saw you, Katrina," he said as he stirred the glass in his hand. "You left school early one day. I watched you walk for three blocks, then you got into that car with those three boys. The four of you went to a house in the city. It was a small house. You all had a few drinks, and…smoked a joint or two. Then you…you decided to remove your clothing. And one by one those guys climbed on top of you and hunched you, and hunched you, until there was blood all over that sofa."

171

Katrina's breathing accelerated.

"I was temped to barge in and stop them. But after I got a good look at your face...I saw a hint of a smile. That's when I knew that you were enjoying it." He sipped on his drink. "I jerked off during the whole episode. After I came I became angry. Not because you were in there getting a train ran on you. No, that wasn't the reason at all."

Katrina stared at him from across the room. "It was because those boys were black, wasn't it?"

David smiled. "Exactly. That's why I called your mom and had her send the police over there."

"You bastard!"

"I guess you have a right to be angry at me for telling on you like I did. It could've ruined the relationship that you had with your father totally. But I guess your mother knew that...that's why she kept it a secret. To this day poor old Michael doesn't know that his precious little girl with the cartoon panties has been sucking black cocks since she was only fourteen."

"Yeah? Well I guess you forgot to tell him because you were too busy playing peeping Tom and jerking your dick off while your lame ass was looking through people's windows." She paused to catch her breath. "But you won't have to tell him." She reached into her purse and pulled out a tape recorder. "Cause I will."

David's eyes zeroed in on the small electronic device. The glass that he was holding fell from his hand.

"See, I've been onto you, Da-vid. Ever since I as a little girl and you used to sit down and show me what accountants do on the computer. And tell me about how easy it was to steal money. And I noticed that every single time you stood up from that computer, you would have a wet stain on the front of your pants. Probably coming on yourself every time our hands touched."

"You little…" he bolted toward her.

Katrina pulled the lamp down in front of him, causing him to trip and stumble, then she shot out the door.

~ ~ ~ ~ ~

"That bitch wouldn't never let me see her while she sucked on this dick for nothing in the world. She would always hide under the fuckin' covers and shit. So we get to arguing in front of some people one day, and that bitch say, 'That's why you ate this pussy.' I said sheeit, bitch, you sucked my dick, so what's the difference? She started tripping and screaming, 'Pussy, you ain't never seen me suck yo' nasty-ass dick.' I said, shit, you must got a hell of a pussy on your face then."

Everybody at the card table started laughing. All night we had been up playing spades and listening to me tell stories. Half of them were lies, but they were some funny ones. It was me, Dre, another nigga named Dre, and Smoke.

Dre looked at Smoke with a big smile on his face while he shuffled the card deck. "Every story this nigga Qu'ban tells us, he eatin' some pussy or ass in. That's why I'm always calling this nigga a maggot. Mutha fuckin' flies love to eat shit."

Once again there was laughter at the table. I didn't find that statement to be funny though.

I said, "If a nigga ain't kinky in some kind of way out there, it's gon' be hard for him to get some pussy. 'Cause niggas is out there eating bitches up. They don't pay a hoe to fuck her no more, they're paying just to eat the bitch. Like the bitch is a fuckin' meal or somethin'…"

"Yeah, nigga, let that be the reason," Dre commented.

"Man, fuck you. Deal the fuckin' cards."

The door to the TV room opened. In walked O'ban carrying a thick-ass book in his hand. He set it down on the table beside ours, took a seat, then opened it up.

Smoke looked at him. "What the fuck you doing?"

"Studying. What it look like?" O'ban replied in a smart tone.

"It look to me like you tryin' to fool yo' mutha fuckin' self. V.T. Auto. Nigga, you don't know shit about no mutha-fuckin' cars, except how to pack it with dope."

More laughter.

"I expect that out of a bunch of niggas in prison who ain't got shit else to do but play cards and tell jokes."

I jumped in. "Whoa! Whoa! Nigga, don't forget yo' brother is sitting at this table."

O'ban peered at me. "Nigga, I'm talking to you, too."

"No you ain't."

"You playin' cards and telling jokes, ain't you?"

I leaned back in my chair. "Nigga, if you gon' be on all that righteous-ass shit, take yo' punk ass up to the chapel or library and get the fuck away from us. We biddin' over here, nigga."

"Yeah," said Smoke. "Convicts."

O'ban closed his book and stood. "And that's all you knuckleheads are gonna ever be." He stormed back out the way he came.

I got quiet as I sat back rubbing on my chin. I couldn't help but wonder was the nigga really trying' to change? Or was he too fucking scared to put that work in on Terry and all this righteous bullshit was really a cover-up? Either way I had lost my faith in him, and came to the realization that I was gonna have to take care of Terry by my goddamn self.

~ ~ ~ ~ ~

Before Katrina went home that night, she put the tape with David's voice on it in an envelope, sealed it, wrote her dad's office address on it, then dropped it in the mailbox.

~ ~ ~ ~ ~

Brianna stood up from the floor where she was playing when she heard the front door open. "Mama!" she screamed out. Then held her arms out to be picked up.

"Heyyy." Katrina picked her up and held her tight against her chest for a long moment. "Mm. I love you, baby."

"You too, Mama," Brianna cooed.

Katrina's eyes focused on her mother who was standing in the hallway with her bathrobe on, holding a teacup.

"Go in the bedroom and ask Aunt Nancy to put you to bed, Brianna." Katrina kissed her, then set her down on the floor.

Brianna stopped and kissed her grandmother before she went into the bedroom.

Kathy sipped her tea. "How are you doing, Katrina?"

Katrina scratched her hand. "Mom? Why didn't you ever tell Dad about what I did that day I skipped school with those three black boys?"

Another sip from her cup. Kathy cleared her throat. "Katrina, I've never told you or your sister this...but there are certain things that can make your daddy turn into a very...violent man." Her teacup started to shake as her hand trembled. "If your dad would've found out that you were down in that ghetto, having sex with a group of ni—those black boys, he would've killed them, and gone to jail. Then where would we have been?"

She hesitated, scratched her hand some more. "Did Dad

175

ever…"

"Hit me?" Kathy finished her sentence for her. She walked over to the window and peered out of it. "Yes. But I took it, because I was promised a future if I just stood by him. At least I thought I was." A tear escaped her eye. She looked back at her daughter.

"Your hand is itching, Katrina."

Katrina gazed down at her hands and flinched as if noticing it for the first time. She stopped and folded her arms across her chest.

Kathy said, "The last time your hand itched that bad was after you'd stolen money from my purse."

"Mom, I was 16."

"That's how I knew when you had stolen something. Your little hand would always itch." She paused. "Katrina, have you been stealing again? I can see it in your eyes that you're into something." Katrina looked away. "Whatever it is, get out of it while you can. I lost your father. I couldn't take losing you, too."

Kathy walked over and hugged her daughter for a long moment, then went to bed.

Katrina stared out the window.

"Is it true?"

Her head snapped to the left. Nah Nah was standing there.

"Is what true?"

"Are you into something?"

Silence.

More itching of the hand.

Nah Nah closed her eyes. "Don't tell me you've been stealing from Terry, Katrina."

"Then don't ask," Katrina replied in a smart tone.

"Now I see why you were so eager to work for Terry and didn't want me involved. You were afraid for my safety. Did you ever think about your own?"

"Look, it really doesn't matter, okay? This will all be over anyway. And we'll be left with a whole lot of money. Terry's money."

"And what the hell do you plan on doing, digging yourself a deeper hole?"

"No."

"So what are you gonna do?"

"You'll see. But I'm gonna need your help."

CHAPTER TWENTY-TWO

David hurried off the elevator and bolted straight toward the receptionist station. The girl sitting behind the desk was busy talking into a headset while typing on the keyboard in front of her.

"Cindy!"

"Hold, please." Cindy stopped talking and looked up. "What is it?"

"Has the mail come in for today?"

"Yes."

He sighed a breath of relief. "Good. Where is it?"

"Mr. Miller picked it up off my desk on his way in."

His heart dropped. David's head snapped to the left, and he focused in on the thick, wooden door that led to Michael's office. Sweat rolled down his face.

"David, are you all right?"

His first thought was to leave. Then he remembered that Michael usually tossed the mail on the table, and wouldn't open it until lunch. He checked his watch. It was fifteen minutes until noon. There was still time.

He left Cindy's work station. One short knock on the door was all he managed to do before he barged in. Michael was sitting behind his desk with his hands together. A peculiar look was on his face. Then David heard his own voice.

"To this day, poor old Michael doesn't know that his precious little girl with the cartoon panties has been sucking black cocks since she was only fourteen."

David stood there panting, trying to figure out what to say, while the tape played on. "Sir, I can explain."

~ ~ ~ ~ ~

"Hi, Katrina," Kortni said with a smile after Katrina walked through the door of Body Workz.

Katrina nodded, but kept on going.

Kortni rolled her eyes. "Bitch."

Inside her office Katrina took a seat behind her desk and started tapping away at her computer. When she was finished she made a phone call. Then she got up and walked to Terry's office.

"Come in."

Katrina stepped inside. Terry was sitting in front of an open wall safe, removing stacks of money, then placing them on the desk.

"Wha' sup?" he inquired.

"Uhh...I...I need clearance to get into the main files."

"Cleaning up some money?"

"Trying to," she said with a nod.

Terry looked at her suspiciously. Suddenly he stopped what he was doing and stood. Katrina could see the bulge in his slacks as he walked up on her.

Terry said, "Have you ever stolen from me?"

It was a trick question that she was prepared to answer.

"Yes. I took some extra cash to pay the insurance on my car. I thought that I was worth that after all I've been doing for you around here."

By the time she saw Terry's face twist up, she felt him bury his fist into her stomach.

"Ahhhh," she uttered as she fell down onto the carpeted floor, clutching her stomach.

Terry took out his gun, grabbed her hair, then stuck it in her mouth. Katrina's eyes grew wide with fear as she peered up at his face.

"Don't ever fuck up and get the notion that I'm soft, Katrina. I don't give a fuck who your daddy is, how white you are, or where you come from. You steal something from me again...and I'll knock yo' fuckin' head off. Right here in this office. 'Cause I don't give a fuck."

He snatched the gun from her mouth and helped her to her feet. Katrina had a sour look on her face.

"You okay?" he asked.

She shook her head yes. Holding her stomach, she turned around.

"Hey," Terry said. When she turned back around he smacked her across the face. Katrina gasped as her hand flew up to her cheek. "Now get the fuck outta here."

Kortni saw Katrina stumble out of Terry's office. She looked to be in pain. She watched as Katrina took a moment to gather herself, then walked back to her own office.

She plopped down in her chair. Through teary eyes she gazed at her computer screen and saw that she had been granted access. A few sniffles later, she began typing away. Another phone call. Twenty minutes later, she folded her laptop and put it inside her briefcase.

As soon as she stepped outside her office, she heard her name being called.

"Katrina."

It scared the shit out of her. Slowly, she turned in the direction that the voice came from.

Terry's head was sticking outside his office door. "You goin' to lunch? Pick me up something." Without waiting for an answer, he ducked back inside and closed the door.

Kortni watched as Katrina strutted past her and out the front door. She saw the big red bruise on her right cheek as she passed.

Outside Katrina jumped into her car and fled the scene. She was back on the freeway, headed toward Kansas when she spotted the blue Chrysler. It was back on her tail. She played it cool and kept driving normal. Occasionally she would bob her head to the beat of some imaginary music in her head. She couldn't turn the radio on for real because she wanted to be able to hear if the driver tried anything.

Terry was hip to what she was doing. It was confirmed by the confrontation that they had inside his office. And it wouldn't be long before he went behind her and checked the computer, and saw what she had done.

Katrina got on her cell phone and called her sister.

~ ~ ~ ~ ~

Terry hung up the phone. Then he and Snatch went into Katrina's office and started searching. They were looking for anything. Something that might prove that she was stealing, or anything else that they might need to know about.

While Snatch continued the search, Terry logged in on her desk computer. He accessed the bank files. The same ones that he'd granted her access to not even 30 minutes before. When he learned what it was she had done, he spoke to Snatch.

"Get yo' man on the phone."

"What hap…"

"Now!"

~ ~ ~ ~ ~

Katrina made an exit off the freeway on Johnson Drive. The Chrysler did not follow. By the time she parked and walked into the bank, she was perspiring enough to have jogged a mile in 80 degree weather.

"May I help you?" the teller asked.

"Yes." Katrina stepped up to the counter. "I'm here to make a large withdrawal."

Thirteen minutes later, Katrina exited the bank with her briefcase in her hand. She spotted Nah Nah's car parked two spaces away from hers. Like a child about to cross a street, she looked in both directions. There was no sign of the blue Chrysler. She bolted over to Nah Nah's car.

The sound of her car door being snatched open scared Nah Nah. She was about to scream until she saw that it was her sister.

"Damnit, Katrina!" Nah Nah screamed. "You scared the living crap out of me."

"Sorry." Katrina handed her the briefcase. "Take this."

Katrina stepped out of the car. Nah Nah backed out of the parking space. She made a right, then a left turn out of the parking lot exit. Everything seemed to be cool, until about three blocks later it happened.

Bam!

Nah Nah got rear-ended. Her head snapped backward on impact, then snapped forward, slamming her face against the steering wheel. Blood and tears covered her face. She peeled her face away from the wheel.

Her door swung open. Assuming that it was the cops or

ambulance workers, she didn't say a word. She was laid out on the concrete road. Through teary eyes she managed to see a bald headed black man get into her car like he was searching it.

Nah Nah sat up. She attempted to speak, but caught a light head-rush. Her hand held onto her forehead. The man backed out of the back seat of her car. She noticed that he had Katrina's briefcase in his hands.

"He...hey!" Nah Nah screamed. "Hey, stop!"

The man approached fast and kicked her in her stomach. She fell over on her side in pain. He walked about ten feet back and got back into the now wrecked Chrysler LHS, the same Chrysler that had been following Katrina. Then he drove away without so much as a glance at Nah Nah, who was trying to get up from the pavement.

From the interior of her car, Katrina watched as the Chrysler pulled out of the gas station across the street, in pursuit of Nah Nah. When they were out of her sight, she walked back into the bank.

The sixty-year-old security guard was standing over two money bags.

"Thank you so much for watching them for me," Katrina said with a false smile. "If you don't mind, could you walk me out to my car?"

"I most certainly will."

The security guard carried her bags to her car and placed them inside her trunk. Katrina removed a $100 bill from her purse, folded it, then slid it into his pocket.

"You're too kind," she said. She climbed into her car and picked up her cell phone. She had two calls to make.

~ ~ ~ ~ ~

Terry knocked the lamp off of Katrina's desk. "Goddamn, that bitch!"

"What happened, man?" Snatch inquired. He walked around the desk to where Terry was standing.

Terry pointed at the computer screen. He was taking slow, deep breaths. "This morning I had one point five million spread over three commercial bank accounts. Five hundred thousand in each one. I'm looking at it now and it's telling me that one hundred and fifty grand has been withdrawn out of each account."

Snatch's eyes narrowed in on the screen. "What kind of sense would that make? Why would she only take $450,000 and leave you with over a million dollars? Why not just take it all?"

Terry was pacing the floor now. "That's what the fuck I'm trying to figure out. I just stuck a gun into that bitch's mouth this morning, so she knows I'm not playing."

"It don't make no sense."

Terry became enraged and swung at the air. "I'ma crack that white bitch's face! And make her shit back out every dime she ever stole from me."

Snatch started typing on the computer.

Terry said, "What're you doing?"

"I'ma transfer these funds into another bank account in case this bitch decides to strike again."

Snatch's cell phone rang. He had barely gotten it out of his pocket when Terry snatched it out of his hand. He flipped it open and answered it.

"Hello." He listened intently to what was being said into his ear. He smiled. "Hurry up then. I got something for you."

He hung up. "Yes!"

"Who was that?" Snatch said without taking his eyes off the screen.

"That was your man. He says he lost Katrina, but he got the briefcase."

Snatch looked at him. "How did he do that? What he do, let the bitch go?"

"Unt unh." Terry placed the phone on the table. "She had Nah Nah playing running back. He intercepted it when she tried to hand it off to her."

Snatch didn't look convinced. "She seems like she's a lot smarter than that."

Terry's face suddenly became serious again. "You better hope she's not," he said coldly.

"What's that supposed to mean?"

"You brought that bitch to my attention, dog. So any debt that this bitch leaves behind will become yours." With that he headed out the office door.

Out of frustration and anger, Snatch slammed his fist down onto the desk. A flashing light on the computer screen caught his attention. His eyes peered at the screen. It took him a second before he realized what had transpired during that quick moment that he had stopped and talked to Terry.

"Shit!" Snatch jumped up out the chair, making a break for the door. "Terry! Terry!"

Terry was sticking his key into his office door when he heard Snatch calling his name. Snatch approached him damned near out of breath.

"What is it?" Terry asked.

Snatch swallowed. "All our accounts...they've just been frozen."

Terry scowled. "Frozen?" The only people who could do something like that were the feds. "Shut everything down. Now! And destroy all the files and disks."

Snatch ran back to Katrina's office to clear out her computer files. Terry practically broke down his office door trying to get to his computer.

The Chrysler LHS pulled into the parking lot of Body Workz. With a big smile on his beefy face, caused by the anticipation of a big pay-off, the big man exited the car. He clutched Katrina's briefcase tightly as he approached the front entrance.

Out of nowhere, two big white boys dressed in back suits approached him. They had badges in their hands that read F.B.I.

"Excuse me, sir," one of them said, "do you mind if we search that bag?"

He looked from one agent to the other, then slung the bag at them. When they ducked, he spun around and took off. As that was happening, three Ford Explorers raced into the parking lot. One of them unintentionally slammed into the fleeing man, striking him on the right side. He flew into a parked car, and fell to the ground where he was apprehended.

~ ~ ~ ~ ~

The front door swung open. Suited men filed into the room one at a time, with guns drawn, swarming the place like ants.

Kortni gasped. "Michael, I…" She stopped at the sight of the P89 that was pointed at her face, "have to go." The phone slid from her hand onto the table in front of her.

All the commotion in the building had the place in an uproar. Girls were cussing and screaming in all sorts of languages that the feds couldn't understand as they lead them all to the front area where they were cuffed.

Terry managed to clear his files and destroy his computer by the time they barged into his office. He already knew the routine and was on the floor with his hands locked behind his head when they came in.

"I haven't did shit!" he pleaded. "This is a legitimate business."

When they brought him out into the hallway, he saw Snatch being held up against the wall while his hands were being cuffed behind his back.

The agents that approached the suspect outside walked in carrying the briefcase that the man had stolen from Katrina. He sat it down in front of Terry and opened it up. Out of it he pulled what Terry thought should've been cash, but was really a laptop computer. The agent typed in a few keys, then showed Terry what had come up on the screen. It was all of the financial data and other incriminating evidence that Katrina had saved to use against Terry and his company. So it really didn't matter that both he and Snatch had destroyed all the evidence in Body Workz. Katrina had provided them with everything they would need to put Terry away for a long time. Terry closed his eyes in defeat.

"Terry L. Finch," one of the agents said, "you're being placed under arrest for so many charges that I can't even begin to name at this time. So for the moment let's just say pandering." He looked at the agents that had Terry secured. "Get him out of here."

CHAPTER TWENTY-THREE

"That should do it," Katrina said after she squeezed the last of the money into one of three safety deposit boxes at the bank. She turned around and faced Nah Nah. "There's a total of $600,000 in these boxes. They're in your name."

"Why?" Nah Nah asked curiously. She was overwhelmed by everything that had taken place. "Why not in your name?"

Katrina sighed. She glanced at her watch. "By now the feds have stormed into Body Workz and arrested everybody. I was involved in that conspiracy, but I'm a government witness. I have to turn myself in. I've already been promised to be granted a bond when the hearing comes up. So don't worry. I'll call you when I can."

Nah Nah showed a look of concern. "Just be careful, Katrina."

They embraced for a long moment.

They departed the bank in Nah Nah's car, headed toward downtown. Nah Nah cried all the way to the station. To her, Katrina had gotten in too deep. For every action there was a reaction is what her mother always told her. It may not happen immediately, but there was sure to be one.

Katrina stared up at the tall building. A feeling of anxiety came over her. She sighed heavily.

Nah Nah placed her hand on her shoulder. "You scared?"

A little shrug.

"Why did you do this?"

Hesitation. "I did this because I wanted to get Qu'ban out of jail early. And I wanted to be able to make up for what I did with Terry." She paused. "We weren't raised to be the women that we became. I realized that by watching you. No matter how wild you allowed yourself to become, you've never let the partying consume you. And I have a lot of respect for you for that. It has helped keep me grounded more times than you know."

Nah Nah reached out and hugged her sister. They both were in tears.

"Take care of my baby," Katrina said.

"Kay."

Katrina broke the embrace and grabbed the door handle. "I have to go." Without another word, she exited the car. She was halfway up the steps when she turned around and waved goodbye to her sister.

~ ~ ~ ~ ~

It took more than an hour for the police at headquarters to get Katrina booked in. After she'd taken a series of finger-prints, she was given a paper towel and led toward the lockup area. Her eyes were puffy as she walked down the hallway. A row of 12 man cells were lined up on her right, and to the left of her was one huge cell that took up the entire side. One TV sat on the middle wall of the cell, and a 10 foot bench sat in the middle of the floor. At least 40 women of all colors and ages were gathered inside there. Katrina knew instantly that this was where she did not want to be.

As she was being walked down the hall, she snuck a glance toward the huge cell called "The Bullpen." She saw most of the girls that worked as escorts at Body Workz inside the cell. They were huddled together, presumably having a conversation about the days' events. Some of them had tears streaming down their faces.

Katrina looked away. They put her in the fourth cell on the right side. She was alone, and separated from all of her co-defendants. In an attempt to pass time, she sat her shoes on the matless steel bunk, then lay down, using her shoes as a pillow.

Fifteen minutes later she was awakened by the loud sound of the cell door being opened. She jumped up. A tall, over-weight man in a black suit was standing there next to the turn-key.

"Ms. Miller. I'm Agent Hobbs. I'll be working with you until this investigation is complete. You'll be receiving a bond hearing as soon as tomorrow. At that time you'll be recommended for release, then we'll go from there."

Hearing what the agent had to say about her getting released made her feel a lot better. "Thank you, Mr. Hobbs."

"Okay." He shook her hand. "I know this is not the best place to stay, but it could be worse."

Agent Hobbs left her alone again. When the cell door closed, Katrina looked across the hall. Standing in the bullpen with her arms stuck outside the bars, staring directly at her, was Kortni. For a second they just gazed at each other without a word. Then Kortni turned and walked away.

~ ~ ~ ~ ~

Michael stepped outside his office and locked the door. Cindy, who was sitting behind her desk, stopped him on his way out.

"Mr. Miller," she called out.

Michael stopped before her. "What is it, Cindy?"

She picked up a stack of mail. "David didn't come in today. I called his home and cell and there was no answer. What should I do with his messages?"

Michael took a deep breath. "Burn them. David no longer works here." Then he walked away.

"Um, Mr. Miller!"

Michael turned around with an annoyed look on his face. "What is it, Cindy?"

"I have a Kortni on line two."

"Oh." Michael went into his office to take the call, closing the door for added privacy. "Hello."

Sniffles. "Baby...I'm in jail."

Michael's heart sank. "In jail? What on earth are you doing there? What happened?"

Kortni explained the entire situation to him, not forgetting to mention the part about how suspicious Katrina had been acting before the raid, and how they had her down there in a separate cell, having private talks with agents. "I just can't help but think she did this because she found out about you and me."

"My daughter did this to you?"

"It sure looks like it." She paused. "The bad part is...I'm officially an illegal alien and there's a strong possibility that I'm going to be," sniffles, "deported." The fact that she had said it out loud made her cry.

"Try not to worry, Kortni. I will do everything in my power to keep that from happening."

"Please try, baby." Sniffles. "I have to go."

191

"Okay. But afterwards, you have a lot of explaining to do."

~ ~ ~ ~ ~

"And if they hate then let 'em hate, and watch the money pile up," I sang along with Fifty as I walked into the TV room with my headphones on. My partnas were at the table playing a game of dominoes.

"Wha' sup, Dre," I said in a loud voice. When we slapped hands it made a loud sound.

This skinny ponytail wearing white boy, Donnie, jumped up and snatched his headphones off his head.

"Goddamnit, Q! We're trying to listen to the movie and you come up in here hollering and screaming all over the damned place."

"If you don't like it, Donnie, just bond out. Get the fuck outta prison if you don't like it."

Donnie bit down on his bottom lip. I noticed that his hands were trembling like he wanted to fire on me. I took off my headphones and set them on the table in front of Dre. I pulled up my sagging khakis as I approached him.

"What the fuck you looking at me like that for, Donnie? Huh?" Before Donnie had a chance to respond, I reached back and slapped the shit out of him. His headphones flew off his head. Everybody in the room gave us their attention.

The entire left side of his face turned red. He looked at me. "Let's take this to the restroom."

"Let's go."

Dre got up from the table and followed us to the bathroom. He was there just in case I needed him. I walked into the bathroom first, followed by a small group of onlookers ready to see a fight.

Donnie walked in a second later. I got in my boxer stance.

He never even put his hands up. After a short glance at me, he shouted, "Don't you ever hit me again in front of all those people!"

It took everything inside me not to laugh. In other words, he was telling me that what I did would've been acceptable, if I would've slapped him in private. It was clear to me that he wasn't trying to do nothing. So I waved my hand at the sucka like fuck it.

Dre had his chest all poked out glaring at every white boy in the room as we walked out. We were halfway down the hall when O'ban came running toward us.

"Wha' sup, man?" he said. "I heard some shit was going on."

"It wasn't nothing. I had to smack the shit out of Donnie's punk ass for mouthing off."

"Is it over?"

"It better be," I stated as I continued on down the hallway.

O'ban followed. We were in our cell when he said, "I just got some fucked up news from Nah Nah."

I jumped up in my bed and lay back on my pillow. "What is it?"

O'ban took a breath. "Terry got raided on. The feds got him right now."

I sat up. "What happened to Katrina? Did they get her, too?"

"Katrina turned them in."

Some people would think that Terry's fall was supposed to make me feel good. But it did just the opposite. I would never be satisfied with him going to prison rather than taking a bullet in his skull. How could I possibly get any gratification out of something that the feds had done to him?

Doing a bid was unacceptable. I wanted him dead.

That whole day after I found out about Terry's capture, I stayed in my cell. The rest of the unit left to go to chow. It was quiet as I sat up in my bunk alone with my thoughts.

I was staring up at the ceiling when I heard the click clack sound of dress shoes walking across the tile floor. Mr. Allen popped up in my mind. I thought about him because I remembered what I saw on him last time he was up here and I had missed chow.

Quietly I slid off of my bunk and stepped into my shoes. I peeked outside the door. He wasn't in sight, but I knew which way he had gone. Down the hall I went. At the end of the hallway I took a left. The area was dark. To the left of me was a cell. Its door was closed. It had a small window in the center of it.

I looked through it and that's when I saw it, the reason why Mr. Allen was up here sneaking around. What I had seen that day was the hard on that he had on. Now as I stood there gazing through the window in disbelief, I could understand why. Mr. Allen was standing up against the wall, eyes closed, his face toward the door. On his knees in front of him was Matthew the Punk, serving him with a vicious blow job.

Mutha-fucka!

I wanted to make my presence known, but decided not to. It was some valuable information that I would keep to myself in case it ever came in handy.

~ ~ ~ ~ ~

"Cut out all the bullshit, Simon, and give me the worst-case scenario. How much time am I looking at?"

Brad peered at Terry through the screen. He took a deep breath while he did some figuring in his head.

"Uhh, somewhere around 30 years."

Terry wanted to faint. He put his head down.

"With that kind of time," Brad continued, "I can almost guarantee that you won't get a bond. There will be a hearing, but I wouldn't expect anything good to come from it. These are very serious charges that you're facing."

After a second or two passed, Terry looked up. "It was that bitch, wasn't it? Why would she do some shit like that anyway?"

"Well, from what little information I've gathered so far, she opted to trade your head in order for a friend of hers to get an early release from prison."

Terry frowned. "A friend of hers? Who?"

Brad licked his finger, then flipped through his note pad. "Umm...Qu'ban Cartez. He's serving a..." Brad paused. Frowned. "That name sounds so familiar."

Terry forced a giggle out. "That's because you were my attorney when I rolled over on his girl after we cut that deal with the feds." He shook his head back and forth. "I should've known."

Brad sat there with his mouth open staring at the pad. "Oh. This changes everything. I forgot you acted as a confidential informant before." Brad closed his suitcase and stood. "Let me see what, or how, I can use this information in our favor."

Terry stood. "You do that."

CHAPTER TWENTY-FOUR

Unfortunately, just like any other federal prisoner, whether they are a witness for the government or not, Katrina had to sit in jail for a few days until her bond hearing was scheduled. Those three days had been the loneliest three days of her life. She attempted to call Michael, her dad. She didn't know why, but she yearned for him. To her surprise, Michael declined her call, saying that she had intentionally ruined his relationship with Kortni. He wanted nothing to do with her.

By the time she was walked into the courtroom in an orange jumpsuit and shackles, she was a nervous wreck. Dark circles had formed around her eyes and her hair was tangled. For three days she had been asking herself what the hell she was doing there.

The bailiff stood. "All rise for the honorable Judge Booker T. Fenner presiding."

Katrina turned around. A warm feeling came over her when she saw her sister sitting in the back of the courtroom holding Brianna. She had almost missed her, but Kathy was sitting beside them. A lot of anxiety was on her face.

No more than 20 minutes later Katrina and her family came walking out of the courthouse. Tears were in everybody's eyes as they walked in silence to Kathy's SUV.

Inside the car, Kathy sat in the driver's seat and looked at Katrina through the mirror.

"So what now, Katrina?" Kathy asked.

Katrina stopped fiddling with Brianna for a moment. "Now," she sighed, "I have to testify against those people in court."

"Then you'll be free to go?"

"Yes...and so will Qu'ban."

Kathy turned around and faced her. "Who?"

"My daddy," Brianna said happily.

"You're going through all this for that...man?" Kathy asked in disbelief.

"Mom, please."

"Don't you, Mom, please me. You're..."

"Not in front of Brianna!"

Kathy closed her mouth, looked at Brianna for a moment, then turned around. Without a word she started the car and drove away.

~ ~ ~ ~ ~

Also on the docket to appear for a bond hearing that day was Terry. When he showed up for court, his lawyer had a big smile on his face. He informed Terry that he had mentioned to the United States Attorney that he had acted as a credible government informant on a prior case. During that time he proved to be a dependable and honest informant.

The prosecutor for the United States didn't argue it. In fact, he did just the opposite, when he recommended that Terry be released on bond and placed on pre-trial investigation.

Terry departed the courthouse a temporarily free man,

along with his lawyer. He settled into the passenger seat of Brad's Lincoln.

"See what you can do about getting Snatch out on bond," Terry commanded. "Meanwhile, I'll work on getting you them ends that I owe you."

"Make that your first priority," Brad stated. "We go back a long way, Terry, but I still gotta eat." He offered Terry a cigarette.

Terry took one out of the pack and fired it up. "Don't worry. I think I know just where to get it from."

~ ~ ~ ~ ~

Katrina spent the entire day with her family and child. They had lunch together at the park while Brianna played. An early movie played at the dollar show, which they saw. Then they all went for pedicures. Even Brianna got a coat of polish put on her little toes.

When nighttime fell, Katrina didn't feel that she or her baby would be safe at home. Who knew who Terry had out there hunting for her? So far she was the only witness for the government's case. Without her testimony, the case could fold. Until the day came for her to testify, she would go into hiding.

They picked up some food from a local Chinese Hut, then drove Katrina to a motel. Cash was paid for her room in the name of Kathy's deceased sister Janet.

Katrina and Brianna exited the SUV in front of their motel room.

"This is it," Katrina said as she grabbed her bag of clothing from the floor of the front seat.

Nah Nah opened the room door for her. Katrina threw the bag on the floor. They embraced in the doorway.

"I'll be back tomorrow," Nah Nah said. "Make sure that you keep the door locked." She gazed down at Brianna. "And you better be good." She tickled her stomach.

Brianna giggled, then ran into the room.

Katrina looked at her mom, who was sitting in the car. She waved her hand. "Bye, Mom."

"See you tomorrow," Kathy replied. "I'll bring more of your things."

"Okay." Katrina returned her gaze to her sister. "Well, I need some sleep. I know Brianna's tired. She been up all day."

"All right. I'll see you two guys tomorrow." Nah Nah looked up into the room. Brianna had kicked off her shoes and was lying in the bed with her eyelids closed. "She is tired."

"Yeah."

"Okay, then. See ya, sis." Nah Nah jogged to the SUV and climbed in. She waved at her sister one last time as they were driving away.

Katrina closed the door, slipped out of her clothes and took a hot bath. Brianna was sprawled across the bed, sleeping on her stomach, when she returned. She gazed at her sleeping child and smiled. How peaceful she looked laying there with her thumb stuck between her lips. Katrina climbed in bed and pulled her daughter close, then drifted off into some much needed sleep.

~ ~ ~ ~ ~

"Look, honey, I'm doing everything that I can to get you out. This won't be a walk in the park. You are an illegal alien facing a serious federal indictment," Michael explained.

Kortni stared crying on the other end of the phone. "I don't know how I got myself into this bloody mess."

Michael sighed heavily. "Try not to worry. I'm doing everything that I can."

Sniffles. "Okay, darling. I love you."

"I love you, too." He hung up the phone. "Fuck."

~ ~ ~ ~ ~

Bzzst. Bzzst.

Terry's hand fumbled around on the nightstand until it located the phone. "Hello."

"It's me, Snatch."

"Snatch?" Terry sat up in the bed. He wiped sleep out of his eyes. "Wha' sup? Where you at?"

"Downtown on a pay phone. I just got out on a signature bond."

Terry began to get suspicious. "Don't tell me you rolled over on me, Snatch?"

Snatch started to laugh. "Hell, naw. I was just kidding with you. I'm with Brad. He got me out this morning. I'm headed your way now."

"Good. 'Cause we got shit to do. See you when you get here." Terry hung up. He gazed over at the woman who was sleeping next to him. "Kizey! Kizey!"

The woman stirred, then opened her eyes. "What?"

"Get yo' ass up. I got some shit to do." He removed the covers from over her naked body.

"Damnit, Terry!" She gazed up at him through narrow eyes.

"Get yo' ass up then." He stood and walked naked to the bathroom.

~ ~ ~ ~ ~

Nah Nah left the house headed for school. She had enrolled in a local college to finish up her degree. She left a little early so she could stop and pick up some breakfast and drive it to Katrina's motel room first. When she left the house, Kathy was on the phone trying to explain Katrina's situation to Michael, with hopes of gaining some type of support from him. But from what Nah Nah overheard, the conversation wasn't going too well.

Nah Nah picked up some scrambled eggs, hash browns, sausage, a carton of milk and a cinnamon roll for Brianna from a nearby breakfast place, then drove out to the motel.

Katrina answered the door with nothing on but a bath towel. "Come in."

Nah Nah stepped into the room carrying white Styrofoam trays. She placed them on the table.

"I just wanted to bring you two some breakfast before I went to school. Brianna gets cranky when she doesn't have a morning cup of milk and roll."

Katrina sat on the bed, rubbed her face, and yawned. "You have her spoiled rotten."

Nah Nah looked at her watch. "Okay. I have to go." She bent over the bed and kissed her sleeping niece, then headed toward the door.

Katrina stood. "Make sure you come back. Don't leave us out here alone."

"I will," Nah Nah replied as she strutted out to her car.

Katrina stood in the doorway watching as her sister drove away. Nah Nah drove right past the white Taurus that had been following her since she left home.

Katrina closed the door and locked it. "Bri Bri," she called out.

"No," Brianna uttered in a sleepy voice. "I'm sleep."

"You better get up. Aunt Nah Nah brought you your favorite—a cinnamon roll and milk."

Brianna quickly sat up. "Huh?"

A smile formed on Katrina's face. "I thought you'd get up." She handed Brianna her overnight bag. "Go into the bathroom and brush your teeth and wash your face."

"I can't reach the sink."

"Do it in the tub."

Brianna rolled out of bed, took the bag from her, then slowly walked into the bathroom.

The phone rang.

Katrina looked down at it.

It rang again.

She walked over to it and was just about to pick it up when she heard a knock on the door.

Katrina gasped as she took a fearful step backward.

The phone continued to ring.

Another knock on the door.

She released a breath of relief when she saw the maid's cart roll to a stop outside the window.

"I'm so fuckin' paranoid," she said to herself. She walked over to the door, unlocked it, then opened it up.

~ ~ ~ ~ ~

About a minute before Katrina opened the door in her motel room, Nah Nah had been driving on the freeway when she received a call on her cell phone.

She cut her music down. "Hello."

"Hey, Nancy." It was Katrina's attorney. "I'm trying to locate your sister if it's possible."

Nah Nah thought that she detected a hint of worry in his tone. "Is there something wrong?"

"Could be. I was trying to talk to her to inform her that somehow Terry Finch made bail yesterday. I just learned about it this morning. I thought she'd like to know."

"Oh my god," Nah Nah uttered. "Thank you, Paul. I'll make sure that she gets the message."

"Thank you, Nancy."

Nah Nah hung up on Paul, then dialed the number to the motel that Katrina was staying in.

~ ~ ~ ~ ~

"Ahh!" Katrina screamed as she backed away from the door.

Terry stepped into the room with a cold look on his face. He pushed the door closed with his gloved hands.

Katrina turned around in an attempt to run, but Terry clutched her blond locks and pulled her back toward him.

"Remember what I told your stupid ass I was gonna do if you ever crossed me?" he whispered into her ear. "Huh, bitch?" He pushed her forward. Katrina fell onto the floor. She climbed up on all fours, trying to crawl away. He straddled her back, pulled her head backward, then placed the barrel of a .38 snub nose flush against the back of her skull.

Katrina cried as she squeezed her eyes tight, waiting to hear the loud popping noise that would put her in an everlasting sleep.

She screamed out in fear when she heard the phone ring.

~ ~ ~ ~ ~

Nah Nah held the phone up to her ear, listening to it ring as she pulled into the parking lot of Rockhurst College. Twice she called Katrina's room and didn't receive an answer after being told by the man at the front desk that she had not left the room.

She finally hung up the phone and threw it in her purse out of frustration. Her right arm reached over and snatched her book bag out of the passenger seat. Her heels tapped against the pavement as she walked at a quick pace up to the front entrance.

~ ~ ~ ~ ~

"You got what you owe me, Katrina?" Terry asked.

Crying, Katrina replied, "In the bank."

"In an account?"

"No. No. It's split up in safety deposit boxes. I have it all."

Terry looked at his watch. "Let's go get it."

"I can't."

"Why not?"

"Because if I do, I know you'll kill me."

Terry snickered, then he reached back and pulled down her sweats, then her panties, exposing her bare ass. He gritted his teeth as he jammed the nose of the .38 into her rectum. Katrina screamed out.

"Ahh! Ahhh!"

"Huh?!" Terry hollered as he twisted the barrel sideways, pushing toward her rectum.

"Okay!" she hollered. "Pull it out! Pull it...uhh."

Terry pulled the barrel of the gun out, then stood up and moved away from her. "Get yo' funky ass up. Make yourself look presentable so we can go get my goddamned money."

Katrina lay flat on her stomach with her arms behind her as she held onto her now sore ass. Her body shook as she continued to release a stream of tears.

Terry gazed at the food on the stand. He noticed that there were two Styrofoam plates instead of one. It couldn't have been Nah Nah's. She only stayed long enough to drop off the food and bounce.

He looked up and toward the bathroom door. It was

closed. He started toward it. Katrina saw the direction that he was headed and suddenly got a burst of energy.

"No!" she said as she managed to get up on her knees, and darted toward him. Her hands clutched his left leg around the ankle. "Okay! Okay! Let's go get the money, Terry."

"Get off me!" He kicked her hand away.

Terry snatched open the door with his gun drawn. Brianna was asleep inside the empty bathtub, her toothbrush in her hand, laid across her chest. He stepped inside.

Katrina climbed to her feet as she pulled up her sweats. "Don't hurt her, Terry. Please!"

Terry scooped Brianna up in his arms. The toothbrush fell from her hand. He turned around and looked at Katrina. "Don't make me hurt her."

Katrina immediately walked over to the sink and cut on the water. Terry exited the bathroom with Brianna in his arms. She was still asleep.

It took her a second to freshen up. After she did she called her sister.

"The boxes are in Nah Nah's name," Katrina explained while the phone rang. "She had absolutely no idea what I was doing, so whatever you do to me…please leave her out of it."

Terry put the gun in his pocket. "You better get that bitch on the phone and get her up to that damn bank within the next twenty minutes, or I'ma do something really fucked up to you, Katrina." He paused. "And this baby if I have to."

The look in his eyes said that he might actually have meant what he said about Brianna. Katrina's hands began to shake.

"Hello," Nah Nah whispered into the phone.

"Nancy. I need you to stop doing whatever you're doing

and meet me at the bank where we stashed that money into those boxes."

"Katrina, I'm at school."

"The bank! Right now! Please."

"I'm on my way."

CHAPTER TWENTY-FIVE

They were inside Terry's car on their way to the bank. Brianna lay across the back seat, still asleep. Katrina stared out the passenger window while tears continuously streamed down her face. Her head snapped toward him suddenly.

"Terry? Are you going to kill me for what I did?"

Terry didn't respond right away. His silence terrified her. She knew if she gave him the money, and with her being the only witness in their case, he was going to rid himself of her. If she didn't give him the money, she would get killed even quicker. She was damned if she did, and damned if she didn't. They were about 15 minutes away from the bank. She had until then to come up with an idea that might save her life.

"Thirty years I'm facing, Katrina," Terry finally stated. "Pretend that you was me, and I was you, and tell me what you would do to me."

The only answer that she could think of would probably trigger his anger enough to kill her before he got the money back. So she chose to remain silent and try to think of a way to save her life.

Terry parked in back of the bank and put the car in park. He looked at her. "After you get the money, just start walking.

I'll pick you up somewhere."

"Okay." Katrina peered back at her sleeping daughter, then opened her door. She grabbed the empty duffle bag from beneath her feet.

Terry clutched her arm before she stepped out. "If you try some bullshit, your daughter's gonna suffer for it."

Sniffles. "I won't try anything." She wiped her eyes, then exited the car. She made it to the front of the building when she saw Nah Nah's car speeding up the street. Nah Nah parked in front of the bank.

She got out and ran up to her sister. "Katrina, what's going on? Your lawyer called and told me to tell you that Terry made bond yesterday. You have to…"

"Nancy!" Katrina said, "Calm down. I'll tell you what's going on later. Right now we need to go up in here and get what we came for."

"Okay. Okay."

They stood in the small room before the three boxes unloading money, and loading it inside three money bags that were supplied by the bank.

Nah Nah had just realized something. "Katrina, how did you get here? And where the hell is Brianna?"

Katrina swallowed. "Umm…she's with my friend at the motel room. Don't worry, she's safe. Now come on, we have to hurry."

Shaking her head in disapproval, Nah Nah said, "I can't believe you just left Brianna with anybody. No wait—yes, I can. You're not even fit to…"

"Nancy, would ya just shut up!" Katrina yelled out. "Jesus! Just do what I told you to do."

Without another word Nah Nah continued to help fill the

bags. When they were finished they placed them inside the duffle bag.

"Let's go."

Outside the bank they both stopped outside the front entrance. Nah Nah attempted to speak, but Katrina dropped the bag and embraced her tightly. Nah Nah could feel her sister's body trembling while she held onto her.

Katrina sniffled as she broke the embrace. "I gotta go." She tucked the can of mace that she had just slipped off of Nah Nah's hip into her sweats. Then picked up the bag.

"Don't worry about me, Nah Nah. I'll be fine." Katrina took off walking around the building. Nah Nah watched her back until she disappeared, then got into her car and drove away. Katrina came back to the front of the building after she left, then started walking down Johnson Drive. Terry picked her up about a block and a half away.

Terry didn't even smile when she threw the duffle bag onto the floor of the back seat, then sat in the front. Knowing how slick Katrina was, he unzipped the bag, then peeped inside. The money was there.

"Fuckin' conniving-ass bitch," Terry stated as he began to drive away. "This still don't change the fact that I'm about to get thirty years all because you wanted to get that nigga of yours out of prison."

Katrina's head snapped in his direction as her heart sank to her stomach.

"You thought I wouldn't find out?" Terry asked without taking his eyes off the road. "Huh?"

"I..." she began to sob.

"Don't cry now. Unt unh." He giggled. "You wanted to be a nigga. You wanted to be in the game. Yeahh, bitch."

Katrina peered into the backseat at her sleeping daughter. "What are you going to do to me, Terry?"

Terry looked at her. "Nothing."

Terry pulled into the parking lot of the motel that Katrina was staying at. He stopped in front of the room.

Katrina nodded. "Go 'head. Take off."

"Mama."

Katrina looked into the backseat and saw that Brianna had awoken and was sitting up in the seat, rubbing her eyes. Katrina reached back and grabbed her. Then she opened her door.

Terry smiled. "You had a beautiful child."

Katrina paused after she heard him use the word "had" in reference to Brianna. She looked back at him.

"Terry, you…"

"Get out."

Katrina exited the car. She took out the key to her room and stuck it into the lock. Before she entered, she looked over her shoulder and saw Terry's car still sitting there. She took a deep breath, then walked in.

"Mama," Brianna called.

"Shh." Katrina sat her down on the floor, locked the door, then pulled out her can of mace.

Terry began to drive away. He went left after he exited the parking lot. About a block down the road he stopped at a parked white Bronco. Snatch had the hood up, pretending to be checking the oil.

Snatch looked to his right and saw Terry sitting in the car. Terry nodded, then drove away.

Terry had snatched the phone out of the socket before they left, and he had taken her purse with her phone in it.

Katrina sat in the room after having fed Brianna the cold breakfast. She had to get out of that room, get to the phone in the lobby, then have Nah Nah come get her.

Brianna was sitting on the bed watching TV. Katrina stood. "Brianna, I have to go to the lobby and make a phone call. Stay right here on this bed. Okay?"

Brianna nodded her head.

"Okay." Katrina held the mace tight in her hand while she peeked out the curtain. She didn't see anyone. "I'll be right back, Brianna."

Katrina walked out the door and closed it. Quickly she ran up the walkway to the front lobby. She didn't have any money in her pockets so she made a collect call to her mother's house.

"Hello."

"Mother."

Kathy could hear the anxiety in her daughter's voice. "Katrina, are you okay?"

"Yes. Mother, could you please call Nancy and tell her to come pick me up at the motel?"

"Yes, of course. I'll do it right now. Are you sure you're okay, Katrina? You sound a bit anxious."

Katrina took a breath. "I'm okay. Just a little nervous about the trial and all."

"Well, don't you worry about that. It'll all be over in no time."

"Look, ma, I have to call you back. Tell Nancy to hurry."

"Okay."

"Bye." Katrina hung up the phone. She hurried out of the lobby and back to her room.

The door was cracked when she got there. She pushed

211

open the door. She gasped at the sight of the big man that stood next to the bed, holding Brianna in his arms.

~ ~ ~ ~ ~

As soon as Nah Nah received the message from her mother she shot straight out to the motel. She noticed her can of mace was missing from her hip. That alone signaled her that her sister was possibly in trouble. She wanted to follow Katrina, but for some reason thought that it would be best if she didn't.

Nah Nah whipped into the motel parking lot. The door to Katrina's room was closed, and the curtains on the window were shut. She pulled to a stop in front of the room and parked. Within seconds she was out of the car and walking up to the door.

"Katrina!" she yelled while she beat on the door. "Katrina!" More beating. "Katrina…"

Someone snatched open the door. Nah Nah found herself standing face to face with a heavyset black woman who appeared to be in her late 40s.

"Yes?" the woman asked.

"I'm here to see my sister."

The woman shrugged. "I don't know who your sister is. Sorry."

"Katrina! Katrina Miller." Nah Nah pushed past the woman and stepped into the room. The only person inside was a maintenance man who looked as if he was repairing the phone. "Katrina!"

"Miss! Miss," the woman called from behind her. "The woman that was staying here turned her key in a little while ago."

Nah Nah spun around and faced her. "Was she with a

baby?"

"I never saw her. She just dropped the key inside the box."

Nah Nah regarded the maintenance man. "What happened to the phone?"

The man signed, grunted, shrugged his shoulders. "Uhh. It looks like it was snatched out of the wall, and the head broke off of it."

Nah Nah walked over to the door, looked out of it. She peered around the parking lot area. There was no sign of her sister, nor her niece.

Her heart began to pound in her chest. When she didn't see them she screamed out, "Katrina!"

~ ~ ~ ~ ~

Knock! Knock!
Knock! Knock!

Terry flushed the toilet inside the bathroom of his posh hotel room in downtown Kansas City. He rinsed his hands, then hurried to answer the door. He smacked the ass of the 21-year-old white girl that lay on his bed, smoking a cigarette as he walked past. He had picked her up after he dropped off Katrina, then checked into the hotel to make sure that he would have an airtight alibi, in case anybody came asking questions.

Terry opened the door wearing nothing but a thick towel wrapped around his waist.

Snatch was standing there. He looked like he had been in a fight. He stepped inside and went straight to the bar.

Terry frowned as he closed the door. "What the fuck are you doing here?"

The young white girl pulled the comforter over her to shield her naked body from Snatch's probing eyes.

Snatch downed a shot of whiskey, then he took a breath. "Man, some fucked up shit just happened."

~ ~ ~ ~ ~

A week later, and there were still no signs of Katrina. Nah Nah and her parents had been all over the news inquiring about the whereabouts of their daughter. No one seemed to know anything. After three days, and after the police found out that she had cleaned out three safety deposit boxes from the bank the morning of her disappearance, they closed the investigation. Katrina Miller was presumed to have ran off. It was just a coincidence that the star witness in a drug and pandering sting up and disappeared the day after the top defendant in the case made bail.

Kathy Miller and Michael Miller were called to the county morgue to identify a body of a white woman who was found in the trunk of a car. Kathy was so sure that the woman inside the cold morgue was her daughter that she suffered a massive heart attack just moments after she entered the county building.

Nah Nah rushed to the hospital as soon as she got the message. When she slowed to a stop inside the emergency room, she saw her dad talking to the doctor. He had tears in his eyes.

"No," Nah Nah said as she started to back away, shaking her head. "No!"

Michael looked in her direction. "Nancy, I'm so sorry."

Nah Nah turned around, bolted out the door, jumped back into her car, and sped away. She drove and drove until she was finally caught by a red light. She slowed to a stop. Tears rushed out of her eye sockets as she began to beat her fists against the steering wheel.

"No! No! Noooo!" She sobbed uncontrollably. "You're all I had left!"

Kathy Miller had died not knowing if the woman inside the morgue had been her daughter Katrina. There was still a possibility that she might be alive.

CHAPTER TWENTY-SIX

"Why do you insist on holding a grudge against your old friend Terry, Mr. Cartez? It's been nine months and no bodies have been found," Dana Lowe spoke.

She was the head shrink at the prison. I had been seeing her twice a week since Katrina and Brianna had come up missing. I enjoyed getting the chance to vent, but even after six months of treatment, I could not shake the anxiety that I had about wanting to get out and end it for Terry. Permanently. It was as simple as that. Why couldn't that woman sitting before me get that through her skull?

I was sitting across from her in a leather recliner, staring up at the ceiling. "Because," I replied, "he killed both my child and my baby mama. And for that he must die."

"Don't you mean your significant other?"

"You're white, and it's black people's slang. So I don't expect you to understand. You can never understand."

Dana referred to her notes. "Isn't it true that the authorities interviewed Terry, and were convinced that he had nothing to do with it? Isn't it also true that they suspected at one time that you might've had something done to her from the inside, because she was dating your ex-friend, Terry?"

I rolled my eyes, then looked at Dana like she was stupid. "The police took everything I had. I don't have a dollar to my name. So how in the fuck could I have had something done to her from here?" I stood up. "This session is over."

"Hey. Hey," she said in a calm voice. Dana removed her glasses, walked around her desk and stood in front of me. "Hey, I'm on your side here."

"I can't tell."

"All these questions that I'm asking is just me doing my job. Off the record, I really feel and have sympathy for what you're going through. Your little girl has been missing for nine months, and could possibly be…dead. And hey, I can't blame you for having resentment toward that man." She paused. "But on the record, I'm here to help you shake that criminal thinking that you have."

I dug into my pocket and pulled out a letter which I handed to her.

"I got that soon after the police stopped investigating my daughter and her mother's case. I'll be back in three days. Tell me what you think. Excuse me, I meant give me your analysis, doctor." Then I left the room.

~ ~ ~ ~ ~

Dana sat at her desk and opened the envelope. She read the letter first. It read:

> *Dear Dog,*
> *What's happening? Been a long time. I'm not too big on writing so I'ma get straight to the point. I'm sorry that Katrina took your daughter and ran off. She was a good fuck. I know you were looking forward to hitting that again, being that she traded my life for*

yours. But since you can't, I'ma give you the next best thing.

Enclosed is a stack of photos of me and her in action. I know you're heated at me, but you remember, that's how we do. L.O.L.

I'll be going to trial on the case within the next few months, so it's a high possibility that we will never hear from or see each other again. So you can either shake that anger that you have in your heart for me, or let it torture you for the rest of your life. Holla!

P.S. Without the feds' star witness, I gotta good chance of getting off.

Sincerely,

T-Hawk

Dana looked through the stack of photos of Terry sticking his short, fat dick into Katrina in every position imaginable. The fuck faces that she wore, Dana presumed, were enough to have crushed Qu'ban's little heart.

Quietly, Dana placed the photos and the letter into her purse, then left work for the day.

What Qu'ban didn't know was that Dana Lowe had been watching him since she had first evaluated him when he first entered the prison. She had read through his file, tapped into his phone calls, and even read his mail coming in and going out. She seemed to be obsessed with him. Several times she wanted to make contact with him, but didn't know how to go about doing it. Until the day his ex-girlfriend and child came up missing. That gave her the excuse that she needed to get him in her office.

Dana was only 26 years old, but over the years had grown

way out of shape. She had been a fox in her teens. But after a bad incident with a man, her self-esteem was destroyed. Then she had to hitchhike on the highway. A passing car accidentally grazed her legs, dislocating her left knee, causing her to walk with a slight limp. But her face, although it was pudgy, was still very pretty.

Qu'ban was at one of the lowest points in his life. That's why Dana felt that it was her duty to reach out to him.

~ ~ ~ ~ ~

After the disappearances of Katrina and Brianna, and her mother's funeral, Nah Nah decided it was time to turn her life around. She re-enrolled in school, then moved into an apartment, all paid for by her new friend, Tremon.

With Michael pretty much absent from her life altogether, Tremon had been helping her cope with her loss. Make no mistake, it did not interfere with her loyalty to O'ban, or the things that she did for him while in prison. But she did have mad respect for Tremon.

The problem was, O'ban was about to come home. And she had to figure out how she was going to break the news to him about Tremon.

~ ~ ~ ~ ~

"Did you read the letter?"

Dana took a deep breath, then released a gust of hot air. "Yes, I did."

"Did you see the pictures?'

"Yes, I did."

"Now do you see why I have so much resentment?"

Dana reached forward, opened her purse, took out the envelope, then handed it to me. She removed her glasses and rubbed her eyes.

"How come…" she paused. "How come you never told me that Katrina was white?"

I shrugged, unable to see the relevance of her question. "Does it matter?"

"Of course it does. Because of some reason white women, myself included, can't help but have an attraction to black men, knowing they're only going to use us, abuse us, or just see us as their sex toys."

I was shocked by her words.

"You've dated a black man before?" I asked curiously.

Dana choked up. "W…well, no. But I am attracted to black men. I've just never actually…been approached by one."

She was lying. I could tell by the way her eyes were avoiding mine.

"I don't believe you. I think you've had a black man before and he treated you badly and now you're scarred for life."

Dana's face became cold. Her eyebrows arched liked a devil. "What the hell do you know? You don't know shit about me, convict. All you see when you look at another white woman is that you might be able to manipulate her like you did that poor girl Katrina. I saw those pictures of her giving your friend a BJ, cum all over her face. It angered you to see that some other guy had done to her what you had been doing to her." Her nostrils flared. "You make me sick. Get the hell outta my office!"

"But…"

"Now!" She pointed her finger toward the exit.

I almost laughed. It amused me how she sat there and did a 360 on me in a matter of seconds.

Without saying another word, I got up and did as I was told.

~ ~ ~ ~ ~

<u>Two Months Later</u>

"You're outta here, dog," I said to O'ban.

He didn't say anything, just made a soft grunting sound.

We were sitting in my cell, both of us on the bottom bunk. I was holding back my tears. Don't get it twisted, I wanted him to go home. But at the same time, I had gotten used to him being around, and it was hard on me to see him go. The drug program that he'd taken knocked a year off his sentence.

We both sat in silence for a moment.

O'ban was the first to speak. "Eh. You ever think sometimes that maybe Katrina just got fed up and ran off? I mean, she did take the money out of the bank. And, I just can't see Terry harming no kid, man."

The very thought of Brianna being dead made my stomach turn, because she was an innocent party in all this. A casualty of war. Caught between me and her mother's bullshit.

I cleared my throat before I answered O'ban. "I know in my heart that Terry did something to Katrina and…" I couldn't even say her name out loud. "It ain't no coincidence that she happened to come up missing right after she hit that nigga for his bankroll and turned him in." I shook my head. "That ain't no coincidence, man."

It startled O'ban when I jumped up.

"Listen, nigga. If you too mutha-fuckin' scared to get at that nigga, being that you're just getting outta jail…if you can't do it, then that's on you. But don't go making excuses about it. 'Cause one thing is for sure. That nigga's ass belongs to me. I don't give a fuck if I throw my whole life away behind it."

The C.O. walked into my cell. "O'ban Cartez, they're call-

221

ing for you. Time to leave." Then he left just as quick as he came.

The room grew quiet again. All that could be heard was the deep breaths that I took while I was calming down.

O'ban stood up. "Look, man…"

"I'll see ya, man," I cut in. "Ain't nothing else to say." I gave him an emotionless hug, then left the cell.

I was standing in the middle of the restroom floor when I heard the C.O. ask O'ban if he had all his stuff.

"Yeah. I got it all."

The C.O. said, "Let's go."

Anger rose from deep within. I clinched my fists tight, ready to attack the tin ass, but I didn't. From wall to wall I paced back and forth cussing at no one. I couldn't believe that my life had come to that point. And although I didn't want to admit it, I had no one to blame but myself.

CHAPTER TWENTY-SEVEN

<u>O'ban Cartez</u>

I walked out of the joint February 2004, a free man. Before serving time in the feds, I had never been in any trouble. Therefore, doing the wrong thing wasn't no big deal to me, because I didn't know what it felt like to deal with the consequences. Now that I had been through it, getting out and doing the wrong things, like killing Terry, were no longer a priority for me.

What was a priority for me was getting my life back on track, having me a shorty and getting myself involved in a few of the business ventures that I studied up on while in prison.

Nah Nah was standing by the front desk when I entered the Greyhound Bus Station in Kansas City. She was looking good, too. She was looking around the building. A tight fitting velour Rocawear suit clung to her body. Finally she spotted me and smiled.

"Ba-by," she said with excitement as she started in my direction.

We embraced in the middle of the floor. For a long while I held her tight, inhaling her feminine fragrance.

"I missed you, baby," she said.

"Me, too."

"Mm. Grab my ass. I know you're horny."

I clutched both of her soft ass cheeks. "Let's get the fuck outta here before I cum down my leg. Do we need to stop and pick up some rubbers first?"

Nah Nah punched me in my arm. "Don't treat me like that, baby."

Hand in hand we walked outside and got into her Jeep Liberty. She peered at me in a seductive way while I sat in my seat, muscles bulging out of my sweatshirt.

"What?" I asked.

Nah Nah smiled. Her hands found my buckle and started unbuttoning my pants.

"Hey. Hey."

"Shh!" She pulled my dick out, looked around to make sure that no one was looking, then went down on me. I tilted my head back against the glass window and closed my eyes.

Her cool saliva covered my shaft as she took all of me into her mouth, a total of six times. Then she licked each side, kissed the head, and released it.

"Put it back up," she said, wiping spittle from her mouth with her hand. "I just wanted to prime you up a little bit before we get to the crib."

I put my little man back up. "After I get them guts I gotta go by Pops' crib and see him and my nephew."

"I gotcha." She put the car in drive, then drove away.

~ ~ ~ ~ ~

"The government has one week from today to turn in its list of witnesses. Then another month from then we'll begin with the jury selection process for the upcoming trial. This court is adjourned." The judge banged the gavel once, then exited the room.

Terry rose from his seat. He and Snatch watched as all of their female co-defendants were escorted out of the courtroom dressed in orange jump suits. Kortni looked back into the crowd of onlookers with a big smile on her face. She had just been granted the right to have her own separate trial.

"I'll give you a call first thing Monday morning," Terry said to his lawyer. They shook hands and parted ways.

As Terry and Snatch walked down the aisle, they didn't pay attention to Michael Miller, who was sitting in the courtroom, watching them.

"Without the bitch, they don't have nothing," Terry said with more confidence than he actually felt. Witness or no witness, the government was going to present their case against them to a 12-man jury of their peers.

~ ~ ~ ~ ~

Pink-nippled jugs bounced around. Sweat dripped from her face onto my body. Baby was in the zone, in her own little world of ecstasy as she rode that dick. Up, down, back and forth, she pounded herself down onto my shaft, while purring like a wounded kitten.

Nah Nah sat straddled across my legs, with her arms stretched out above my head. Her fingers interlocked with mine. She planted wild kisses on my upper body. I reached down and clutched her little pink ass, guiding her up and down. Nah Nah bit and licked my nipples.

"Ooh," she moaned. "I wanna have your...babyyy, O'ban. Come for mommy."

She sat all the way down on me, letting my Johnson marinate inside her pussy. She sat up, then stretched her arm backward until she had a grip on my skins. Slowly she started rising her body up to the top of my shaft, then back down.

I stared up at her bouncing titties. She gazed down at me with a black look in her eyes.

"Uhh! I love black dick," she howled.

"Say it again. Say it again, baby," I commanded.

"I love black dick!" she screamed.

I rolled over on top of her. She licked her lips while gazing up at me.

"Tear this shit up," she challenged.

I planted my hands flat on the bed, then planted myself deep inside her guts. Her legs spread wide. She held onto my shoulders and tightened her muscles. I humped to a rhythm. The pussy was too good to go fast. There was no need to rush. She had to come before I did.

"*Slow is the way to go,*" Ron Isley crooned from the radio that sat atop her dresser. "*Hold on. Hold on. Girl, you gotta hold on. Let's make love. Let's make love, girl. The whole night long.*"

"Uhh," Nah Nah moaned. My strokes were calculated and delivered at just the right pace. Our faces touched, and our lips locked for just a second. Nah Nah licked the sweat from my chin. "Mm. Shiiit!"

Nah Nah reached up and grabbed her ankles. "I'll do anything to be with you, ohhh."

I bit down on my bottom lip as I drove into her, full length. Her back arched. Her mouth opened and released noises of passion. My dick began to jerk. She could feel it inside her. Simultaneously her body was going through a thing of its own. I could feel her body quivering beneath me. Her fingers were locked onto my back.

Nah Nah started to cry when she realized that we were

coming together as one.

I saw the tears in her eyes and smiled. It took me back to that night when me and Qu'ban first fucked them. Qu'ban had made tears come from Katrina's eyes. I finally did it. Victory was mine.

A moment passed before I began to stroke again. Nah Nah rotated her hips as she pushed her back toward me.

About 15 minutes later I found myself coming again. Again I shot my thick load into her. I rolled over on my side. Nah Nah grabbed the remote and cut down the volume on the radio. Beyonce was singing about being "free."

Nah Nah flung her hair back out of her face, then placed her head on my chest.

She kissed my nipple. "I hope I get pregnant."

I dry swallowed. "I shot enough nut up in you to give you a little nigglet."

She smiled and scratched her head. "Our baby won't be no nigglet." Suddenly and slowly a smile began to form on her face. Then came a tear. "I miss Brianna, baby."

I held her tight, then kissed her forehead. "I know you do, baby. I'm glad that you brought her up to visit me that day. I had a good time with her."

"Wherever she is, I hope she's happy." She sniffled.

"Me, too," I answered slowly.

A moment passed without any conversation.

"Baby."

"What?"

"What are you gonna do now that you're out? Are you gonna go after Terry?"

Silence.

"I don't know what I'm gonna do. I do know that I don't…"

I heard the sound of light snores, then looked at her face and saw that she had fallen asleep. I hadn't realized that she had a hold of my dick until I tried to slip out of the bed.

"Where you going?" she mumbled.

"To the shower."

"Want me to come?"

"I got it."

Nah Nah curled up under the covers. I grabbed a towel from the closet and then hit the shower.

As the water began to run down my back, soothing my muscles, my mind started wandering. I was finally free. I was going to go back to school, start my own business, and live the square life like I had promised Nah Nah that I was going to do, while I was in the joint. Fuck doing anything to Terry. I didn't have to. The feds were about to take care of him for me.

Ten minutes later I stepped out of the shower. I toweled myself dry as I looked into the mirror. My skin was already starting to look ashy.

"Fuck the lotion at in this mutha-fucka?" I opened up the cabinet. Wasn't nothing inside there but a bunch of feminine shit. When I closed the cabinet back, my reflection came back into view. What scared the shit out of me was the fact that this time I was staring at two reflections instead of one.

Somebody was standing behind me.

I tried to turn around, but was smacked upside the head with something that felt like steel. Initially my eyes began to tear up with blood and water.

"What the fuck are you doing in my crib, nigga?" the person yelled at me. "Huh?"

I heard footsteps traveling at a fast pace outside the door. They must have been Nah Nah's, because I heard her scream out the name, "Tremon!"

"What the hell are you doing?" Nah Nah shouted.

Tremon looked toward her. I used that opportunity to jump at him and tackle him to the floor. Quickly I clutched the wrist of the arm that held the gun, then hit him in his face, repeatedly.

Surprisingly it only took two hits for him to release the gun. I picked it up, then rose to my feet. From experience I knew to back up out of kicking range. I pointed the gun at Tremon while wiping the bloody fluid from my eyes. When my sight was clear again, I got a good look at the big light-skinned nigga with the long cornrows that was laid out on the floor. That's when I came to the realization that Tremon was a woman.

"Don't shoot her, O'ban," Nah Nah pleaded.

My chest was heaving up and down as I began to relax. Now that I knew that Tremon was a female, I felt like I was in more control of the situation.

"What the fuck is goin' on, Nah Nah?" I asked.

Tremon slowly rose to her big feet while she held onto her jaw. "Tell 'em, Nah Nah."

Nah Nah said, "O'ban, this is Tremon. Tremon has been my...friend ever since Katrina and Brianna disappeared."

Tremon added, "I think we've been more than just fuckin' friends. You let friends stick a foot of dick up yo' ass until they come all over the goddamned place?"

"Tremon, just shut up!"

"Nah, you shut the fuck up!"

I grabbed Tremon by her braided hair and pulled her toward me. "Look, you big bitch! I'm home now. So I don't wanna catch yo' big stupid looking ass around this mutha fucka again. You hear me, bitch?"

I took the gun and slapped her upside the forehead with it. She screamed and grabbed her face. Then I kicked her in the back with my foot, pushing her out the door. Nah Nah stepped out the way. I shot daggers at Nah Nah as I passed her in the hallway.

Tremon was leaning against the wall, holding her head. I pushed her toward the door.

"Get yo' fat ass out of here!" I yelled at her.

Tremon stumbled out the front door. I kicked her in the ass on the way out, causing her to trip down the short case of stairs. Nah Nah was leaning up against the wall looking stupid when I slammed the door.

"You're dead, pussy!" I could hear Tremon shouting. "You and that white bitch!"

I snatched the door back open, pointed the gun toward her, then fired several shots over her head. Her fat ass took off running for her car. She dove into a '97 Lexus LS400 and sped away.

Nah Nah had tears in her eyes now. "What the fuck is you crying about? And who the fuck was that?"

"Tremon is…"

"Why the fuck didn't you tell me about Tremon?"

"Because I…

"Does she live here or what?"

Nah Nah didn't respond.

I frowned. "Bitch, you don't hear me talking to you?" I stepped toward her. "Huh?"

"Every time I try to answer, you keep…ow!"

I slapped her across her face. Her lip and teeth started to bleed.

"I'm sorry," she cried. "I'm sorry."

I waved my hand at her. "Sorry? Bitch, you could've gotten a nigga killed his first night out." For a moment I just stood there watching her sob. After a moment, my heart began to feel guilty for what I had done. I reached out and pulled her close to me, and wrapped my arms around her. Her face was buried inside my chest.

"I'm sorry," she mumbled. "I'm sorry."

Although I believed her about being sorry, I couldn't help but wonder at what point while I was gone did she start having a thing for women? I also wondered what price, if any, was I going to end up paying for what I had just done to Tremon. I mean, the bitch did walk up in there and smack me with a gun, so she did have heart.

CHAPTER TWENTY-EIGHT

<u>Qu'ban</u>

"I want to apologize for the way I acted the other day. That was totally unprofessional of me to do that to you."

I shifted in the leather chair. "I accept. But for a minute there I thought you had turned into Kathy Bates. You scared the shit outta me."

Dana giggled. "Not Kathy Bates. You're crazy." She took the top off her pen, then flipped through her notepad. "So what's new."

"I'm fucked up as usual."

"Would this have anything to do with your brother being released recently?"

"It has a lot to do with it." I sat up and leaned forward, toward her desk. "The truth is, Ms. Lowe, I need to leave this place."

"Like escape?"

"Naw. Not like escape. I just need a change of environment. I think I'd be happy if I could get sent outside the gate to that camp outside. Being behind these fences and locked doors is adding more stress to my emotional state."

Dana signed. "Well, I'm not sure how much of an influence that I have regarding that situation. But it's funny that you mentioned going to the camp outside. I act as a C.O. out there some nights when I feel like doing overtime."

Of course I already knew that. That was the very reason why I even brought it up. I was sure that Dana had a thing for me, I just wasn't sure how to approach her about it. Or if I should approach her at all.

Dana scribbled something down on her pad. "Let me see what I can do about getting you out there." She finished writing. "Now, let's get back to the subject of your brother."

I said, "All I expect out of O'ban is for him to get out and take care of business like he's supposed to do."

"The kind of business that you expect for him to take care of, is it illegal?"

"No."

Dana sat back in her leather chair and crossed her legs. She stared at me. "If you were able to go home tonight, what would you do?"

"Honestly?"

"Off the record."

"I'd go straight after Terry."

~ ~ ~ ~ ~

Tremon whipped her Lexus into Terry's driveway. Steam was coming from her head as she rang the doorbell. Within seconds she was greeted by Snatch. She stormed past him on into the house.

Terry was sitting at the kitchen table having breakfast while he conversed with their lawyer, who was sitting across from him typing on his laptop. Tremon stormed into the room.

Tremon said, "I've been trying to reach you all goddamned

weekend. Where have you been?"

Terry dropped his fork, "Girl, if you don't get somewhere with all that damn screaming in my goddamned house. Don't you see an important person sitting across from me?"

Tremon glanced at the lawyer briefly. "Anyway."

Terry took a good look at her. She looked like she had been in a fight. "What the fuck happened to you?"

Tremon rolled her eyes and sighed heavily. "That's what I'm trying to tell your ass. That nigga O'ban got out Friday. I caught his bitch ass over Nah Nah's apartment. I slapped him upside the head."

"Then why the hell you got all the bumps and bruises upside your head?" The three men laughed.

"Man, you know I can't whoop no real man. The nigga took my gun, cracked me upside the head, kicked me in my ass and some mo' shit."

Terry sucked his teeth. "He say anything?"

"Hell yeah. That nigga stood over me talking shit about how he's back and a lot of nigga about to die," Tremon lied. "That pussy even shot at me. When we first started this thing, you pointed Nah Nah out at that gas station. All you said to me was get to know her and keep an eye on her for you. You didn't say nothing about no nigga getting out of jail and throwing me down no fuckin' steps."

Terry said, "When I told you to keep an eye on Nah Nah, all you were supposed to do was befriend her during her time of need, hang around and catch what information that you could about her sister's investigation. You the one that ate the pussy and fell all in fuckin' love an' shit. So don't run to me crying about her nigga whooping yo' big ass."

Tremon pouted. "I don't even know why I bothered. Just

pay me my money and let me get the fuck out of here."

"I ain't paying you shit, and you don't have to leave on your own. Snatch, throw this big bitch outta my crib."

Tremon frowned. "Huh? Terry, you some shit. I…"

Snatch grabbed her by the back of her neck. Pain shot down her spinal cord. She whined as he pushed her through the house and out the front door. When they reached the stairs, he pushed her down. She fell and rolled down three concrete steps, until her arm got caught in the handrail.

"Ouch!" she screamed out.

Snatch gazed up and down the block before he went back inside. Terry was now standing up staring out the patio windows into the back yard. He ran his fingers through his curly hair.

"Damn, Snatch. This nigga can't be out on the streets running around. I don't feel safe. Especially not while we're concentrating on going to trial. Hell nah."

Snatch said, "O'ban ain't as crazy as that goddamned brother of his. That fat bitch could be lying on him for all we know. I mean, ain't no doubts about him beating her ass, but I don't get him saying all that other dumb-ass shit."

Terry faced him. "Well, I'm not gonna be able to rest until I find out. I'll do my whole life in prison before I let a nigga put me in that pine box." He paused. "Get Erica on the phone."

~ ~ ~ ~ ~

O'ban

"Your first priority is to seek full time employment, Mr. Cartez," the probation officer, Ms. Cannon, stated. "And we will be coming by your residence to check up on you from time to time."

"What won't y'all be doing?" I complained as I scanned

over the long list of rules on the form that I held in my hand. "I might as well be back in jail. Damn."

She glared at me through piercing blue eyes, then removed her glasses. "We will not be using that type of language in this office, Mr. Cartez. If you'd rather go back to jail than abide by my rules, then by all means, be my guest."

About five minutes later I stormed out of her office mad as hell. Never in my life had a bitch talked to me so bad. Nah Nah was sitting in the waiting area when I gestured for her to come on.

"These bitches got my life for the next five years," I told Nah Nah after we were back inside her Jeep.

"All you can do is live with it, baby." She reached into the back seat and grabbed her book bag. "It's about time for my class to start."

After I dropped Nah Nah off at school, I went and picked up Pops so he could ride with me while I went to go find a job. It must have been my lucky day because I got hired at this construction company right on the spot. They needed somebody to help build scaffolds and haul away trash. Twelve dollars an hour was a great place for me to start out, considering that I was a felon with no actual work experience.

~ ~ ~ ~ ~

Qu'ban

Two weeks had passed. I hadn't been summoned to Dana's office for my counseling, so I was starting to get worried that another inmate had come along and stolen my bitch. A couple times I was temped to barge into her office and see what the problem was.

I was coming from my job when I heard my name being called over the loud speakers. The case manager, Mr. Allen, wanted to see me in his office.

"What the fuck this gay mutha-fucka want to see me for?" I mumbled to myself as I was heading in that direction.

No one else was in his office when I walked in. He was sitting behind his desk going over my file.

"You wanted to see me, Mr. Allen?" I asked.

He nodded toward a chair. "Have a seat." I did. He took a deep breath before he began. "Your psychiatrist, Ms. Lowe, has made a recommendation that she deems will be a necessary part of your treatment. She is asking that you be removed from the security of this institution and placed outside in the camp. Now, it is true that you have been managing to avoid trouble since you've been here. However, I'm reading through your paperwork and I can see where you were in the act of shooting a man during the time that a warrant was being served at your residence. Not only that, but there's also a lot of speculated incidents of violence inside your file. None of it you were convicted of, but obviously you were involved in it to a certain extent." He paused to close the file. "So I'm denying her request to send you out to the camp."

I was heated. This tight-uniform-wearing-ass cracker obviously had no sympathy for what I was going through. But he didn't know that I had a trump card, and was 'bout reveal my hand.

Calmly I stood up and walked over to the door. I noticed that he didn't even look at me, neither did he do so during the meeting. Which showed me how irrelevant I was to him.

Finally he shifted his gaze back toward me when he heard me closing his door. Then I sat back down in my chair.

"What the hell are you doing?" he asked suspiciously. "If you think you can intimidate me, then you're wrong."

"Am I?" I crossed my legs. Then I proceeded to tell him what I had seen him doing with another inmate while the rest of the unit was at dinner. I also explained to him that it was not my intention to make any trouble, I just wanted to get outside to a place where there was no fences, bars, and only one officer to watch over the 30 inmates that were being housed there. Without waiting for an answer, I got up and walked out of his office, confident that I would be contacted by him at a later date saying that I had been approved to transfer.

~ ~ ~ ~ ~

O'ban

For almost three full weeks I had been showing up for work every morning at 7:30 a.m. and clocking out at 4:00 p.m. Nah Nah helped me get a student loan so I could enroll into college the following semester. During the past weekends I had been keeping my nephew, trying to establish a relationship between us.

I was on the right track. But I couldn't help but think that I wasn't meant to live the square life—going to work, having kids and throwing barbecues on holidays. And that trouble was waiting for me just around the corner.

It was my fourth weekend as a free man. I had done enough fucking on Nah Nah, spent quality time with my people, and I hadn't had any fun since I'd been out. It was time for me to unwind. So I finally got on the horn and called Jawan, informing him that I was out, and had been out for close to a month. He immediately stopped what he was doing and told me that he was on his way.

Jawan picked me up, took me to get a few outfits, a couple pair of kicks, then handed me $800 for my pocket. Three hundred of that I planned on sending to Qu'ban's books. I had to remind myself to send some pictures and a letter to him soon. I knew he hadn't called because he was still holding resentment toward me because I hadn't gotten at Terry like he wanted me to.

When I walked into the club I felt like I was back at home again. Just being in this atmosphere, around all these fine looking ladies and players, made me think twice about living the square life. I belonged in there macking hoes and throwing money. But after I stopped and really got a look at all the faces up in there with bright smiles, I started to realize that this was the new breed. Sooner or later these same faces were gonna start popping up in the obituary section of the newspaper, and inside the walls of multiple prisons. It was just a matter of time.

It was that rational thought that I had that made me order a glass of cranberry juice rather than a shot of cognac. I was determined to stay focused, no matter what kind of environment I found myself in.

Jawan and I partied for over three hours, mingling, dancing, shooting pool and just remembering old times. Then Nah Nah called. She and Qu'ban Junior were up playing Nintendo and wanted me to join them.

I alerted Jawan and told him that I had to leave. He was disappointed, but he was an open-minded person, so he understood. He was drunk and stumbling all over the place when we stepped outside.

There was a tall, leggy white girl walking ahead of us. She was probably the only white girl in the club that night. I hated her from the moment that I saw her, because lusting after white women was one of my greatest sins.

The white girl made a left outside the front door, then suddenly stumbled. I ran to her aid and caught her by the waist before she had a chance to fall.

"Whoa!" she said with a drunken smile. "Thanks, mister." She looked down and noticed that she had broken her left heel. Her hand flew over her mouth. "Whoa!" She giggled, then looked at me. "Um, can you please carry me over to my car? Because I don't think that I can make it."

"I got chu." She bent down and took off the broken shoe. I scooped her up. "Which car is yours?"

She pointed a long, slim finger toward the parking lot. "The purple 4Runner over there."

I started in that direction.

The girl hollered over my shoulder at Jawan, "Bye-bye."

Jawan said, "Come and get me up outta here if you need me."

The girl fished her keys out of her purse, then opened the front door. I placed her inside. She leaned over and started patting the driver's seat.

"Get in, talk to me for a minute. I won't bite."

I smiled, look at my watch, then figured what the hell. Baby reached over and unlocked the door so I could get in.

Suddenly she started to feel her chest, then pockets, then rambled through her purse. She gasped. "Oh, my god! I left my fucking phone in the goddamn club." She took off her other heel, tossed it into the back seat, then slipped into a pair of flip flops. "Don't move! I'll be right back, okay?" Without waiting for a response, she was out of the car and running back toward the club.

For a brief second I closed my eyes and yawned. Then I heard the driver's side door being snatched open. My eyes opened. I saw Snatch's bald headed-ass getting inside the truck. Before I could move, I felt somebody's arm shoot from the back seat and lock around my throat.

"You lookin' for me, nigga?" I heard a strained voice whisper into my ear. "Huh?"

I grabbed his forearms. Snatch closed the door. I nearly threw up when he hammered his huge fist into my stomach. My hands clutched my midsection. A burning sensation shot through me, but I couldn't pay much attention to that, because I couldn't fuckin' breathe. My eyes felt like they were about to pop out of my head. My feet were kicking at the floor in front of me.

"Answer me, bitch!" The voice belonged to Terry. "Tremon said that you was looking for me. Talk to me like you talked to her."

I grunted, snorted, gritted my teeth, but not a legible word came out. Although I couldn't see it, I heard the frightening sound of a gun cock. Shortly after I felt the barrel being jammed against my temple.

I tried to speak. "T...T...Terr..."

Terry squeezed harder. And harder. He squeezed me so goddamned hard that his arm started shaking. I was a second away from passing out, but luckily he released me.

My head snapped forward. I gagged as I tried desperately to catch my breath. I held onto my neck as slobber dribbled down to the floor.

There was the sound of laughter. Then someone slapped me in the back of my head.

"Shake it off, bitch!" Snatch commanded. More laughter. "You been looking for us? C'mon, now, O'ban. You don't say something convincing, then your head is gonna go back in

Terry's vice."

I grunted and spit on the floor. They had caught me fucked up. I didn't know what to do. As far as I knew, I wouldn't survive through the night.

Terry said, "I don't want to kill you, nigga. But I'd rather see you dead than me. So you got about 30 seconds to tell me what you plan on doing."

Finally my breathing began to stabilize. I lifted my head up. "I don't." I dry swallowed. "I don't want to...beef with...you, Terry."

"Why the fuck not? I'm the reason you just did all that fuckin' time in prison. And you expect me to believe that you ain't got no beef with me?"

"I swear. I swear, man," I uttered softly.

"Un huh. Okay." Terry sucked his teeth. "Well, I'm not convinced. Snatch, you convinced?"

Snatch hit me in my jaw. It sounded so loud that I thought he shot a gun inside the truck.

"Nah, I ain't convinced," Snatch replied. "The nigga's face is too tense."

A blast from Terry's fist hit me in the back of my head, and my face flew forward toward my knees. I couldn't see it, but Snatch had the gun pointed toward my head.

"Wait," Terry said.

I could hear people walking outside the club. It sounded like the club was letting out. During that time I eased my head on the door handle. The noise from the crowd began to fade.

"Go 'head," Terry commanded.

Just in the nick of time, I turned my head to the left.
Pow!

The bullet grazed my ear and lodged into the front door. I

pulled the handle and ducked outside the truck.

Pow!

Another bullet struck me in my arm as I took off running up the parking lot. The loud blasts that echoed inside the car had my ears ringing and my heart thumping. Ahead of me I could see females running around in circles, ducking behind cars, as they screamed for their lives.

I ducked in between cars, running in a zigzag pattern until I made it out on the main street. Then I just started running north. My adrenaline must have kept me from feeling the pain from the bullet that was in my arm.

The loud roar of an engine was coming from somewhere behind me. I didn't bother to turn around and look. Instead I kept on running. A short distance later, I heard it pull up alongside of me.

"O'ban!" somebody called out.

I immediately stopped running after I recognized the voice as Jawan's. Then I jumped into the truck with him.

I waited until my breathing slowed. "Take me to the hospital."

CHAPTER TWENTY-NINE

Inside the emergency room at Research Hospital I was led into a cold room, placed on a steel table and patched up. One of the nurses who worked there knew me from back in the day. While I was waiting on the doctor to bring me the prescription for the pain medication, she hurried into the room and told me that the police had been called and were on their way.

I didn't waste no time. With my shirt in my hand, I snuck out of the room, onto the elevator, then outside to the parking lot. I found Jawan asleep in his truck.

He jumped awake when I got in.

"Take me home."

~ ~ ~ ~ ~

Both Nah Nah and Qu'ban Junior had fallen asleep waiting on O'ban to come home. Both of them jumped awake on the couch after they heard someone beating on the door. Flashlights could be seen through the window.

"Open up! It's the police."

"Just a minute." Nah Nah opened the door.

Two out of the three officers stepped into the apartment and began looking around.

Nah Nah was baffled. "What the hell are they doing?"

"Calm down, ma'am," the remaining officer said. "We're here to serve a warrant for O'ban Cartez."

Nah Nah raised her brows. "O'ban? For what?"

"About an hour ago he showed up at Research Hospital with a gunshot wound to the arm and right ear. But he disappeared before we could arrive to interview him. We ran his name, contacted his probation officer, and she gave us this address."

"I don't know anything..."

"He's not here," one of the officers yelled from behind her.

"Let's go." He handed her his card. "Call me if he comes home. And please urge him to turn himself in."

"There has to be a good explanation for all this. I'm sure of it."

"I'm sure there is, too," he said in a sarcastic tone. "Good night."

~ ~ ~ ~ ~

We were bailing up Troost Avenue when I called Nah Nah to tell her that I was on my way. She countered, explaining to me that the police had been there, and a warrant had been issued for my arrest.

"Fuck!" I shouted. "Look, pack up a bag and meet me at the Long John Silver's on Bannister Road."

Nah Nah said, "I'm on my way."

~ ~ ~ ~ ~

Nah Nah hung up the phone and looked out the window. A patrol car was sitting in the parking lot next to her neighbor's van.

She packed an overnight bag with clothing and cosmetics and she and Qu'ban Junior left the apartment. At the end of the staircase she encountered the apartment complex manager, Ms. Alexander.

"Ms. Miller," the manager called out.

Nah Nah stopped, sighed and rolled her eyes. "What is it?"

"When you first moved into this complex, you were warned that there was not to be any reason for the police to be called to your residence for reasons other than an emergency."

"I know, Ms. Alexander. And believe me, there is a good explanation for all this. But unfortunately I don't have time to explain it to you right now. Goodbye." Nah Nah hurried down the walkway with Qu'ban Junior in tow.

~ ~ ~ ~ ~

Jawan put another $500 into my pocket before I departed from his company. Pops had met us up there so he could pick up Qu'ban Junior. I left with Nah Nah in her Jeep.

"Baby, what happened?" Nah Nah asked with concern.

"Just drive, and let me think."

Like I had said before, I knew that trouble was waiting for me around the corner. If I kept going down the right path, I would've missed it. But I had to go left by going to that club, and as a result, all hell had broken loose.

I had been hoodwinked by a white bitch into getting in her truck, who was obviously in cahoots with Terry, and his plot to kill me. Trouble seemed to be following me like a contagious disease that I couldn't get rid of ever since I got out of prison. Now I was on my way back to jail—amongst thieves, suckas and all of the other bad element that flooded that place, all because of the love that I had for the streets.

"Stop at a motel," I told her. "I need some pussy."

~ ~ ~ ~ ~

Qu'ban

Finally I was called into Mr. Allen's office and notified that I was being transferred to the camp outside. I was so happy about the news that I went to Dana's office unannounced and knocked on the door.

"Come in."

She was sitting behind her desk, typing on her computer when I walked in. She sighed when she saw my face.

"Mr. Cartez," Dana said.

"Hello. I was just wondering why I haven't heard from you. You haven't placed my name on the call-out sheet or nothing."

Dana said, "Well, I talked to Mr. Allen, and he denied my request to have you transferred out to the camp. So..." She paused as she watched me remove the papers out of my pocket. I handed them to her.

A smile appeared on her face halfway through the letter. "This is great. I'm so happy for you. Congratulations."

I took the paper back. My heart was pounding as I prepared to have a conversation with her that I wasn't sure was safe. But fuck it. I had to go for mine.

"You know the real reason that I want to get out there, Ms. Lowe. And it ain't got nothing to do with no goddamned treatment."

"Careful, Mr. Cartez. I am a government employee, sworn under oath."

I nodded my head. "I know that. But I also know that you believe in what is right, Ms. Lowe. And in this case, I think you know that I am. That's why you asked me that question that day."

"What question?"

I snorted. "Do you really want me to answer that?" I

247

winked my eye at her. "See you outside." Then I left her office.

~ ~ ~ ~ ~

O'ban

I spent the rest of the weekend fucking the hell out of Nah Nah in an attempt to get her pregnant, and thinking about what the hell I was gonna do about my situation. It didn't come to me until about 4:00 a.m. Monday morning. I didn't have no money to be going on the run. At most I was only facing a 9 month violation. I could do that standing on my head. But before I went, I was about to kill two ducks with one stone, and rid myself of all my problems. Because the only way I was gonna be able to duck trouble was to eliminate it.

My eyes opened on that Monday after the weekend.

Nah Nah was on the phone, talking in a loud, teary voice. "I understand Ms. Alexander. All I'm saying is that there is no drug activity going on at my apartment." She listened for a moment. "My ex-housemate is just acting out because she's trying to get me evicted." She sniffled. "So I've got 30 days to get out?"

I reached over and took the phone out of her hand, then leaned over and hung it up.

"Ain't no use in arguing with her, baby," I said. "What's done is done. So…"

Nah Nah jumped up, ran across the bed, then dashed into the bathroom, slamming the door behind her. I could hear her loud cries through the door. I wondered if she blamed all of her problems—her sister and niece coming up missing, her mother dying suddenly—on the fact that she had met me?

While she was busy doing her thing, I started getting dressed. She could cry all she wanted to. I had shit to do. I snatched the keys up off the dresser, then stood outside the bathroom door.

"I gotta go, girl! What you gon' do?"

"Just a minute."

Nah Nah came out the bathroom, grabbed her bag, then went back inside. Ten minutes later she was dressed and ready to go.

She had already missed work and gotten evicted from her apartment behind me, but she was not about to fuck up her education again. So Nah Nah had me drop her off at school while I went to take care of whatever business I had planned.

"Take care of my Jeep," she said as she exited the Jeep in the parking lot of her school. "It's all I got left."

"Shut the fuck up," I mumbled under my breath. Then I drove away before she got a chance to say another word. I reached the end of the parking lot before I realized that I had forgotten something. I backed up.

Nah Nah was still standing there looking at me like I was stupid. She handed me the piece of paper that was in her hand through the window. We kissed.

"Be careful," she said.

"I will."

I stopped by Pops' house where I was supposed to meet Jawan. He had some heat for me that I could throw away after I used it. It just so happened that Qu'ban called while I was there.

"Bro!" I yelled into the phone. "Long time, man."

"How you holding up out there?"

"Shit's fucked up right now," I answered honestly. Then I told him what all had happened since I'd been out.

Qu'ban grunted. "I can't believe you. No, I can believe you. You wasn't built for this shit for real." My grip tightened around the phone. "But you don't have to worry about it no more, because I'ma handle it for both of us. So just lay on back and live the square life that you been living with Nah Nah. I gotta go. Stay up."

I hung up the phone feeling less than a man. The only way that I was gonna regain my brother's approval and restore confidence in myself was to put Terry's ass to sleep.

Jawan arrived a short while later and gave me a throw-away .380 automatic. He didn't ask any questions or offer any advice. He just shook my hand and rolled out.

I said my goodbyes to Pops, then got into Nah Nah's Jeep. The address on the paper Nah Nah gave me read "3912 Forest," Tremon's mother's house. I put the gear into drive and headed over there.

Tremon just so happened to be walking out of her mother's house when I turned onto the block. She walked down the walkway, pulling up her sagging jeans. She stopped suddenly and turned around as if someone had called her. She yelled something, then walked back into the house.

I parked the Jeep, then ran down the block and hid on the side of a brown Buick that was parked on the opposite side of her Lexus.

A minute later she came skipping back out the house. She popped the locks. Just as she was entering the front seat, I came up behind her and struck her in the back of the head with my fist.

"Ow!" she screamed as she fell into the front seat.

Using the door to brace myself, I started kicking Tremon in her legs. "Get over! Get…over! Move!"

Tremon hollered and grunted as she crawled over into the passenger seat, desperately trying to escape the blows from my foot. I hit the locks, then pulled out my gun. I pointed it at the side of her head.

Tremon's face was twisted up as she held her leg where she had been kicked. "Ouch! Shit, O'ban, I ain't did shit!" She continued to rub her leg. "Owww! Oww!"

I clutched her throat, then pressed the barrel of the .380 up to her face. "You told Terry that I was on some bullshit, huh?"

"O'ban, man…"

"Where that nigga stay at?"

Tremon started crying. I laughed at her. "I thought bitches were tougher than that, Tremon. I put this pistol in yo' fuckin' mouth, then all the bitch comes outta you." I clutched her jaws tight and squeezed until she screamed for me to stop.

"Okay! Okay!"

I released her face. "Take out your phone, call Terry and tell him that you're on your way to his house. And make it sound urgent."

Reluctantly she removed her cell phone from her hip and dialed his number. She spoke to Terry for a moment, then hung up the phone.

Tremon said, "We gotta hurry up. He said that he has to be in court in an hour."

~ ~ ~ ~ ~

A bright red Porsche 911 pulled into the parking lot of Rockhurst College on 52nd and Troost Avenue. The large white man that stepped out of it shook the wrinkles from his dark blue slacks. He thumped his cigarette onto the pavement as he walked toward the building.

Nah Nah was inside her Language Arts class trying to concentrate on her work. She had just picked up her pencil when she heard the classroom door open. When she looked up she saw one of the school counselors, Mr. Rosenberg, coming toward her. Quickly she put her face in her book, trying to look busy. He stopped next to her and whispered something into her ear. His breath smelled like alcohol and coffee.

After he said what he had to say, he turned and left. Nah Nah closed up her book and exited the classroom behind him. Michael was waiting for her in the hallway.

"Hi, Dad," Nah Nah said in a low voice.

"I showed up at your apartment this morning. As I was leaving I ran into your landlord. She said that you were being evicted."

Nah Nah lowered her head.

"God, Nancy, what is wrong with you?" He stood towering over her with his hands on his hips. "Your mother…"

"Don't you talk about my mother," Nah Nah said, raising her voice. "You were the one that left her alone. Her heart had been shattered long before Katrina and Brianna disappeared." She paused to catch her breath. "You can miss me with all that bullshit, Dad."

Michael glared at her. "Look at you. Dressing like you're hip and talking all that jive. I might was well have put you in the microwave as an infant and cooked you brown."

Nah Nah's eyes narrowed on him. "You're a goddamn hypocrite. How dare you speak to me like that!" Her eyes became moist.

"Because you're not in control of your life."

"I am, too."

"Well, why is it that when I talked to your landlord I was informed that you were evicted because of suspected drug activity? Do you sell drugs, Nancy?"

"No! It was a mis…"

"I don't think so. You're probably strung out on dope and being pimped by some black guy."

Nah Nah grunted. "Well, I guess the apple don't fall far from the tree, because that black bitch that you left us for sure was draining your wallet."

Michael lost control of himself and smacked her across the face.

Nah Nah wiped blood from her lip while she fought to hold back her tears. "You didn't come here to find out what was going on with me, Daddy, or even if I needed your help. Instead you came here to talk down on me and make me feel worse than I already feel. If that's the kinda father that you are going to be, then I don't need you in my life."

With that being said, Nah Nah walked back into her classroom.

Michael stood there with his hands on his hips and his nostrils flaring.

Chapter Thirty

<u>O'ban</u>

I pulled over on the back road a couple blocks from where Tremon told me that Terry stayed.

"Get the fuck out," I commanded.

Tremon frowned. "What?"

I stared at her. "Get…the fuck…out."

Tremon pushed her door open and followed me to the back of her car. I lifted the lid on the trunk. Before she had a chance to react, I grabbed her by her cornrows, pulled her head down, then hit her behind her ear with the gun. She slumped over halfway into the trunk. I lifted her legs up, then tucked her entire body inside.

Out of my pocket I pulled a pair of latex gloves that I had swiped from the cleaning lady at the motel. I put them on, wiped the gun down with Tremon's T-shirt, then placed the gun inside her hand. When I was satisfied that the gun was covered with her prints, I removed it and put it back inside my pocket.

I closed the trunk, got back inside the car and drove the short distance to Terry's house. Since Terry was already expecting Tremon, I parked her car in his driveway. I checked the chamber and the clip from the gun before I got out. I had to be careful. Fucking with Terry, I could end up leaving in a body bag.

Casually I approached the front door and rang the bell twice. Someone peeped out the curtain. My hand made a fist around the gun in my jacket pocket. My heart was beating through my chest.

Suddenly the door swung open. Standing before me in an oversized Mets jersey and a fitted ball cap was a kid I recognized as Spin, Terry's 20-year-old nephew. Obviously he had no idea about the beef between me and Terry, because he greeted me with a smile.

"Wha' sup, O'ban?"

I shook his hand. "Long time no see. Man, you don' grown a foot since I seen you last."

"Yeah. I'm playing basketball for Highland Community College in Texas."

"Yeah? That's good, man." I looked beyond him into the house. "Terry here?"

"Yep. He's downstairs."

"So it's just you and him?"

Spin regarded me curiously. "Yeah. O'ban, why you asking all…"

I pulled my gun from my pocket and forced him back into the house. "Move, nigga!"

Spin was frightened. "O'ban, man…"

"Move!"

"Don't kill me, O," he begged as we stepped into the house.

Without taking my eyes off him, I reached back, closed the door and twisted the lock. "Show me where he at."

Spin led me downstairs into the studio. I didn't know

much about music, but I could tell that a large amount of money had been spent on equipment. It sounded like Terry was somewhere playing a keyboard. We turned a corner, and the back of Terry's head came into view. He was sitting down fingering a keyboard.

Without looking up he asked, "Is that Tremon?"

I rushed up on his chair and locked my arm around his throat. "You looking for me?" I whispered in his ear. He gagged, choked and made loud grunting noises. "Huh?"

Spin backed up against the wall, looking like a child who was about to receive an ass whooping. I choked Terry as hard as I could, then slung both him and the chair onto the floor. Just for the fuck of it, I slapped him across the back of his head as he was getting up.

"What the fuck you want?" he hollered.

I kneeled down to his ear and said, "Break yo'self, nigga." Then I stepped back away from him. "Take me to it."

Terry took his time getting up from the floor.

"If you fuck around with me, T, I'ma kill you, Spin and anybody that decides to show up at that door."

"Aw, man," Spin cried. "Terry, give it to him."

Terry glared at me with his face twisted up. He was so angry that he was nearly in tears. But he didn't want to chance anything. So he did as he was told.

I followed them both into the basement bathroom. Spin was told to stand up against the wall with his nose in the corner. Terry got down on his knees and opened the cabinet door under the sink. He wasted no time reaching into the cabinet where the safe was, and started punching in code numbers that opened the lock. After he typed in the five digits, I heard a beeping sound.

Then it hit me—the reason why he was suddenly so eager to open the safe for me. Terry was fast. Before I had a chance to react, Terry had already reached into the safe and pulled out the gun.

I heard a blast.

Pow!

Out of reflex my eyes closed and my finger automatically started pulling on the trigger.

Pop! Pop! Pop! Pop!

I heard Spin scream, then I heard something that sounded like a gun falling onto the tiled floor. I released the trigger at the same time as I opened my eyes. There was a thin cloud of smoke.

Spin was on the floor, sitting with his back up against the wall. The single bullet hole in his nose was leaking blood. Terry had turned around and was slumped over the toilet. Blood soaked his jacket. Just to be safe, I pointed the pistol at the back of his head and was about to pull the trigger again until I heard a woman yell, "Terry!" from the top of the stairs. I became still.

"Terry!" she yelled again.

A child's voice came out of nowhere. "Mama, I…"

"Shut up!" the woman yelled at the child. "Go outside and wait in the car."

I recognized the voice as Terry's sister, Te Te. She must have flown in from Texas to support Terry during his trial.

"Terry, are you okay?"

I picked up the empty wastebasket from the floor, then scooped the money from the safe into it. Clutching the wastebasket under my free arm, I tiptoed up the stairs. As I was nearing the doorway, I heard footsteps coming toward me.

Shit. I hid around the corner. The footsteps came closer.

"Terry, quit playing so much!" Te Te shouted. "You're scaring me. I thought I heard gun…"

I pushed the door into her, knocking her into the wall. Before she could open her eyes, I darted through the house and out the front door. The kid who was on the porch saw me, but not enough to make a positive I.D.

I jumped into Tremon's Lexus and smashed out. Shit hadn't gone as planned, but at least I had gotten the job done.

~ ~ ~ ~ ~

Once Terry was sure that O'ban was gone, he turned around and slid off the toilet onto the floor. The one shot that he was hit with had hit him in the shoulder. After O'ban started firing, he realized that the best thing for him to do was play dead. It worked.

"Shit," he cried as the pain in his shoulder shot through his body. He looked to his right and saw Spin sitting up against the wall with a hole where his nose once was. Instantly Terry vomited.

He wiped his mouth with his sleeve. "Not my ne…" he began to sob. "Spin." It hurt like hell, but Terry managed to get to his feet. While holding onto his shoulder, he glanced around the bathroom. That's when he saw three bullet holes in the wall behind where he was standing when he had been shot. O'ban had only fired four shots, Terry was sure of that.

That could only mean one thing. Spin had been killed by the hands of his own Uncle Terry. It all happened so fast. Terry had pulled the .45 automatic from the safe, swung it around and fired wildly. Now that same .45 was lying on the floor outside the safe.

"Terry!" he heard Te Te yelling. She was coming down the

stairs at a fast pace.

Terry hurried up and picked up the gun, then set it inside the toilet and let the lid fall. Then he rushed over to the stairs to prevent Te Te from coming down and seeing her son in that state.

Te Te saw blood all over Terry and went hysterical. "Where's Spin? Where's my son?"

"Calm down, Te Te," Terry said.

"You're bleeding. Why is blood all over you? I thought I heard gunshots. Then somebody tackled me and ran out the house."

Terry grimaced from the pain. "Did you see what he was driving?"

"Umm. I saw a black Lexus in the driveway."

"A black Lexus?"

Te Te tried to push past him. He stopped her.

"Move, Terry! Where is my son?! I want to see my son," she stated firmly.

Terry stared at her for a moment, then allowed her past. He took off up the stairs. He had just picked up the phone when he heard his sister scream at the top of her lungs.

"Noooooo!"

After he dialed Tremon's number, he put the phone up to his ear. He noticed that his vision was starting to blur. His body swayed forward, but he caught himself. Tremon's phone went straight to the voicemail. He never got a chance to hang up the phone because he fell to the floor right there in the dining room.

~ ~ ~ ~ ~

I parked Tremon's Lexus a few blocks away from her house. From inside the car I popped the trunk and got out.

Tremon was still unconscious when I rolled her heavy ass out of the trunk, then placed her into the front seat of the car. I placed the gun in the glove box, shut the door, then walked back to Tremon's block where Nah Nah's Jeep was parked.

~ ~ ~ ~ ~

Nah Nah walked out of school early. When she got outside she saw Michael's car sitting in front of the building. She adjusted her books in her hand as she walked over to the car.

Michael was sitting in the front seat staring out the window. Tears were in his eyes.

"Dad?" Nah Nah said with concern.

He sniffled. "Kortni was found guilty today. She's being deported."

As if Nah Nah really gave a shit about the woman who helped cause her dead mother so much grief.

Nah Nah didn't know what to say. "Wanna take me home?"

Michael cleared his throat. "Sure."

Not a word was said as they drove out to the motel where Nah Nah was staying temporarily. Michael parked outside the room door. His head fell back against the headrest. A second later he was crying again.

Nah Nah sat there gazing at him, becoming angrier by the moment. If there was anybody who he should've been shedding tears for, it was his family—Kathy, Katrina and Brianna.

Nah Nah spoke up. "Look, Dad. I can't sit here and express my sympathy for your current situation. If I did I would be lying."

Michael's head snapped in her direction, glaring at her through a set of angry red eyes. "Yes, you would be lying, wouldn't you? It's partially your fault what happened to Kortni," he snapped.

"My fault?"

"Yes, your fault! You knew what your sister was up to. In fact, I truly believe that this whole plot was set up so you two could remove Kortni from my life in spite of what happened with me and your mother."

"Dad, you…"

"Just shut up, Nancy! You don't care about me or my well being. All you care about is being happy with the fact that you've made my life miserable, and chasing after your little nigger boyfriend." He turned his head away from her. "Get the hell out of my car. I don't know why I came to you anyway."

Nah Nah's face twisted into a sneer as she raised her fist and hit Michael upside his head.

"Don't you ever talk to me like that!" she screamed as she got out of the car. Then she slammed the door hard enough to crack the window.

Michael stared at her in disbelief as she stormed up to her room door. He continued to stare at her until she disappeared inside the confinement of her room.

~ ~ ~ ~ ~

Before I returned to the motel for the night, I stopped by a few supermarkets and purchased $5,000 worth of money orders, which I dropped into the nearest mailbox addressed to my brother Qu'ban. Then I snatched up a bottle of Patrón and headed on in.

Nah Nah had cleaned the room and was in bed listening to music in the dark. I gave her a kiss on the forehead on my way to the shower. The money that I had transferred into a bag, I put into the room's safe.

I returned to find Nah Nah lying on the bed naked with her legs spread. I was naked as well. Beads of water covered my body. I got onto the bed, where she rolled over on top of me, planting kisses on my face. Slowly her lips made their way down to my hard swipe. With one quick stroke, she licked me from my balls to the tip of my dick. I loved getting head from white girls, because to them it was more than pleasing the man, they actually got off on it. It was like a science to them.

The more I moaned and whispered the name, "Nah Nah," the deeper she took me into her mouth. Then she'd take it out and lick the saliva off the sides.

"I love you, daddy," she whispered as she rubbed the head under her chin and across her lips. Pre-cum hung from the tip of her chin. She jacked the long, black pole a few times while staring up at me, then she tucked me back inside the soft, warm confinement of her jaws.

~ ~ ~ ~ ~

From outside the window, Michael glimpsed though a crack in the curtain as his daughter committed what was to him the ultimate sin. His breathing became heavy and deep, like the life was being choked out of him. Not long ago he had come to her seeking comfort, and received just the opposite. Now there she was catering to the needs of a nigger, like he was more important than her own father.

"Stained cotton," he said to himself as he walked away, on the verge of vomiting.

~ ~ ~ ~ ~

"So you didn't get a look at his face?"

"No," Terry replied to the policeman that stood beside his bed. "The man wore a Halloween mask."

The officer said, "You didn't recognize the voice either?"

"No."

The officer raised his brows as he closed his notebook.

"Interesting. Look, if you think of anything, be sure to contact me at the number I gave you. A kid has been murdered. Your nephew, in fact. And we're gonna do everything we can to bring his killer to justice."

"I want the same," Terry replied. But justice for him was totally different than the type of justice that the cop was referring to.

Terry was forced to stay until the next day because they had to run a few tests and take some X-rays. The doctor authorized his release the next morning. Snatch escorted him out of the hospital.

They drove away in a rented blue Dodge Intrepid.

"You all right?" Snatch asked.

"Fuck nah. This nigga done killed my goddamn nephew, man!"

"I know," Snatch said in a sympathetic tone. "I know. We gon' get him."

Terry dumped the actual murder weapon into the sewer, down the street from his home, before the police arrived.

Terry took a Glock 40 and a 9 mm from the glove box. He placed them both in his lap. "Tremon was involved in this shit, too. She's the one that called me and told me to stay at the house, then drove the nigga out to my crib." Terry fumed. "Both of 'em gotta die today."

"I got plenty of gas." He removed a freshly rolled cigarillo from the ashtray. "Here. Sooth your nerves."

Terry took it from him. "Head north."

~ ~ ~ ~ ~

Tremon hadn't awakened until about 4 o'clock that morning. She was in so much pain that she had to go the emergency room. She had found her keys lying on the floor by the door. Truman Medical Center was on the north end of town, about two miles from where she was.

After a five hour wait, she was finally released. The first thing she did was grab herself two number threes at McDonald's. She ate her food as she was driving south on Troost Avenue, contemplating what she was gonna do about O'ban. So far, nothing came to mind.

~ ~ ~ ~ ~

I kept $3,000 in my pocket for me to take to jail with me. The remaining $79,000 I gave to Pops to put up for me. I was planning on turning myself in to the authorities because I did not want to be around for the murder investigation of Terry and his nephew Spin. The further I could get away from that, the better. Then I would return in nine months after the heat wore off.

At Nah Nah's request, we stopped by her school on Troost Avenue. She wanted to inform her professor that she had an emergency in the family and would miss class.

She returned 15 minutes later with her homework assignment in hand. I made a left on Troost, headed north.

~ ~ ~ ~ ~

"Stop at the gas station on 63rd and Troost and get me something fruity to drink," Terry commanded Snatch. "Then head north to 12th Street. I wanna stop and holla at that punk-ass attorney." He touched his wounded shoulder. "Just because I got shot don't mean that this case we're fighting is gonna go away."

~ ~ ~ ~ ~

It took us a little while to reach 12th and Locust, police headquarters. Instead of getting out and walking into the front door of the police station, I drove into the parking garage. Wasn't no use in walking up when I could use the elevator.

I parked in front of the elevator doors that led upstairs to booking. After I put the gear in park, I faced Nah Nah. She took off my red ball cap and placed it on her head.

I took some Motrin from her purse and swallowed four of them. Two days later and the pain my arm was becoming unbearable.

"I'ma wear this hat around representing as your girl, since I don't have a ring yet," Nah Nah said.

I wrapped my arms around her, "You'll get one when I get out."

"I better." She moved her head back and studied my face. "You are so handsome."

"I know."

She giggled. "Gimme kiss."

I leaned in and planted a kiss on her wet lips. When our lips unlocked, I froze and studied her face. Nah Nah deserved much better than me. Hopefully when this was all over, I would get out and actually marry her and be able to remain faithful to her.

"Okay, I gotta go. Love you." I opened the door.

"You too. Take care of yourself in there, O'ban."

"You too. I don't want you looking all fucked up when I return," I joked.

"What if I get into a wreck and ended up crippled? Would you still be with me? Hmm?"

"I'd love you even if you had to shit out your mouth." I stepped out and closed the door.

"Unn, you nasty."

Nah Nah slid over into the driver's seat, then let down the

window. "Well you should, because your mouth smelled liked shit this morning, and I still love you." She found that hilarious.

"Forget you." I kissed her once more, then walked away. She blew me a kiss just before the elevator doors closed.

~ ~ ~ ~ ~

Nah Nah let her window back up before she pulled back out of the garage. She headed back toward Troost. When she reached the avenue, she placed Fat Joe's CD into the deck. Seconds later as she was making a right turn, she heard Lil Wayne start rapping, "*I'll make it rain.*"

~ ~ ~ ~ ~

Snatch was traveling north on Troost Avenue when he heard Terry shout, "Ain't that that bitch right there?" He clicked the 9 mm off safety and jumped into the back seat, behind Snatch.

"Slow down a lil' bit." He let down the window.

~ ~ ~ ~ ~

"*I'll make it rain. I'll make...make...make.*"

"Shit!" Nah Nah exclaimed after she heard the CD start skipping. For a brief second she took her eyes off the road to fix the radio.

That's when the shots rang out.

Pop pop pop pop pop pop.

The first two shots made her body tense up. The next entered her window, grazing her head. The fourth entered the door, lodging in her dashboard. The fifth made her scream when it pierced her back. And the final shot penetrated the window and entered her face, knocking her unconscious.

"Go! Go! Goo!" Terry commanded. Snatch drove at full speed, then made a quick left turn, just barely missing a speeding car.

They stopped about two miles away from the crime scene, where Terry got out and tossed the pistol into a manhole. Then he casually walked back to the car and got back inside.

They never saw the man who had been following them since they had fled the scene.

CHAPTER THIRTY-ONE

<u>O'ban</u>

I hadn't been inside of the holding cell an hour when the turnkeys came into the bullpen and snatched me out the cell, then sat me down inside the interrogation room.

Then two black detectives, one light skinned with a silver tooth, one dark skinned with a nappy beard, came into the room. Both were eyeing me like they hated me.

They sat down and explained to me that my listed girlfriend, Nancy Miller, had been shot quite badly less than a mile away from the jail, and had been placed in the ICU at a nearby hospital.

She was wearing my jacket and hat, and they concluded that it had been a mistaken identity. The bullets had really been meant for me. I was shocked when they told me that they believed that it was a retaliation move by Terry Finch, who had been shot inside his home the day before.

Light-skinned leaned forward until our noses touched. "Did you kill that child when you shot Terry, son?"

"Fuck naw!" I said in a convincing tone. My eyes began to water because I was thinking about Nah Nah. But I didn't allow my inner pain to cause me to break down during this punk-ass interview.

"Terry helped start the case that put you and your brother away!" he yelled into my face.

"Tell me something that I don't know," I replied in a forced even tone.

"That's right, you know. And you expect us to believe that you didn't get the urge to retaliate since you've been out?"

I said, "Terry's already facing a lot of time from a fed case that he's fighting. In a few months he won't even be on the streets. So why would I risk my life goin' after somebody that's already goin' down?"

The dark man with the beard smiled. "Because you can't get no gratification if the feds take him out. Plus you'll be known as a coward on the streets. Whatever your fuckin' reason is, boy, I want your confession and I want it now!"

"I'm sorry, but I can't help you. What I do know is, before I got out, Nancy's sister and niece had been suspected as being murdered by Terry. His trial is getting near." I shrugged. "Maybe he was trying to clean house."

The detectives both looked at each other.

For two more long hours I was held up in that room getting drilled by those two pricks. And in the end, I still stuck to my guns, by continuing to say, "It wasn't me."

~ ~ ~ ~ ~

Qu'ban

Word about Nah Nah getting shot up in her Jeep because she had been mistaken for O'ban came down through the wire. But you know how niggas are. One person gets the news, then tells another person, who tells two more people, and so on, and so on. By the time the story got to me, it had been revised to make O'ban look like Terry had been giving him the blues out there. It was also said that Terry had shot O'ban at the club, and that was the reason that O'ban intentionally violated his probation to flee from Terry's wrath.

"They even said that some dyke bitch named, uh uh, Tremon had been found shot to death inside her car," Mike told me. Mike was the same person who had told me about Nah Nah. "The police is trying to link that shit to Terry. They say that he's trying to clean house before he goes to trial, which I also heard got rescheduled for an early date. I mean like soon." He shrugged. "Of course I only heard all of this shit. Who knows how much of it's true or not."

"Yeah," I said. "Look, I gotta go think a minute. I'ma get up wit' you later. Aight?"

"Cool."

We shook hands and I departed from the yard back up to the camp. I had made it outside the prison gates. It was a lovely place to do time. Instead of a big scary looking-ass institution, we were housed in a small building that resembled a house. Four TV rooms, two weight piles, a pool table and vending machines were present to accommodate us. But the best thing about it, and the only reason why I was there in the first place, was that there was no fence.

Some nights I would sit outside on the steps with my headphones on, watching the cars drive up and down Kansas Avenue. It was a beautiful spot, true enough, but just seeing the scenery was the farthest thing from my mind. I was plotting, mapping out my route. Which way I'ma go. What's the best time to go? How will I get out without being seen? How will I return without being seen? Being in this camp will be my alibi. If I got caught out of bounds, and

Terry was found dead, I would definitely be their first suspect.

I didn't know if Dana was gonna ride with me on this or not, but even if she didn't I was gonna go for it anyway. I had to, not only for me, but for O'ban, Nah Nah, Katrina and my precious baby girl. Terry would be going to trial soon, and would more than likely end up in prison. After that there would be no chance for me to get my revenge. It had to be done soon. And I was ready.

The following week Dana was going to be transferred out as the third shift C.O. for the week. That gave me five whole days to try to persuade her to help me.

Three days. It took me three days and the $5,000 that O'ban had sent to my books for me to persuade Dana to go along with my plan. The funny thing was, some time during our meeting that night, I got the feeling that she wanted me to get revenge for my daughter. Why did I think that? Because she already had the plan thought out for me.

We were inside the C.O.'s office when she said, "You run across the south side of the field until you reach the street where my car will be parked. You would have the keys. You drive to Kansas City, locate Terry, then do your thing. Then you'll return as if nothing ever happened."

"Okay. What about count time?" I inquired.

She smiled. "This entire facility is family oriented, goofy. My cousin Megan is the C.O. who helps me do the midnight, 3 o'clock and 5 o'clock counts. She knows we're friends. I'll just tell her that I let you sneak off to go visit a strip club or something. People sneak off from camps all the time, Qu'ban. You know that."

I studied her face. "Why?"

She leaned back in her chair. "Because I want to see you get revenge for your daughter. I've seen you cry, I've felt your pain in my office while we were processing your story." She shrugged. "And I wanna help."

"And your cousin Megan? She's gonna look out for me because you said so?"

Dana peered at her lap. "I also promised her the five grand that you're giving me."

I nodded my head up and down, up and down in thought. "We'll do it Friday night."

"It's your call."

I rose from my seat and walked around my desk to where she was sitting. I looked at her. She looked at me. Then I leaned in and kissed her. She immediately pushed me away.

"Hey! This is not what you think it is, Mr. Cartez."

I backed away. "I'm sorry."

"I know I'm chubby, but I'm not gullible," she stated. "You wouldn't want me if you met me on the street, so let's not go there."

Embarrassed, I left her office without another word.

~ ~ ~ ~ ~

From the prison wire—Mike—I had gotten word that Terry's nephew, Spin, was being laid to rest. That meant that Terry and his entire family would be at his mother's house, celebrating Spin's homecoming. So I knew exactly where he would be.

It was Friday evening. I planned on making my escape after the midnight count. It would take me around 4½ hours round trip. I had to be back by 7:30 a.m., by the time Dana's shift ended. Which meant that I had under three hours to locate Terry, and then do what had to be done. Then I would return as if nothing happened.

It was indeed the perfect plan.

And I was gonna pull it off.

CHAPTER THIRTY-TWO

As soon as the midnight count cleared, I casually walked out the front door and across the dark field. The two white Dodge trucks that usually patrolled the perimeter were nowhere in sight. Probably parked somewhere and fell asleep.

My shirt was soaked with sweat by the time I made it to the road. Dana's '97 Sebring was sitting there as promised. I found the keys in the ashtray. As the engine purred I hoped that it was in good enough condition to make the journey.

Two hours and forty-five minutes later I was in Kansas City. Just as I suspected, Mama Fanny had a house full of mourners when I slowly drove past. All the lights were on. Music was going. People were on the porch chatting with drinks in their hands, and all out in the front yard.

I was driving so slow that it looked like I was parked. Suddenly out of nowhere I saw Snatch step out in front of me. I hit the brakes.

Errk!

The car stopped just before hitting Snatch's long legs. With a big frown on his face, he peered into the front windshield. The bright headlights prevented him from seeing my face.

Snatch slammed his hand down on the hood of the car, then

continued on across the street. I drove up the street, keeping my eyes on him in the rearview mirror.

He climbed into a silver Chrysler 300C. I pulled over and let him pass, then pulled out behind him. Snatch led me to an all night party shop four blocks away. There was only one car in the parking lot when he entered it. Judging by where it was parked, I would say that it belonged to the owner.

Snatch walked into the store before I drove up into the lot. I walked over to the dumpster and fished out an empty bottle of Vodka. It was a fifth.

Six minutes later he exited the store with a brown paper sack in his hand. He got into the car and set the bag on the driver's seat, then closed the door.

The interior light came back on when I snatched the door open. Snatch's head snapped toward me. He had about a half a second to holler before the vodka bottle that I swung smashed into his nose. The bottle broke on impact.

Blood streamed down his face. His narrow eyes locked in on me. He looked as if he he'd seen a ghost. He recovered quite quickly. That's when I saw his hand going for his waist.

"Pull it!" I bellowed. "Pull it, you," I brought the jagged bottle down hard on top of his head, "bitch!"

"Ow!" he screamed as he fell over toward the passenger seat. "Owww! Qu, please!" His face was covered in blood.

I reached around his waist and removed his gun.

"Don't kill me out here, Qu!"

I got into the back seat and sat directly behind him.

"Shut yo' big stupid ass up," I said. "Now take me back around there where Terry is." I slapped him across his bald head. "Hurry up!"

He drove away. I sat low in the back seat and pulled the clip

275

from the chamber. The .45 automatic that I held had a full clip. I put it back inside.

The people that were outside had disappeared, presumably back inside the house. Snatch parked on the opposite side of the street. There was a minivan parked outside Mama Fanny's house that shielded our view.

"Call'em," I commanded.

Snatch's hand trembled as he held up the cell phone and began dialing numbers.

"Terry," he said into the phone. I leaned forward and pressed the gun against his temple. "Come outside, man. I'm sitting in the car across the street." He listened. "Huh?" More listening. "Just come out. I got something I want you to see." He hung up. "Here he comes."

Snatch hissed as he clutched his bloody nose. "Sss...Owww!"

"Give me yo' belt. Hurry up."

Snatch removed his leather belt from his slacks, then handed it to me. The front door to the house opened, but the van shielded my view.

I looked at the back of Snatch's bald head, then swung the gun and hit him upside his temple. He slumped over toward the door. Terry was standing in front of the minivan looking both ways before he crossed the street. He had the sleeves of his dress shirt rolled up to his forearms.

His eyes narrowed on the car as he approached. I hit the locks. He climbed into the car and shut the door before he looked over at Snatch.

"What the..." I threw the belt over his head and pulled it back toward his throat. Before he could react, I had him in a choke hold. His mouth opened wide. "Gggggg."

I pulled the belt tight, cutting all the oxygen from traveling to his lungs. I reached my head around him until I came into view of his beet red left eye. It nearly popped out of his head.

Out of the window a little boy appeared. He had a phone in his hand coming toward us. When he was about six feet away from the car I released his neck. He fell forward coughing and gagging, desperately trying to get some oxygen to his brain. I pulled out the gun.

"Send him away, T," I commanded. "If you don't, I'ma start firing until everybody is dead. Including him."

Still coughing, Terry let down the window. "Wha…wha…wha…"

The boy held up the phone. "Somebody's on the phone for you." The boy cut his eyes toward the back seat and saw me through the window.

Terry said, "Tell 'em I'll call 'em back."

"But…"

"Go 'head, Jason. Now get outta here." The boy ran away. Terry coughed some more. "How did you get out?"

"I'm Qu'ban Cartez, nigga. If I can make babies, make it rain and take lives, what can't I do?" I looked at my watch. Time was running. "Wake his ass up."

Terry shook Snatch's arm. "Snatch! Snatch! Get up!" He slapped him on the head. Snatch grunted as he started coming around.

"Huh? Huh?"

"Start this car up," I said, "and drive away."

Snatch started the car, took the time to wipe his face with his sleeve, then pulled away. "Where we goin'?"

I looked at Terry. "To wherever y'all hid Katrina and my daughter."

Terry looked back at me. "Huh?"

"You'd better not have killed them, Terry. Or I'ma bury you with them."

"I'ma lot of things, Qu," Terry explained, "but you know that I would never kill no kids, man. You know me, Qu!"

"Shut up!" I shouted. "I'm not playin' with you, Terry. For over a year now I've been haunted by my daughter in my dreams. And they won't stop until I find out what happened to her."

"Qu, look, man," Terry said. "When I got out, I found Katrina at the motel. I took her to the bank to get my money, then I dropped her back off. True enough, I told Snatch to go over there and kill'er, but he didn't do it."

I looked at Snatch. "Why not?" Sweat was running down my face. "Huh? Why didn't you kill her, Snatch? She turned you mutha-fuckas in. She stole your money. Then you get out and don't cause no physical harm to the bitch or my daughter what-soever? That's bullshit."

Pow!

I fired a shot straight through the radio. Snatch flinched and swerved into the other lane.

"Where are they, goddamnit?"

"We don't know!" Terry shouted back.

Silence. The thought of me never finding out the truth filled my body with anxiety.

I looked at Snatch. "Snatch, he said he sent you over there to kill her…what happened?"

Snatch had told me something that sent a chill through my body, temporarily causing me to shiver. For a moment we rode in silence as I sat there taking it all in.

Both men in the front seat were so scared that their entire bodies were spasming. They knew it was over. They knew they would never stand trial, and that the next homecoming that would be celebrated at Mama Fanny's house would be in honor of them.

We were driving down the nearly deserted James A. Reed Road. I pointed the gun at the back of Terry's head. He didn't even know it was coming. I held the trigger.

Boom!

We had been struck from behind by another vehicle. The impact caused me to hit my head up against the headrest. The car rolled onto a parked car. I heard a car approaching, but I saw no lights. A door opened. Footsteps. Terry's door snatched open and he was being pulled out. Doors slammed. I heard a car speeding away. I gathered myself, then kicked open the door on Snatch's side and crawled out. Snatch wasn't conscious.

~ ~ ~ ~ ~

Terry lay across the back seat when his cousin started backing away. His little cousin Jason had seen Qu'ban's face when he brought the phone out to the car for Terry. Then he alerted his daddy inside the house about what he had seen. Terry's cousin Eddie left the house as soon as Snatch pulled off, and he followed.

"Hold up," Terry mumbled. "Hold up!"

Eddie looked back at him. "What?"

"Stop the car."

Eddie huffed, but did as he was told.

"You gotta gun?" Eddie nodded. "Give it here, and go back. I'ma put an end to this shit right now."

~ ~ ~ ~ ~

I heard the car with no headlights approaching. They had

undoubtedly come back to finish me off. I crawled up under the parked car. The car stopped. The engine was still running when I heard doors opening. Footsteps came toward me. Then I heard shots being fired.

Pop! Pop pop pop pop pop pop!

The loud gunfire said hello to the silent night.

Terry was firing into the back seat. I crawled up under the car that we had collided with, then came out on the opposite side. I was already up and had the gun on Terry before he finally saw me.

Pow! Pow!

Terry ducked away.

I came running around the car with the gun drawn. He was running for the car.

Pow! Pow!

"Ah!" he screamed as he fell onto the pavement. The gun fell out of his hand.

Eddie made it to the driver's seat. I pointed the gun at him and fired. *Pow!* One single shot to the head. Terry was still breathing when I approached him. The cops would be there soon, so there was no time for a long send off.

I stood over him with my gun pointed at his face.

Pow! Pow! Pow!

What I left behind did not look like any human being that I knew. Before I fled the scene, I planted the last hollow tip 'round somewhere inside of Snatch's skull.

I had someone else to visit, but there was no time. I would have to put it off until it was safe to escape again. So I traveled on foot back to the store where Dana's car was parked. I cleaned up the gun, then tossed it into the dumpster.

After I got back into the car, strangely enough, I didn't feel any relief by taking Terry's life. If anything, my craving for blood had become even more intense, because I knew that my job wasn't finished, and that I wouldn't sleep well until it was.

I entered onto Highway 71 headed south. Two hours and forty-five minutes from now and I should've been home safe. Instead I heard the frightening sound of the ghetto bird hovering in the sky above me. Then the spotlight shone on my car.

But that didn't stop me.

What did stop me was the road block that I encountered about a mile up the road. The entire section was barricaded with police vehicles. At least ten armed police were standing about, and all of them had their weapons pointed at me.

What could I do?

I did what any nigga in their right mind would've done. I pulled over and waited for instructions.

"Put your hands up!"

"Step out of the car!"

"Down on your stomach!"

"Lock your hands behind your head!"

"Now kiss the ground because this will be the last time you'll ever see it again, you fuckin' idiot!"

Three hours after I had left the prison, Dana placed the letter that Terry had sent me on my bed, as well as the photos. Then she beat her face until it bled. When her supposed cousin Megan came down for the 3 o'clock count, she found Dana face down in her office, faking unconsciousness. After finding the pictures on my bed, the police figured that I had been enraged enough to attack Dana, steal her car keys, then drive to the city seeking revenge. They had motive, bodies and a blood stain on my left shoe.

CHAPTER THIRTY-THREE

Three months later I was sitting in the hole doing pushups when Dana came to visit me. I didn't ask, but she knew I wanted an answer for her setting me up like that. She informed me that back in '99 she and some friends had driven to Kansas City from Springfield, Missouri for the weekend. They went to a club where she met me and agreed to go to a motel with me. After I peed in her that morning, took her cell phone and left her stranded, she decided to hitchhike a ride on I-70, back to the motel where her friends were. She ended up being struck in the leg by a passing car. While her leg was out of commission, she gained 60 pounds, which also helped destroy her self-esteem.

Now fat and disabled, she gave up the party life and started working at the prison, where any woman was beautiful. The occasional compliments from inmates about how sexy she was made her days. But she still wasn't happy. Until the day that she saw me step foot on her unit.

"Stained cotton," Dana said. "That's what my dad called me after I told him what happened." She smiled weakly. "I won't ask you why you did what you did, because I don't even think that you know. I was just a stupid white girl, trying to be down. Thought I'd try something new by sleeping with a black man." She shrugged. "Look where it got me."

And the truth was, I didn't know why I had done her that way. Being ornery got me two life sentences added on to the time I already had. Which was really fucked up because three days after I killed Terry, I received a letter from the courts stating that my sentence had been vacated due to Katrina's deal that she cut that had helped bring down Terry's organization.

If I had only known.

~ ~ ~ ~ ~

O'ban

Ten months had passed and I walked out of jail a free man again. So much had happened while I was on the inside, to Nah Nah, to Terry, and to Qu'ban, that I didn't know how to cope. Or what I was going to do with myself. It was no surprise to me when Nah Nah wasn't waiting at the bus station when my bus arrived.

Nah Nah had written to me once while I was in prison, but I never responded. I copied down the address and threw the letter away. I caught a cab out to her new address. When I pulled up I saw a gray minivan pull up in front of the house. Nah Nah climbed out and opened up the side door. She pulled out a baby carriage. A newborn. The reason I guessed that she had written me, to inform me about the arrival of our new baby.

She used a pair of metal crutches to help her walk. Even with the aid of the braces, just getting from the van to the porch was a struggle. I felt sorry for her. But I wasn't sure she was someone I could live my life with anymore.

"Where to?" the cabby asked.

I peered at Nah Nah one more time. She took a deep

breath before attacking the stairs. Then I instructed the driver to pull off.

I used the money that I'd taken from Terry to open my own body shop, got me a new Charger, and a down payment on a crib. While I was in the process of repairing my life, I couldn't help but think about all the things that I'd done to help destroy Nah Nah's.

Then one day Pops, Qu'ban Junior and I went out to eat at Applebee's. We were sitting at our table chattering over a basket of hot wings.

Nah Nah and the baby walked into the restaurant. When I spotted her, I wasn't even sure that it was her. She had a small scar on the left side of her face, but she was laughing like she was happy. It wasn't until I saw the braces leaning against the wall behind her, was I sure it was her.

She gazed in my direction as if she felt me watching her. Her smile vanished instantly. Then she looked away and resumed playing with the baby.

I got up and walked over to their table.

"I just wanna speak to you for a moment."

Nah Nah avoided eye contact. "What do you want?"

I sat down. "You," I replied.

"Don't play with my heart." A tear rolled down her cheek. "I'm crippled. I'm ugly. Why would you want to be with me?" She sniffled. "Why would anyone want to be with me?"

"You're not ugly. And you must've forgotten the promise that I made before I left you that day."

"I didn't forget." Her voice was soft. "There's nothing I can do for you anymore."

"Does that thang still get wet?" She smiled. "Can you have more babies?"

"Yes and yes, but the second child would be hell."

"Then forget everything else." I wrote something down on a napkin, then gave it to her. "It's my phone number and address. You should use it."

"I can't. It wouldn't work." She put the napkin in her purse and grabbed her crutches. Trying to lift herself up too quickly, she almost fell. I hurried to her aid.

"Just promise you'll think about it, mama?"

She silently nodded her head.

I walked back over to my table and joined Pops and my nephew.

Pops said, "It'll be okay, son."

That night after I put my nephew to bed, I had just stepped out of the shower when I heard the doorbell. I answered the door in my robe. As soon as I opened the door, the lightening from the coming rain flashed. I blinked, and Nah Nah was there standing before me. She had on makeup. She was dressed in a skirt and flat shoes.

"I love you," she said.

Ten minutes later we were naked, and I had her up in the air with her legs around my waist, hitting her to the beat of the rain. Two weeks later and we were roommates.

~ ~ ~ ~ ~

It was Christmas night. Against Nah Nah's wishes, O'ban invited Michael to dinner. It was Christmas after all. After a tearful party at the Cartez family home, where O'ban and Mr. Miller finally made amends, Michael left drunk, claiming to be on his way to his Catholic church.

As he was driving his Porsche along the road, his mind began to reflect back to the day that Katrina and Brianna came up missing. He saw himself sitting in his car inside the motel room when Katrina walked out and went to the lobby. Then he saw Snatch approach the room door. It took some force for Snatch to force his way inside.

Michael picked up a crowbar, got out of his car, then ran up to the room. Snatch was hovering over the baby, who was sitting on the bed. Snatch heard the door being pushed open and turned around. But it was too late. He had caught a glimpse of the man that held the crowbar above his head, right before he got knocked out.

When Katrina returned, she found Michael standing over Snatch, while he held Brianna in his hands. Katrina saw Snatch lying on the ground and gasped.

Michael said, "It's not safe for you here. We have to leave."

Michael's mind flashed back to the present. He pulled into the gravel driveway of an old house. He parked with his headlights still on. As he stared at the front door, his mind began to reflect again.

He pictured himself driving up to that house with Katrina and Brianna in the car.

"Where are we?" Katrina asked.

"Some place where you'll be safe."

Katrina carried Brianna inside. The interior of the home was empty. Michael had his back to her.

"You disappointed me," he said. "You just had to go and ruin it for me, didn't you? Didn't you?"

Katrina held Brianna in her arms as fear began to consume her.

"You took my Kortni away from me." He glared at her. "But you'll never be able to testify." He disappeared into the kitchen.

"Dad!" Katrina screamed out. "Dad!"

Suddenly Michael came running out of the kitchen with a pot in his hand, then dumped its contents on both her and Brianna.

Katrina cried. She soon came to realize that he had thrown wet dog food onto them. Michael snatched Brianna from her and ran into the basement. Katrina followed.

"What are you…"

Michael sat Brianna at the bottom of the staircase. Katrina ran after her. When she reached the bottom he hit her in the head, knocking her down. When her eyes fluttered open she focused in on a pair of cufflinks that she knew had once belonged to Michael's co-worker David.

The door was closed and locked.

"Mama," Brianna uttered.

Katrina looked in the direction that her child was staring and she saw something so frightening that she released her bowls.

Three hungry, growling dogs stalked toward them.

Michael's mind came back to reality again. He grabbed his bottle of Jim Beam and exited the car. He unlocked the door and went inside. In his head he heard his daughter and granddaughter's screams. The door was shut. He went into the kitchen and removed a can of dog food from the shelf, opened it, then he opened his bottle and took a swig. He looked out the window and his mind began to reflect again. This time it was on the day that Nah Nah got shot.

He'd been following O'ban and Nah Nah from the minute they left their motel room that morning. He followed them all the way to the police station. When they pulled into the garage at the station to drop O'ban off, he waited down the street. He wanted to catch Nancy alone. When the Jeep pulled out of the parking garage 10 minutes later, he recognized his daughter's silhouette as the Jeep passed. She was finally alone. Nah Nah had become obsessed with black people, and loved them more than she did her own father, was his belief. She had to go.

Michael followed the Jeep as it headed east. The Jeep stopped at the intersection of 12th and Troost. That's when he picked his gun up from the seat. But before he could pull alongside of her, she made a right onto Troost, and he followed. Now that the gun was in his hand, he was even more determined to kill.

Nancy slowed down to almost a complete stop and leaned over toward the radio. He let his passenger side window down, and drove up next to her Jeep. He raised his gun…and fired on his own daughter.

After that he sped up Troost. That's when he saw two men in a blue Dodge Intrepid up ahead of him, firing shots into a Lexus. The car bolted away, then made a sharp turn. Michael had to swerve to the right to avoid a collision. He followed them. A few blocks down the car stopped. The passenger got out and tossed the weapon into a manhole. Michael waited until they were gone, wiped his gun down, then threw it in with the other.

The truth was, it was Michael's influence that helped both Terry and Snatch get a bond. He did that so they would be immediate suspects when Katrina and Brianna came up missing, and when Nancy got shot.

Michael snapped back to reality. He grabbed the bottle of Jim Beam and took another drink. The floor creaked. He could feel the presence of someone in the room with him.

"I knew you'd come," Michael said without looking at the person. "I know that those two guys that your brother killed revealed to him that I had taken Katrina and that little nigglet daughter of hers." He sighed. "Like I said, I knew that your brother gave my name to you anyway, because I tapped your home phone. So I wrote a little confession note and placed it in your jacket pocket, knowing full well that after you read it, you'd keep quiet about it, so you could follow me out here and kill me."

O'ban stepped from the shadows. He held a gun down at his side.

Michael turned around slowly. In his left hand was a .357 revolver. "But my plan was to kill you."

O'ban dropped the gun that he was holding.

"Now step forward. You're going to experience death in one of the most horrible ways imaginable. Just as they did."

O'ban walked forward while Michael backed up toward the basement door.

"Stop right there!" Michael commanded. "Now pick up that can of dog food and pour it over you."

"No."

"Huh?" Michael said as his head snapped toward the doorway where the voice had come from.

Pow! Pow!

Michael fell back against the wall, dropping the gun in the process. Nah Nah stepped into the kitchen. She had a crutch in one hand and a smoking .25 automatic in the other. Tears were in her eyes.

"How could you, Dad? Your own flesh and blood."

Michael was silent as he stood against the wall, leaking from his stomach.

O'ban picked up the huge can of dog food, then threw its contents onto Michael's body.

"Wait!" Michael exclaimed. "No! Please."

O'ban opened the basement door, then grabbed Michael by the arms and slung him down the stairs. Before he closed the door, he caught a glimpse of a ripped up piece of a child's bloody clothing sitting on the steps.

Soon they heard Michael's loud screams.

Before they closed the door on that old house for good, O'ban doused the place with the bottle of Jim Beam, then struck a match.

He now understood that you couldn't associate yourself with negative people and expect to get a positive outcome. Bad company is bad company, no matter what ethnic background you come from.

ORDER FORM

Triple Crown Publications
PO Box 6888
Columbus, Oh 43205

Name: _____

Address: _____

City/State: _____

Zip: _____

	TITLES	PRICES
	Dime Piece	$15.00
	Gangsta	$15.00
	Let That Be The Reason	$15.00
	A Hustler's Wife	$15.00
	The Game	$15.00
	Black	$15.00
	Dollar Bill	$15.00
	A Project Chick	$15.00
	Road Dawgz	$15.00
	Blinded	$15.00
	Diva	$15.00
	Sheisty	$15.00
	Grimey	$15.00
	Me & My Boyfriend	$15.00
	Larceny	$15.00
	Rage Times Fury	$15.00
	A Hood Legend	$15.00
	Flipside of The Game	$15.00
	Menage's Way	$15.00

SHIPPING/HANDLING (Via U.S. Media Mail) $3.95 1-2 Books, $5.95 3-4 Books add $1.95 for ea. additional book

TOTAL $_____

FORMS OF ACCEPTED PAYMENTS:
Postage Stamps, Institutional Checks & Money Orders, all mail in orders take 5-7 Business days to be delivered.

ORDER FORM

Triple Crown Publications
PO Box 6888
Columbus, Oh 43205

Name: _____

Address: _____

City/State: _____

Zip: _____

	TITLES	PRICES
	Still Sheisty	$15.00
	Chyna Black	$15.00
	Game Over	$15.00
	Cash Money	$15.00
	Crack Head	$15.00
	For The Strength of You	$15.00
	Down Chick	$15.00
	Dirty South	$15.00
	Cream	$15.00
	Hoodwinked	$15.00
	Bitch	$15.00
	Stacy	$15.00
	Life	$15.00
	Keisha	$15.00
	Mina's Joint	$15.00
	How To Succeed in The Publishing Game	$20.00
	Love & Loyalty	$15.00
	Whore	$15.00
	A Hustler's Son	$15.00

SHIPPING/HANDLING (Via U.S. Media Mail) $3.95 1-2 Books, $5.95 3-4 Books add $1.95 for ea. additional book

TOTAL $_____

FORMS OF ACCEPTED PAYMENTS:
Postage Stamps, Institutional Checks & Money Orders, all mail in orders take 5-7 Business days to be delivered.

ORDER FORM

Triple Crown Publications
PO Box 6888
Columbus, Oh 43205

Name: _____

Address: _____

City/State: _____

Zip: _____

		TITLES	PRICES
		Chances	$15.00
		Contagious	$15.00
		Hold U Down	$15.00
		Black and Ugly	$15.00
		In Cahootz	$15.00
		Dirty Red *Hardcover Only*	$20.00
		Dangerous	$15.00
		Street Love	$15.00
		Sunshine & Rain	$15.00
		Bitch Reloaded	$15.00
		Dirty Red *Paperback*	$15.00
		Mistress of the Game	$15.00
		Queen	$15.00
		The Set Up	$15.00
		Torn	$15.00
		Stained Cotton	$15.00
		Grindin *Hardcover Only*	$10.00
		Amongst Thieves	$15.00
		Cutthroat	$15.00

SHIPPING/HANDLING (Via U.S. Media Mail) $3.95 1-2 Books, $5.95 3-4 Books add $1.95 for ea. additional book

TOTAL $_____

FORMS OF ACCEPTED PAYMENTS:
Postage Stamps, Institutional Checks & Money Orders, all mail in orders take 5-7 Business days to be delivered.

ORDER FORM

Triple Crown Publications
PO Box 6888
Columbus, Oh 43205

Name: _____

Address: _____

City/State: _____

Zip: _____

		TITLES	PRICES
		The Hood Rats	$15.00
		Betrayed	$15.00
		The Pink Palace	$15.00
		The Bitch is Back	$15.00

SHIPPING/HANDLING (Via U.S. Media Mail) $3.95 1-2 Books, $5.95 3-4 Books add $1.95 for ea. additional book

TOTAL $_____

FORMS OF ACCEPTED PAYMENTS:
Postage Stamps, Institutional Checks & Money Orders, all mail in orders take 5-7 Business days to be delivered.